"MOVE, AND I'LL BLOW YOUR BRAINS ALL OVER THE STREET!"

"Mister, I got a few coppers, that's all," Howie said carefully. "You're sure welcome to 'em. I ain't looking for any trouble."

"And I'm not looking for any coppers, Howie Ryder. What I'm looking for is you."

Howie's heart nearly stopped. He cursed himself for a fool. He'd never caught the trooper looking at him at all; the man had never once given himself away.

"Guess you got the wrong man," Howie said, forcing an easy grin. "Name's Cory, and I—"

The barrel of the weapon was a blur. Howie tried to jerk away and the iron struck him hard across the brow. He went to his knees and doubled over with the pain.

"Sit up," the trooper said harshly. "I ain't going to kill you lyin' down. . . ."

DAWN'S UNCERTAIN LIGHT

by

Neal Barrett, Jr.

A SIGNET BOOK

NEW AMERICAN LIBRARY

A DIVISION OF PENGUIN BOOKS USA INC.

NAL BOOKS ARE AVAILABLE AT QUANTITY DISCOUNTS WHEN USED TO PROMOTE PRODUCTS OR SERVICES. FOR INFORMATION PLEASE WRITE TO PREMIUM MARKETING DIVISION, NEW AMERICAN LIBRARY, 1633 BROADWAY, NEW YORK, NEW YORK 10019.

SIGNET TRADEMARK REG U.S. PAT. OFF. AND FOREIGN COUNTRIES
REGISTERED TRADEMARK—MARCA REGISTRADA
HECHO EN DRESDEN, TN.

SIGNET, SIGNET CLASSIC, MENTOR, ONYX, PLUME, MERIDIAN and NAL BOOKS are published by New American Library, a division of Penguin Books USA Inc., 1633 Broadway, New York, New York 10019

First Printing, July, 1989

1 2 3 4 5 6 7 8 9

PRINTED IN THE UNITED STATES OF AMERICA

PART ONE

South by Southeast

CHAPTER ONE

THE CREEK WAS NO DEEPER THAN SPIT, A SLUGGISH course that scarcely seemed to move under an August sun that drank the land dry. Along the red clay banks the earth had crumbled and given way, loosing chunks of dirt into the bed.

Howie Ryder studied the land with a farmer's practiced eye. Nothing stirred in the thick oppressive air. Rain hadn't touched this place in a year, maybe more than that. The fields were parched, the soil cracked and sere. The land was more than dry. It was plain used up. Rain wouldn't likely bring it back. Too many generations had squeezed a living from the ground and there was nothing left to give.

The house stood beneath a dead oak, a one-room shack with the paint sucked off by the sun. Howie stood well out of sight in a stand of trees. The dirt yard was empty, but he knew someone was there. A cane chair stood on the porch, the bottom freshly patched. A cornshuck doll lay on the steps. There was sun-bleached wash on the line—a woman's dress, and smaller garments cut from the same faded cloth. A man's shirt and coveralls. A sheet and rag towels. There was still wear left in the coveralls and shirt, and they'd be nice to have. Howie left them where they were. If the man here had kept his family safe in such times he had a gun. And if he did he was in there now, waiting for the stranger to leave or come close enough to fire. It wasn't smart to waste lead. The way to get it back was to hit a man square and dig it out.

Howie knew there might not be a man at all. A woman with her man off to war or maybe dead would have the sense to leave his clothes on the line. That would be the smart thing to do.

Howie left the dry fields and started walking east again. Stopping for a look was just a caution; he hadn't figured on going any closer than the trees. Even if the folks in the house had come out and asked him in, he wouldn't have come nearer than the creek. There wasn't food to spare these days; if you had any sense you knew that. A friendly invitation wasn't always for supper and a bed. At Dan's Crossing three days back, Howie had seen a man and his wife and two grown-up girls all hanging from a tree. The woman and the girls were stripped bare, and they had plainly been used. A man who'd lost both arms in the war told Howie the family had been buying a lot of goods, and they hadn't had a crop in three years. Some men got together and went out to the house; a little persuasion and an afternoon's digging turned up ten bodies buried shallow in the yard. The two girls were real pretty. That's how they'd gotten strangers in.

And that was how things were, everywhere he had been. The fighting hadn't come to the South; there weren't any Loyalists or Rebels about, there wasn't any shooting going on. But the war reached out and found you, no matter where you were. There was hurt everywhere, and the misery that went with empty bellies and the fear that went with that.

Late in the afternoon, Howie found a burned-out house and a barn that had collapsed on itself, one wall standing and halfway holding up the rest. Anyone could see it was a good place to hole up for the night, and a man would be a fool if he did. Before he left the barn, Howie kicked around and found two ears of dried red corn and took them off in the woods a good quarter mile south. Dried corn was hell to chew, but once you got it down it swelled up and seemed close to a meal.

When night came he worked on the corn and drank from the glass jar of water he had dipped out of the creek. The water tasted better if you let the silt settle, but he never had the patience for that. When the water was gone he leaned back against the tree and thought about where he might be, and how much more he had to go. Howie didn't like the night. The night was real bad. In the day you had to look what you were doing, and there wasn't time to think. The night put pictures in your head, and showed you things you didn't want to see. The thing to do then was just think about dark. Dark and nothing else at all. Sometimes it worked and you went right to sleep. Sometimes it didn't and the bad stuff came and took over in your head. Howie could see that's the way it might be this time, and there was nothing you could do about that. If it came it just did.

The men came at him just before first light, making little noise, working up to him on the ground. He could smell their sweat and knew they weren't afraid. Howie figured they'd done this once or twice before. They came in together, the second man holding a knife, just behind the first. They stopped still to listen for a while, then the first man crawled up slow and grabbed out at Howie's arms to hold him down. Howie rolled to one side and came up in crouch; the man with the knife looked surprised because Howie wasn't there and then he was. Howie thrust his own blade in belly-deep, sliced up quickly to the breast, and jerked free, all in a move too fast to see.

The other man cried out in fright, crabbed away and tried for the weapon at his belt. His eyes told Howie this wasn't the way it ought to be. It was his job to hold; he hadn't ever had to do this. He could see that a man who wasn't ready was a man already dead, and he wouldn't have to think of that again.

The men had been doing something right up to now. Howie found a bag of copper coins, a pistol, and some shells. He kept the best of the knives and a good straw hat, and a better pair of boots than his own. A slit on one side and they fit just fine. The men were likely deserters, unless they'd stolen the pistol too. Howie followed their tracks out of the woods in case they'd left packs somewhere, but there was nothing else to find. Neither of the two had any food.

Howie started walking east, chewing corn along the way. He left the men where they were. He didn't look back, and didn't think about them after that.

For some time after Mexico, Howie had walked north and east, finally running flat out of land and coming up against the sea. He marveled at the great blue expanse that seemed to stretch out forever to the sky. Ma had shown him a picture in a book one time, an ocean and a boy in a boat. The water in the picture looked flat and painted on; it didn't look a thing like this.

Howie liked the sand and the shells and the curious things that washed upon the shore. The beach was thick with tiny creatures that scuttled along the sand; they were easy to catch and good to eat. Storms came in off the water now and then, and he had enough to drink.

He followed the coast for some time. It was the easiest thing to do. Twice he saw the ruins of old cities and quickly passed them by. He tried to draw a map of the country in his head, and decided the big stretch of water was the Gulf.

The coast seemed to go on forever. Finally he began to find settlements on the beach and headed north. The land changed to pine trees and farms. Small towns, and people with hollow eyes. At the Big Muddy River, a man kept a large raft. It cost a small coin or real goods to get across. Howie didn't have either at the time. He waited till dark and then stole a small boat and rowed to the other side.

He knew he was getting close. Crossing the river told him that. The map in his head said the country made a narrow little tail to the east. Silver Island lay somewhere south of the tail. His thoughts didn't go beyond that. He didn't see another Howie going somewhere else, doing something he wasn't doing now. Silver Island was enough.

Half a day after he left the men in the woods, he found one of the old stone roads and followed it east. A hundred summers and winters had done their work. The road was buckled and overgrown; tall trees split the man-made surface and thrust slabs of rubble aside. Howie could smell salt air and knew the Gulf was not far to the south. The trees were full of white birds. He even saw a little game, snicks and two rabuts, and some creatures he couldn't name, the only animals he'd seen since Mexico.

By late afternoon he smelled stock. The odor sent a sharp wave of nausea through his belly. Pictures appeared in his head, things he didn't want to see. Howie stopped and drank from a clearwater stream, cooled his face and thought about what he ought to do. Stock meant a town up ahead, and a fairly good-sized one at that, if they had enough men to guard meat. He didn't want to see the town, but he knew it was something he had to do. There were things he didn't know, things he had to find out.

It wasn't a real big operation; meat was scarce as it could be, and nearly every head went to feed the troopers fighting in the war. Howie wondered if there would ever be another great herd like the one he had helped drive west. Most likely not; the army was simply eating up stock too fast.

Two men with rifles watched Howie as he passed. Their eyes said keep walking by. That was fine with Howie. He picked up his pace and walked as quickly as he could. The stink was overpowering. The pens were set up in a clearing, on the bank of a sandy river that likely ran down to the sea. With a river close by you could dump all the waste from the stock and the organs nobody liked to eat. If the river was deep enough, shippers could barge the herd down to market and save money on feed. A herd on foot liked to eat, and that cut profit to the bone.

The cutting plant was silent, and that told Howie a lot. The lack of noisy clatter said meat was being shipped out live; the price was too good to sell to folks who couldn't match the army buyers.

As ever, there was slow, constant motion in the pens, stock shuffling aimlessly about. Howie passed the breeding sheds, keeping his attention straight ahead, trying to ignore the growing knot that cramped his gut. He walked by a high board fence, past gateways and ramps, and came right on the mares. Howie stopped, too shaken to turn away. Sweat cold as ice stung his face. They were young, no more than fourteen, each one gravid and heavy-breasted, nearly ready to foal. One looked up, a mare with matted yellow hair, looked right at him with dull, incurious eyes, grunted in her throat and clutched her breasts. Bile rose up in Howie's throat and he turned away and retched.

"Hey, you," one of the guards called out, "what the hell you think you're doin'?"

"You can't hold it, don't drink it," the other man said, and both the guards laughed.

Howie swept a hand across his mouth, staggered through the brush and ran blindly through the trees. Thorny branches ripped at his flesh. Terrible pictures filled his head, visions bright and sharp as colored glass. Howie ran until his lungs caught fire and then dropped to the ground. An awful cry escaped his throat, a cry of sorrow and anger, a pain that cut and slashed at his soul. All the pictures in his head turned red. Howie let them come. He didn't try to fight them anymore.

It was close to night when he walked into the town. The storefronts were closed up tight, and there were very few people in the streets. Howie heard a woman laugh. Two men squatted beneath a tree. One shook a handful of stones and then tossed them on the ground. The other man groaned.

Lamps in the tavern cast pale yellow squares on the street. Howie walked through the open door and found a table in the back. The air was thick with the overpowering smell of cooked meat. Howie's stomach threatened to revolt, and he fought the sickness back. He had to eat, get something down. He tried to remember when he'd had real food. Counting back didn't work. The weeks and the months swam together, one long day and night. Grubs and dried corn. Wild onions and nuts. Stale creek water, and those animals he had sucked from their shells on the beach.

"What'll it be, mister?"

The voice started Howie out of his thoughts. He looked up to see the old man. Gaunt, narrow in the chest; frazzled silver hair and livered flesh. The smell of sour sweat.

"Bring me something to eat," Howie said.

"How you want that done?"

"*No.* No meat."

The force in Howie's voice brought a frown to the old man's eyes. "Listen, the meat here's good. And you ain't goin' to find a fairer price."

Howie didn't look up. "Bring me something else. Whatever you got. And something to drink."

The old man muttered to himself and walked away.

Howie drew in a breath, tried to relax. Hunger was working on his nerves. There were six or eight men in the room. He knew they were looking at him. He could feel them at his back. Two men stood and left their table by the door. Howie knew they were coming his way. He didn't look up until they stopped. The first man limped. His eyes were dark as stones, his beard tangled red splashed with black. The second man was shorter, broader in the chest. His face was peppered with powder burns.

The first man grunted, an easy smile that was a lie before he spoke. "Where you from, friend? I don't guess I've seen you in town."

"West," Howie said.

The man laughed and winked at his friend. "Hell, I reckon everyone's from there. Me and Ben here fought ol' Lathan 'cross the Colorado Mountains and back. That's where Ben got his fine purty face. Rifle blew up in his hands. Me, now, I got my toes shot off. Near took the whole goddam foot. Where'd you say you lost that eye?"

"I don't guess I did."

The man's expression didn't change. The smile was still there, and Howie knew this was how the man wanted things to be; now he had the reason, the excuse he'd come to find.

Howie didn't move. "Go ahead," he said quietly. "Do whatever you've got to do."

The man seemed startled. Howie's challenge brought anger to his cheeks. He looked into Howie's good eye, looked for a good long time. Then something in his face went slack. He blinked, as if he'd seen something he didn't want to see. He turned and laughed harshly at his friend, and it was clear that the laugh wasn't real.

"Hell with it, Ben," the man said. "Man don't want to talk, there isn't no law against that."

Ben looked puzzled. The man gripped his arm and urged him back across the room.

Howie was vaguely aware that the room had gone silent

for a while. Now the tavern was full of talk again. He forgot about the men. A platter appeared and a cup of cool ale. The aroma made Howie want to cry. He dug into hot boiled onions and potatoes, a loaf of dark bread, pausing now and then to wash it all down with drink. The plate was empty in an instant, and Howie asked for more. He knew what the unfamiliar pleasures were doing in his belly, that he ought to have the good sense to stop. Howie didn't care. Eating roots and bugs didn't make sense, either. If he threw it all up, well, hell—he'd thrown up worse about a dozen times before.

CHAPTER TWO

HOWIE FELT A LITTLE WARM, AND FIGURED THE ALE WAS likely going to his head. Shoot, he could soak that up with more potatoes and bread. That'd work just fine. He turned and watched as the old man crossed the room with another heaping course. As the platter reached the table, a man dropped quickly into the chair across from Howie, arriving precisely with the meal.

"Mister, I didn't ask for no company," Howie said.

"Oh, now, I'm not company, son," the visitor protested. "You just go right ahead. Don't bother 'bout me."

Howie wasn't sure what to do. The man had a broad and easy smile, not mean underneath and maybe hiding something else. He wasn't like the other man at all. Howie guessed he was forty, or somewhere about. He had a nearly bald head and no beard, pale blue eyes that never seemed to sit still. The thing that struck Howie, and nearly brought chewing to a stop, was the fact that the man was so *clean*. The room was full of lean and sullen men with tangled hair and ragged clothes, and here was this stranger all shaved and spanking new. Good clothes and smelling like soap, and a little extra fat on his ribs. A man like that would have money in his purse, and Howie would have bet a whole copper that his boots were new, too.

Howie shook his head and stuffed bread in his mouth. It was a wonder this fellow was still alive. Any man here would stick a knife in his throat and strip him bare before the poor bastard could turn around.

"You look like a man who hasn't seen a good meal in some time," the man said. He smiled at Howie's plate.

"You might be right," Howie said.

"I'm guessing that you fought in the war. If you did, why you know full well what hunger's all about. Nothing I could tell *you* about that. Men cold and starving and too weak to fight. Crying for a single crust of bread. Famine and disease across the land, sorrow and pain in every home. And is hunger the cause? Is that what the war's all about? No sir, it surely is not. Avarice and greed is what brought this nation to its knees. One man wants what another man's got. And when he gets it, then what? Why, he wants something more. Lust of any kind is never satisfied." The man stuck out his hand. "Son, I'm Brother Ritcher Jones, and I didn't get your name."

Brother Ritcher Jones. That explained a lot. Howie stared in irritation at the hand, clean and new as baby's skin.

"Mister, I don't want to talk," Howie said. "I sure don't want to talk to no preacher."

The man beamed, pleased as he could be. Howie wondered if he'd said something nice, and couldn't figure what it might be.

"Right talk can do a man a lot of good," Jones said. "Clear the air and get his spirit working right."

"I wouldn't know about that," Howie said.

Ritcher Jones gave Howie a solemn look. "Son, I don't mean to preach at you at all. It's just that I see a hungry man here filling his body's needs. And I know full well that a belly's not the only empty place a man's got. There's other parts need filling, too. A man can eat a sack of potatoes every day and still walk in the dark, alone and sore afraid."

"I already done that," Howie said.

"Oh, I see that you have," said Ritcher Jones. "I can

see that right clear.'' His eyes seemed to blur, as if he might really know, as if he might understand Howie's pain. Either that, Howie thought, or he wanted you to think that he could.

Ritcher Jones stood, smiling at Howie like church was letting out, folding his hands the way preachers liked to do.

"Think about that empty place, son," he told Howie. "Think about a man's inner needs."

Jones walked away; Howie didn't look up. He ran a crust in a circle around his plate, mopping up the juice. He could feel his belly cramping something fierce, sweat getting cold on his brow. Howie swallowed hard and forced the food back down where it belonged. A good meal had been too long coming, and he was damned if he'd throw it up now.

The clown was funny as he could be. He stumbled in the tent in a lopsided hat and a baggy old patchwork suit. All the children laughed, and the grown-ups, too. A trooper played his fiddle and the clown began to dance. He whirled and leaped about, sweating so hard that the paint rolled off his face. He leaped so high that he flipped over neatly in the air, and when his feet hit the ground, a bunch of long silver ribbons was in his hand. He pranced and danced about, stopping first before one child and then another. And sometimes when he stopped, he pinned a long silver ribbon to a lucky boy or girl, then laughed and danced away. And when all the silver ribbons were gone, he bowed and threw a kiss to one and all. More than half of all the children were Chosen, more than any other year. Mama cried and then laughed, and Papa wiped a tear away too, and Howie ran and hugged Carolee. It was a real fine thing to get picked for Silver Island; he was glad that his sister would get to go, but he would miss her some, too. She looked so pretty in her brand-new dress, just as happy as she could be, and Howie wondered why her hair was all tangled and matted when Mama kept it brushed real good, and then Carolee looked at Howie with pale and empty eyes and tore the nice dress away and Howie saw her belly all swollen up hard, saw her legs cut and scabbed, saw her whole body crusted in filth, and then Carolee screamed and her belly went flat, and something red and ugly dropped down between her legs and began to squirm and cry. . . .

Howie woke up rigid, a hoarse cry stuck in his throat. He felt as if his belly were ripping apart; he jerked up straight and then everything was rushing up his throat and streaming out of his mouth and his nose. He leaned across the bed and watched his supper spew out onto the floor, then fell back and trembled, gasping for air, too weak to move away from the smell. The room was smudged with dawn, the moist air heavy with the promise of heat to come.

The porridge was lumpy and tasteless but he forced a little down, then chewed on a piece of dry toast. Filling up his gut had been a fool thing to do, and when you did something foolish you had to pay.

He tried not to think about the dream. It had been bad this time, real bad. He dreamed about the war now and then, the fighting and the killing, and Colonel Jacob cutting out his eye. But the Carolee dreams were the worst. They stayed on and wouldn't go away.

A few men were up and about, and Howie listened to them talk. Lathan had broken through and was leading a great army to the east. The government had beaten Lathan back in a big fight north of Colorado and the Rebels were on the run. War talk was always like that. You could hear every kind of tale there was, and there was no way to say what was true. Howie even heard both sides were ready to call it quits, that they might start talking peace soon. That was one rumor he didn't believe at all.

The town had looked bad the night before, and it was worse in the full light of day. Tired, and beat flat to the ground, like the people Howie saw on the streets. The man who ran the tavern told Howie it was called Tallahassee, named for a place that had once been farther to the north. Howie was surprised to hear that. It wasn't good luck to use a dead city's name. Maybe the folks here didn't know that, or didn't care.

Walking down the dusty street, he saw farmers gathered in quiet little groups, men with empty pockets and hopeless eyes. They stood before storefronts and taverns and looked at the ground; no one had the coppers to buy what was offered inside. They had nothing else to do except talk about rain and better years. It was easy to spot the men who'd fought in the West. The older men were whole; the young men were frequently missing limbs or bore terrible scars of the war.

More than once, women and young girls showed Howie a weary smile, and he knew they were offering themselves for money or a meal. It was clear they were finding few takers.

At noon, Howie saw a hanging in the square. Word had gotten around somehow, and everyone in town came to watch. The hanging was quick, with no ceremony or fuss. A rope was tossed over a big oak limb and a towheaded boy was led out through the crowd. He seemed no more than seventeen, and showed no expression at all. He simply stood on a box as he was told, and paid no attention to the noose around his neck. One man kicked the box away and that was that. The crowd hung around for a while, then decided there was nothing else to see.

A smith had a shop across the square; Howie wandered over and offered two knives to be sharpened, and asked what the boy had done.

"Beats me," the smith said. "Might've been a Rebel spy. We been gettin' some of those." He gave Howie a narrow look. "Where are *you* from, mister? You don't mind me asking."

Howie forced a smile. "Up north of here a ways. And I ain't a Rebel spy."

"Didn't figure you was." The smith shrugged and pumped his sharpening wheel, sending a shower of sparks from Howie's blade. "Most of them Rebels has got a look. You know? Sorta squinty-eyed. From lookin' in the sun out West, I suppose. You can tell 'em right off."

Howie wondered what a spy could find out in this town, but didn't ask. He gave the man a small copper coin and wandered back in the direction of the tavern. His belly was sending two different messages to his head: Eat, and don't eat anything at all, and Howie knew which one he'd have to heed.

The tavern was full, and Howie recognized faces he had seen the night before—a man with one arm and a yellow beard, the pair of men built thick as oaks who sat alone in the back. It struck Howie then that there was a reason why the tavern's clientele stayed the same. The town was dirt-poor, but there was plenty of food and drink to be had if you could pay. And what kind of man could do that? Men who sold meat, Howie decided, and men who stole what they got from someone else. Like preachers and other damn fools. There sure weren't any farmers or storekeepers here drinking ale and eating meat.

Howie ordered potatoes and bread, promising himself that he wouldn't overdo it this time. The sack of coins he'd taken from the men who'd tried to kill him in the woods was growing light. When that was gone, he would be right back where he'd been. And what then? He wouldn't kill a man to get his purse. He might do a lot of things, but he wouldn't do that.

Ritcher Jones appeared with two mugs of ale, placed one before Howie, and quickly took a seat.

"Well now, I trust you had a fine night," Jones said. He wore a smile wide as a barn, and a clean blue shirt. "A man needs his blessed sleep, and that's the truth. Sleep cures a man's ills and prepares him for the day's work ahead. Rest is precious food and drink for the soul."

Howie looked straight at Jones. "Listen, what the hell do you want with me, mister?"

"What do I want? What do I want with *you?*" Jones spread his hands wide. "Why, not a thing, son. Not a thing except the chance to share drink with a friend."

"I don't recall you and me bein' friends."

"Well, now. That's the truth. It surely is. But you never can tell. That's the thing, you see. You simply never can tell."

Howie didn't touch his ale. It was clear plain talk didn't

bother Jones at all. The man's fine manner and easy ways made it seem as if you'd welcomed him to sit all along, and that irritated Howie no end. He was about to tell Jones to take his drinks and walk away when a crowd burst in through the door.

There were five bearded men, all wearing torn bits of uniform they'd saved from the war. Howie recognized them all from the night before, including the two who had tried to pick a fight. The sixth man was a stranger, and not like the other men at all. Shorter than the rest, he had a nearly square head, and features squeezed tight on his face. He wore a clean pair of butternut pants, a green army shirt with a sea-blue-and-white shoulder patch, and new boots. His hair was combed straight back, and his beard was neatly trimmed.

Several men rose at once to shake the stranger's hand. His friends called for drink, and soon there was a large crowd of admirers gathered about a table in the front.

"Who you reckon that might be?" Howie asked, then remembered that he hadn't asked Ritcher Jones to leave.

Jones raised a brow. "That, I believe, would be the famed Anson Slade. A local hero of sorts." The preacher took a deep healthy swallow from his mug and carefully dabbed the corners of his mouth. "A survivor, it would seem, from that terrible massacre to the south."

Howie looked puzzled. "What massacre is that? There isn't no fighting 'round here, or none I heard about."

Jones hesitated, then seemed to understand. "Ah, of course. I forget you just arrived. It wasn't a *fight,* so to speak. No, sir. Plain slaughter is what it was. And innocent youngsters at that." Jones looked solemnly at his hands. "God rest their souls. Those fine boys and girls all killed or carried off and Silver Island burned to the ground. The whole place just—Good heavens, boy, are you all right?"

Howie couldn't move. He felt as if a big fist had reached in and ripped out his heart.

"What—what happened?" He strangled on the words. "What happened to Silver Island?"

Ritcher Jones gave Howie a curious look. "Why, it's just like I said. It's all gone. The whole thing. Rebels took the place by surprise, though God knows how they got this far east. Here now, you drink some of this ale—"

Howie struck out at the mug, came to his feet and sent the stool clattering across the floor. Ritcher Jones backed off in alarm. Howie couldn't breathe. The room was veiled in red, and he could feel the rage and sorrow welling up inside, hear the curses in his path as he staggered blindly for the door. Something rose up in his path; Howie's fist struck out and found a startled bearded face and he could feel the dark sky, feel the welcome sultry night, feel the cry in his throat and the tears that began to scald his eyes. . . .

CHAPTER THREE

HOWIE FELT AS IF THE NIGHT HAD SURROUNDED HIM with peace, healed him of his sorrows and his fears. There was no more hatred in his heart, no shadow of the raw and terrible anger that had nearly consumed him in the tavern, the fury that had threatened to explode like broken glass in his head. All that was gone, washed and purified in the silence and the dark. Now he didn't feel the rage or the sadness or regret. He didn't feel anything at all. . . .

The spring he was fifteen, he found brand-new thoughts to think about. Things that had seemed important once didn't matter anymore. Sometimes he woke up from dreams he couldn't name, and there were nights when he couldn't sleep at all. The days were as restless as the nights, and sometimes he'd simply have to run, fall to the soft high grass and lie there letting blue sky whirl around him overhead until the storm within him passed.

He drew in a breath and smelled the dust of the earth, smelled the hot salt air from far away. The town was nearly quiet. Men drifted into the streets, talked for a while before the tavern, then went their own ways. A man laughed. A bottle shattered against a wall. Four men came out together, framed for a moment in yellow light. Three stumbled off on their own. The fourth walked away by himself. Howie stayed in shadow across the street. The man headed toward the east end of town. Storefronts soon gave way to a row of small houses set back among the trees. The man turned up a gravel path, humming to himself.

Howie moved swiftly across the street, keeping to the shadow as best he could. When the man reached his door, Howie's arm went tight across his throat. The man jerked violently and tried to cry out, clawing at Howie's hand. Howie let the man see his knife.

"You do that again," Howie whispered, "and you're dead right here. You got that straight?"

The man nodded eagerly, gasping for breath. Howie slid his free hand past the man's waist and pushed the door aside. The house smelled of whiskey and sweat.

"Anyone else live here beside you?"

"No, just me," the man said hoarsely. "God, don't kill me, just don't do that. All right? I—I got money. It's in my coat. Take it, take anything you want!"

Howie loosed his grip slightly, turned the man around and hit him squarely in the jaw. The man's face went slack. Howie lowered him roughly to the floor. He moved quickly through the house. There were only three rooms—a parlor, a small bedroom, and a kitchen. Howie pulled the shades and dragged the man into the bedroom. He pulled a shirt off a chair and made a gag, stuffing the cloth into the man's mouth. In the kitchen, he found a coil of wire, brought it back, and wound it tightly about the man's wrists and his ankles. The man wasn't lying; he had quite a few coins in his coat, more silvers than coppers, and Howie hadn't seen a lot of those. He searched the house and found a rifle in a closet. He couldn't find shells anywhere and left the rifle where it was.

Howie lit a lamp and turned the wick down low and

placed the lamp on the floor. Then he sat down, and waited for the man to come around.

Howie decided that he'd dozed. He knew he'd been gone a long time, and that Papa would wonder where he was. He heard the voices then, and worked his way down past the big oak tree through the grass. There were three men, not many yards away, stock tenders who worked for his father. Three men, and a girl was with them, too, a girl with a— Oh, Lord God, it wasn't a girl at all—it was a mare! A young mare with yellow hair, and the men were—

Howie couldn't breathe. He thought his head would split open. The mare lay in the soft high grass. Her legs were spread wide and she grinned up vacantly at the men. One of the men touched himself and laughed. His big shaft was stiffly erect between his legs. In a moment he was down on the mare, his hands clutching at her breasts. The mare groaned and engulfed him, thrusting her belly up to meet him. Her eyes were closed and her head arched back until the veins stood out in her throat. The man breathed hard, pumping himself into her. His companions watched, laughing and calling out advice.

Howie couldn't hear what they said. He couldn't hear anything at all. His head throbbed as if there were a million angry bees caught up inside.

Help me! he cried out to no one at all. Help me, help me, help me!

The man's face began to move, and Howie jabbed him once in the ribs. The man's eyes went wide; a frightened cry was muffled in the gag.

Howie leaned down close. "You're Anson Slade." It wasn't a question at all.

Slade nodded frantically.

"I'm taking off this gag," Howie said. "You want to yell, why that's up to you. I ain't against bringin' blood."

Howie stripped the gag away. Slade drew in a breath.

"Who the—*hell* are you?" Slade said angrily. "Dammit, I'll have your—"

Howie touched Slade's cheek with his knife. Slade went silent at once.

"What happened at Silver Island?" Howie said. "I want to know about that. I don't want to hear nothing else."

Slade looked surprised. "Everybody knows about that."

"Well, you pretend I ain't heard."

Slade let out a breath. "Them Rebels landed guerrillas somehow. At—at night. It all happened real fast. They killed all the younguns they could catch, and lined up the troopers and shot 'em dead. Wasn't many of us got away. The Rebels took off in the 'glades."

" 'Glades. What's that?"

"Everglades. A big swamp down south. We know they got that far, but there ain't no way to smoke 'em out. Listen, what you want to know all this stuff for? Take whatever you want, I don't care. You want more money I can get it."

"How do I get to Silver Island?"

"Now why would you want to go there? There ain't a damn thing to see, just—" Slade stopped. He stared at the scarred, hollow socket of Howie's eyes. "It's—hell, it's four hundred miles down there or maybe more. Bad country all the way, even if you stay to the coast. You pass right through the 'glades—only Silver Island's farther down than that. There's a whole string of keys and Silver Island's way down on the tip."

Howie frowned. "What's that mean? The tip of what?"

"The keys. They're a bunch of little islands." Slade wet his lips. "Used to be a kinda bridge road, but that's a long time ago. Storms maybe took it all out. You got to have a boat."

Howie thought about that. He stood and went back to the kitchen, recalling where he'd seen a scrap of paper, a pen, and some ink. He came back and loosened the wires from Slade's wrists and laid the paper and the pen on his lap.

"I need a map," Howie said. "You draw me a map."

Slade rubbed his wrists and tried to grin. "I'm not any good at drawin' maps."

"Mister, I'd sure try if I was you."

Slade muttered under his breath, then picked up the pen and began to draw. Howie asked questions: Where did this path go, and where did the swamps begin and end. Slade could be making the whole thing up, Howie knew, but he couldn't do much about that. When Slade said that was all there was, Howie wired him up again and stuffed the gag back in his mouth.

Slade looked relieved. The lines relaxed around his eyes. Howie grabbed the front of Slade's shirt and slammed him hard against the floor. Slade groaned and tried to fight. He seemed to sense that he was wrong, that the man with one eye wasn't through. When Howie sat down on his chest, all the color drained from Slade's face.

"I want you to hear all this," Howie said calmly. "I want you to know. And I want you to think about it, too. There isn't no Rebels down there, or even anywhere near. The gov'ment itself done the killing. You know that the same as me. I don't know why, and it doesn't much matter anymore. 'Cept you was right there, and now you're right here."

Howie looked at Slade a long time. "Mister, I know what Silver Island was for. I know what you was doin' down there. Now this is what I want you to hear. One of those girls was my sister. Her name was Carolee. You think about her. Carolee Ryder. You just keep thinkin' on her."

Howie leaned down and picked up Slade and carried him over his shoulder. The kitchen had a small back door, and a path outside led directly into deep stands of oak. Even with the gag thrust deeply in Anson Slade's mouth, Howie could hear him screaming inside all the way into the woods. . . .

The three men hung from a high branch, their faces nearly black and their tongues thick and swollen.

"We had to butcher the mare," Papa said.

"Sir?"

Papa nodded to himself, and scratched at a stone with his boot. "Howie," he said carefully, "she might have had seed."

Howie was startled at that. A man was a man, but his seed in an animal . . .

"You're wrong," Papa said, guessing Howie's thoughts. "The thing is, boy, that's something where people and stock is alike. Seed don't know whether it's goin' into man or beast. What you got to see, Howie, is there's no sin greater than the one you seen them men do. A man's got a soul, and when he puts his seed into stock, it's the same as giving part of his soul to a beast. Do you see that, Howie?"

"Papa, I—" Howie's voice choked in his throat. "Papa, the mare didn't look like a mare. Not then. When—when they were doing what they did. She looked like a—girl. Oh, God, Papa, I wanted to do that to her too!"

"Howie . . ." Papa's big hand covered his shoulder. "Howie, men are weak, and they'll get such thoughts in their heads. Things can kinda look the same when they ain't, and you got to understand that's so. She wasn't the same, boy. You remember that. She was meat, and meat hasn't got any soul. . . ."

When Howie was through, he found a shallow depression in the woods where a creek had come by some time in the past, then dried up and gone another way. He rolled Slade in and spent a good long hour kicking at the bank with his heels, loosing chunks of dirt, then tossing in leaves and dead wood after that. It was too dark to do the job right, but he figured it was good enough to pass, even in the full light of day, unless someone started looking close. He brushed more leaves around the place where he'd worked and dropped the knife in a hollow tree and started back, taking the long way back to town. In his room he lit a lamp and stripped down, carefully going over all his clothes to make sure they weren't soiled. He went to sleep at once. In the morning he ate a loaf of fresh-baked bread and thick porridge with honey on the top, and paid his bill for the room. The day was sullen hot and the sky was bright as lead, but there was nothing real new about that. Howie left town and started walking south.

CHAPTER FOUR

THERE WERE FEW SETTLEMENTS ALONG THE WAY, AND none of them overly friendly. Howie quickly learned to pass them by. When he could, he followed the Gulf, keeping to the beach, where it was easiest to walk. Half the time, this wasn't possible to do; sometimes the beach disappeared under the dense tropical growth that pushed right up to the sea. Then he was forced to move inland, following the ruins of ancient roads that had all but vanished under a choking carpet of green.

Slade's map was true as far as it went, but Howie found it wasn't much help. On paper, the western Florida coast curved gently southeast in an unbroken line. In fact, that line was notched by countless small inlets and several enormous bays. More than once, Howie found himself at the end of some long finger of land, with nothing but water ahead. Then he would have to backtrack, following the long miles he had already covered.

Ruins of old cities clustered about the larger bays, awesome, crumbled towers of stone and rusted steel, strangled under greenery that softened the horror of what had happened to the world long ago.

There were plenty of animals about—snicks and rabuts everywhere, and birds of every kind, and now and then creatures with things like branches on their heads. In the swamp, he saw terrible animals that looked like rotten logs, monsters with great jaws and sharp teeth. Howie decided animal life had never really disappeared down here, as it had in the rest of the country. It had simply retreated to a place where no one cared to go. Plenty of bugs had decided to live here too, he thought dismally. There was certainly no lack of mosquitoes, and every other insect he saw had a sting.

The 'glades were the worst. There was simply no way to get through. Howie finally walked back to a settlement he had bypassed three days before. When night came he stole a small boat. The boat had oars and a sail. He tried the sail the first day and gave it up, after nearly capsizing in the sea. After that, he simply kept to the edge of the swamp, and followed the coast south.

Finally, his southeastern path gave way, and Howie knew he had reached the tip of this long stretch of land. Now the sea was due east, peppered with dozens of small islands. The fourth day he followed this course, he found the narrow strip of rock and sand curling back southwest and out of sight, and knew this had to be the "keys" Slade had drawn on his map. He turned and rowed in this direction at once. Now and then he saw traces of the bridge-road Slade had talked about. There was not enough left of it to count, and Howie kept to his boat. Sometimes there were places where he could go ashore for the night. The keys were an empty place to be, nothing but the water and the sand. Howie didn't care about that. He scarcely noticed anything at all.

Six days after he reached the keys, Howie found Silver Island. He had tried to keep count in his head. As near as he could tell, it was forty-nine days since he'd killed Anson Slade and left the place called Tallahassee.

The Bluevale Fair was a wondrous thing to see. The town square was lit bright as day, more lanterns than you could count, all strung out on wires across the street. Blues and reds and yellows and greens, every color you could name.

"Couldn't we stop? Just a minute? Just one minute, Papa?" Howie begged.

Papa grinned and winked at Howie's mother. Carolee was asleep in her arms. "You'll get plenty of fair come morning," Papa said. "Does sound like they're having fun, now don't it?"

Howie scarcely slept. And Papa was right. The fair was even finer than he'd dreamed. There were booths and stands everywhere. They sold metal knives and bright clay dishes, glass buttons and bolts of patterned cloth. And the smells! There were things

Howie had never smelled before. Pepper and cinnamon, tarragon and sage. There were fruit pies and red candied apples and cakes with white sugar on top. There were the Gardens, where you ate without cooking yourself. People just brought things to you, whatever you wanted to have. And at the end of the day there was the parade, with government soldiers and real horses, the first horses Howie had ever seen. Papa promised later on they'd see the pictures of Silver Island pasted up by the courthouse. You might even recognize someone who'd gone there, a boy or a girl you knew. Kids from everywhere were Chosen all the time, and it might be someone from Bluevale, or a farm right next to your own.

Everyone said Silver Island was a lot like heaven. Nobody knew what heaven looked like unless he'd died, but Howie couldn't see how God could come up with anything much better. Papa had seen the pictures before, and said they were something fine to see. There were big white houses under great broad trees. Every window had glass and fine curtains, and the grass came right down to bright blue water. Sails colored bright cherry red dotted the bay. And the best thing of all was you didn't have to worry about a thing. There was plenty to eat and you never got cold. Children who got picked for Silver Island were the luckiest children in the country, Papa said, because they were the start of a brand-new America, the way the whole country would be someday.

"Everybody can't go," Papa said, "and that's a shame. But that's what Silver Island's for, to make a start. To get things going right again. . . ."

The fire had burned everything right to the ground. Still, Howie could tell where things had been and imagine how it was. He followed the squares of rubble and saw how they had laid the buildings out. It wasn't hard to figure. Anywhere you put it, a stock operation was the same, on the banks of a river or here on a white spit of land. And that's what it was, Howie knew. It was the government's big lie, and hadn't ever been anything else. He saw where the breeding pens had been and where the mares raised their young. Burned stubs in the ground, in a place set off from the rest, told Howie there had been a high fence. They'd likely kept the young bucks there. There was a dock, still pretty much intact, a landing big enough for barges where stock could be loaded and taken back to the mainland. On the far end of the island he found the remains of the buildings where the government troopers and officials had stayed. Anson Slade had lived here, and come back a hero of Silver Island.

There were bones everywhere, picked clean by the birds. Bits of crockery and tools. A rusted pistol and a lantern on a pole. Broken glass. Howie bent down and picked up a piece of faded calico. He looked at it, held it in his hand a long time, then gently put it down, as if it might still harbor some shadow of the life it had touched. He looked at the flat desolation, at the white coral ground so bright it hurt his eye. He tried to feel something inside. Sorrow, or hatred or regret. But there was nothing there at all, and he turned and walked back to the beach to find his boat.

When Howie reached the mainland again, he dragged the boat onto dry land and slept for two days. A strong wind came in from offshore and kept the mosquitoes away. The old road that had linked the keys to the land was still partially visible ashore. A road sign, nearly rusted through and fragile as a leaf, said "1." He followed the road a few miles until it disappeared again, then set up a camp. There were hammocks of dry land in the swamp. He walked as far as he could through tangled growth, then tore a piece of cloth from his shirt and stuck it on a tree. He pinned the shoulder patch he'd taken from Anson Slade on the cloth. Then he gathered all the dry wood he could find and walked back to the old road. When night came he built a large fire, and kept it going till the dawn. He caught fish during the day and found some eggs in a nest and ate those. He kept the fire going every night. Four days later they came, creeping up on the camp just before first light.

Howie knew they were there. He was certain that they'd watched him since at least the second night. They stepped out from cover, five of them, four young men and a girl. Howie didn't move.

"You ain't asleep, I know that," the boy said. "Just sit up slow and keep your hands up high."

Howie did as he was told. The tallest boy there had the rifle. The others had longbows, aimed at Howie's heart. The girl came in from behind and pressed her hands quickly down his chest and his sides and down the legs of his trousers.

"Glory be, Jack," she called out, "he's got a pistol. Looks to work good, too. Couple of blades and some money. That's it."

The girl stepped away. She knew what to do, and never let herself get close enough to grab. Howie thought she was pretty.

The tall boy's eyes never wavered. The rifle was steady in his hands.

"What you want here?" he asked Howie. "Who are you?"

"I'm alone. You already know that," Howie said. "You've had time to look around and see there isn't anyone else. You found the patch. It came off a man named Anson Slade. He worked at Silver Island. I killed him up north. A place called Tallahassee."

The tall boy's expression didn't change. "Mister, who you been killin' don't mean a thing to me. You haven't said why you're here."

"They took my sister to Silver Island," Howie said. "I know what they did down there. I reckon you know, too. You want to shoot that thing, go ahead. I'm tired of standing out in the sun."

"I reckon I can fix that," the boy said.

"Jack—" The girl touched the boy's shoulder and looked at Howie. "Listen, what's your sister's name?"

"Shut up, Janie," the boy said.

"Carolee. Carolee Ryder. She was nine when they took her. She'd be about fifteen now."

Howie saw something in the girl's eyes—scarcely anything at all, but enough. She didn't look at the boy, but he lowered the rifle, maybe half an inch.

"Let's move," the boy said flatly, "I don't like stayin' 'round here."

* * *

The camp was three hours into the 'glades. Howie tried to remember how they'd come, but he was lost after the first quarter mile. The morning had started out hot and sultry. By noon, the air was a nearly visible pall, a veil of green. The woods were thick with tupelo and water oak, great cypress trees that perched on tangled roots in black water. The camp was on a dry hammock of land. Hanging moss bearded thick and ancient trees, whose branches bent nearly to the ground. There were nearly thirty people in the camp, children, most of them from twelve to fourteen, a few younger than that. Only the tall boy and the girl were older; around eighteen, Howie guessed, near his own age. When he looked at the young ones he wanted to cry. They were children, but none of them had children's eyes.

Howie searched their faces quickly. He knew Carolee wasn't there. He had known that right from the start.

The children looked fearfully at Howie, keeping their distance, yet curious as to who he might be. Jack spoke to them firmly and told them to keep away. He left Howie completely alone; he hadn't spoken since they'd left the old road.

"Don't pay him no mind," Janie said. "That's just Jack's way." She sat with Howie by the water near the edge of the camp. Howie wolfed down a bowl of soup that smelled strongly of wild onions, and ate some fried fish. The fish had a slightly muddy taste, but Howie didn't mind.

"He don't care for people," Janie said. " 'Cept for us. He's got good reason to watch for anyone that don't belong."

"I guess he does," Howie said. He liked to watch the girl, liked to have her close by. She was nearly as tall as he was, but thin as a rail, like everyone else in the camp. He liked her dark hair and the way the sharp bones in her cheeks drew the flesh across her face. Her eyes were dark, vibrant and intent, as if fear couldn't touch her at all. Howie guessed there was very little left that could frighten this girl, after what she must have seen.

"None of us would be here now," Janie said, "if it hadn't been for Jack." She looked past Howie, her thoughts somewhere beyond the still dark waters of the 'glades. "It was him got us out. All the little ones was cryin' and plain scared to death. Everyone was dying all around, and Jack got together as many as he could and led us out. It all happened so fast there wasn't many had a chance. The troopers just come out fast one night and started killing. People, stock, it didn't make no difference. We was all the same to them. They used guns for a while, walking in a line and just shooting, backin' everyone up till there wasn't no place left to go. Then they came in with clubs and finished anyone off that looked alive. I saw some of the troopers up close. They was the worst kind of men or they wouldn't have been there. But a couple of 'em was crying, I know that. They couldn't take what they was havin' to do.

"Jack got a bunch of us out through a hole in the fence. He'd been working some time on that hole; it was right near the end of the shed where they kept all the younguns. The guards was too busy killin' to see. Jack got us all in some boats. I think there was five, maybe six boats. Only two of 'em made it up here. The boats wasn't much good. I reckon the rest of them sank, or maybe got lost out to sea. I don't know. We never saw no one else."

Janie hesitated, then looked curiously at Howie. "You figured if anyone was still alive he'd be here. That this is where we'd have to come, the closest place to hide."

Howie nodded. He told her what people were saying, that the Rebels had somehow got over east and done the killing at Silver Island, that some of them were hiding in the swamps.

"There's something else, too," Howie said. "Something you ought to know. I saw eight of your folks, down in Mexico. I don't know how they got that far, but they did. They was wandering around, and a black man was keeping them fed. Hell, I thought they was stock. Only, one of 'em could talk. Not real good, but he could talk. They hadn't cut his tongue right."

"My Lord!" Janie's eyes were bright with hope. "Did they give you any names? Did they tell you who they were?"

"No, but they was from Silver Island, all right." Howie looked at his hands. "The one who talked—he'd known Carolee. He said that. He told me—what it was the government did. That Silver Island wasn't what folks thought it was at all. That it wasn't any *new* America they was making; they were doing something awful down there—''

Janie shook her head quickly, cutting Howie off. She closed her eyes an instant, then the moment passed. She reached out and touched Howie's hand.

''Howie, listen,'' she said gently. ''Maybe you don't want to know this at all. You haven't asked, and maybe that's why. But I guess I got to say it. I knew her. I think you figured that. Carolee was like me and Jack. She was good with the younguns. If you was useful that way, they didn't cut your tongue.'' Janie paused. ''Don't go on lookin' for her, Howie. She— I saw her. Back there when it happened. She didn't get away, and you got to stop thinking that she did. That isn't goin' to stop the hurt. Nothing's goin' to do that. You can't bring her back, and that's what you got to know. Just hold on to what you've got and keep thinking how she was before. That's all you can do.'' She looked toward the camp. ''That's all anyone can do.''

Howie couldn't look in her eyes. He felt her hand go away. He felt something die inside, and he knew it was something that he couldn't get back; that it was gone and Carolee was gone too. He felt a sudden, strange sense of relief. Janie had released him from a burden he had carried too long. Only now he didn't want to let it go. It was gone, and there was nothing else there. He was alive; his breathing and his heart hadn't stopped. He wondered why his body couldn't figure what his head already knew. That there was nothing else to do. No place else to go.

Jack came to him in the morning. He had a clay bottle of water and some food, Howie's pistol and his knives, and the handful of coins Janie had taken from him the day before.

''I'm letting you go,'' Jack said. ''That's what Janie says we ought to do. Get yourself some breakfast. There's an easy way out up north. 'Gator Alley. Don't anyone know it's still there. It'll take you due west out of the 'glades. I'll go with you partway. Listen, you don't ever want to come back here. I don't want you doin' that."

"All right," Howie said.

"Is that true what you said? You really kill Anson Slade?"

"It's true."

"That's good." Jack nodded and kicked at the ground. "That's real good." He turned and walked away through low-hanging moss.

"Why'd they do it?" Howie said. "Why'd they go and murder everyone like that? They must've had a reason why. You don't go and do a thing like that, you haven't got a reason why."

Jack didn't answer. Howie didn't know if he heard or not. Howie turned at a soft explosion of sound, a muffled noise in the trees. Birds white as bone rose up into the air.

CHAPTER FIVE

HE GAVE TALLAHASSEE A WIDE BERTH, WALKING WEST and keeping to the coast. There were fine dark forests that came down nearly to the sea, tall pines that filled the air with sweet and pungent smells. As soon as he saw the woods he started north, glad to get away from the water for a while. The sun had baked him dry and he felt as if his teeth were grinding sand. The forest was thick with ferny growth, and the tiny leaves brushed him with water as he passed. The woods reminded him of the place just behind Papa's farm, near the wheat fields past the barn. The growth here was somewhat different, but the feeling was the same. He found familiar plants that he knew were good to eat; toward evening, he discovered a patch of blackberries the birds had miraculously left alone. The ferns hid a small stream, and he stopped near there for the night. He thought about the girl named Janie. She stirred up feelings he hadn't felt in some time, and when he slept he didn't dream.

He studied the river, looking for the places where shallows might let him get across standing up. Earlier he had caught the faint smell of someone's breakfast fire; there was no way to tell how close it might be because the wind was running strong. It might not be near at all, but Howie didn't want to chance that. There wasn't anyone he cared to see.

The river was nearly fifty yards wide. That meant a great deal of time in the open. The best thing to do was get across real fast, back to good cover in the thick stand of trees on the other side. A man wading shallow could maybe fight back; a man up to his neck was as easy to hit as a turtle on a log.

Howie sat in the brush a long time, listening and watching the river. He watched the crows in a tall tree thirty yards away to his right. The crows seemed content. Crows liked to squawk and raise hell if there was anything around. Howie sat still for a while, then walked out in the sun to the water.

The first shot took off his hat. He was halfway across. The second shot came on the echo of the first and went wild. Howie didn't wait around for the third. He thought about the smoke and how it must've been closer than he thought and how careless was the next thing to dead. He thought about the goddam crows, and how they'd let him down.

He ran as erratically as he could, churning up water and slipping into holes. The men were on the far bank, and that was bad. The only good thing was they'd been careless too. They were still up the river a ways, and they had started firing much too soon. If they had sneaked on down through the trees where he had to come out of the river, they could have walked up and shot him in the ear.

Howie made the shore and started scrambling up the rocky bank, slipped and felt the sharp stone rip down the side of his leg. He cursed aloud and bit back the pain. A shot plowed into the earth half a foot from his head. Howie dropped back. There was no use trying to climb the bank. He'd have to stay and fight them right there and that was no good at all. They could come from two ways and he wouldn't know where they'd appear.

Two rapid shots rang overhead and plunked into the river. One of the bastards had a rifle. The sharp, clean sound bounced back and forth across the water.

One of the men yelled to the other. Howie crawled low beneath the cover of the bank, trying not to think about his leg. Worse than that, something was wrong with his foot. It burned like he'd stepped in a fire. There was no time to look. The bank had caved in just ahead, leaving a tumble of dirt and rock. Howie felt a surge of relief. If he could climb up that, he could shoot from good cover. If they were both still close together—

Howie cried out as his foot gave way. He reached up desperately and grabbed for the top of the bank. One of the men shouted and fired wildly at his hand. Howie held on and peeked over the top. Hair crawled the back of his neck. God A'mighty, they weren't ten yards away! He snapped off two quick shots. The man on the right hesitated, slapped at his arm as if a bee had climbed his sleeve, then loosed a shot in Howie's direction. Howie ducked, shifted his aim quickly at the other man, squeezed the trigger too fast and knew at once he hadn't hit a thing. He fired again. The pistol gave a hollow click, the worst sound he'd ever heard.

The man with the rifle laughed. He looked right at Howie, as if he'd never seen anything funnier in his life. A blue hole appeared between his eyes. He sank to his knees, taking plenty of time, taking the laugh with him to the ground. The second man seemed amazed. He looked past Howie at something else. This time Howie heard the shot. The man's right eye disappeared; he turned around twice, looking for somewhere to go.

Howie turned and saw the preacher on a horse. He was sitting in the cover of the trees, forty yards to Howie's back. He grinned at Howie and waved. He held a bright silver pistol in his hand, the barrel fully twelve inches long. Howie could scarcely believe this was happening at all. He'd never seen a preacher with a gun; he had sure never seen one who could shoot like that. It didn't seem right. At least he had an answer as to why someone hadn't cut Jones's throat. You'd have to get past that gun, and it clearly wasn't easy to do.

Ritcher Jones kicked his mount and started toward Howie. He looked like a man on a Sunday-morning ride—a fine straw hat with a red feather stuck in the brim, boots polished up and a crease in his pants, a new white shirt with white ruffles on the sleeves.

Jones tipped his hat and looked solemnly at Howie. "It appears to me you've been having a troublesome morning, son. Troublesome, indeed. You give any thought to what I said, how a man ought to find proper food for the soul? That's mighty sound advice, I'll tell you true."

"I'm sure obliged for the help," Howie said. It didn't seem like the time for a sermon, but maybe preachers went on like that all the time. He walked over and took a look at the dead men, favoring his bad foot. Even from a distance, with no time to stop and study features, Howie had felt he knew the pair. The man with the hole between his eyes had tried to push him into a fight, his first night in Tallahassee. He didn't know his name, and couldn't remember what the fellow had called his friend.

"If a man bears hatred in his heart," Jones said behind him, "so shall that hatred turn and quickly smite him down. Vengeance is the Lord's, and this is as fine an example as you'll see."

Jones squatted down and studied the man with the ruined eye. "I surely didn't mean to do that." He shook his head and frowned. "Low, and a half inch off to the right. I abhor the sin of pride, but a man likes to do a thing right, even if it's something he didn't want to have to do. You better sit, boy. I'll see these sinners off, then take a good look at your foot."

Ritcher Jones grabbed the first man's legs and dragged him down the bank, then out into the shallows. Then he went back and got the other. The slow current caught the two bodies and drew them toward the center of the river.

Jones watched them go, then closed his eyes and clasped his hands. "Lord, have mercy on these thy children, for it's clear they were ignorant of your ways. Forgive me if you will, as I don't see burial as prudent at the time. Gunfire tends to draw a crowd, and there might be other unbelievers near about. I sure don't want more violence to mar this lovely day which thou has fashioned for our benefit and joy. Amen."

The preacher stepped gingerly back to shore, then drew a large kerchief from his pocket and carefully wiped his boots. He picked up the weapons the men had left behind and carried them to his horse.

"Get up in that saddle if you can," he told Howie. "We'll go a little ways in the woods. It's feeling mighty open out here."

Howie started to protest, but he could feel something wet inside his boot; he wouldn't get far unless he patched himself up, and there wasn't any reason not to ride. Besides, arguing with Jones was a good way to tire yourself out, even if you weren't flat worn down to start.

The foot wasn't bad. A bullet had gone through the boot and gouged some flesh from Howie's heel, but there was more blood than anything else. Howie limped down to a creek that fed the river and eased down on the moss-covered bank. He cleaned the wound and the scrape on his leg, then washed all the blood from his boot. Jones had a strip of clean cloth in his pack, and Howie used it to bind his foot tight. Then he leaned back and watched Ritcher Jones prepare lunch.

It was an awesome thing to see. Jones had more in his pack than a good-sized tavern might supply—and better than you'd likely get, too. There were jars full of powders and spices, peppers and pickled fruits. Things in paper packets Howie couldn't identify. Jones found some strips of fish that looked dried and shriveled-up. Then he dropped them in a skillet of hot oil, sprinkled peppers and odd powders all about; the withered strips began to swell up fine, releasing an aroma that made Howie want to cry. From somewhere in the miraculous pack, Jones found a loaf of bread that resembled a club. There were tin plates and cups, knives and even forks. Wine in a pretty green bottle with a cork. Howie tasted some, and thought it left his mouth dry. Jones smiled when he told him that.

"Now that's what a good wine's supposed to do," Jones said.

When the meal was all over, Jones washed everything clean, then put his goods back where they belonged. There were soft leather pockets in his pack, each one the shape of a certain jar or sack, an eating utensil or a plate. Once Howie saw how it was done, it was easy to see how so much could emerge from an ordinary pack. Still, Howie shook his head in wonder. There were tastes in his mouth he'd never thought about before. He had never eaten finer in his life—and here they were out in the middle of the woods. Ritcher Jones clearly wasn't a man to let the famine and hardship of the land get in his way. He had fine clothes and food, a good weapon and a horse. The horse—now that was something Howie found hard to believe. He hadn't even *seen* a horse since he'd left the war in the West. Jones hadn't kept the mount close to Tallahassee, Howie was certain of that. He'd stashed it out of town somewhere for sure. The preacher might be good with a gun, but they'd have killed him real quick if they knew he had a horse.

Howie watched as Jones cleaned his weapon, wiping it with oil and running patches down the overlong barrel. Light filtered through the trees and made a hundred tiny suns on the bright silver surface. The grips were something white like bone, and there were squiggly lines etched into the metal.

Jones caught Howie's eyes and grinned. "You like that, do you? Here, see how she feels."

Howie was astonished. Pleased that he could hold such a weapon in his hand, and surprised that Ritcher Jones would let him do it. Even if a weapon wasn't loaded, you didn't hand it over to a man you hardly knew. Not if you had good sense.

"I never seen anything like it," Howie said, hefting the gun in his hand. In spite of the length of the barrel, the weight was centered firmly in his palm, the way it ought to be.

"It looks to be brand-new," Howie said. "It sure ain't from long ago. Not still lookin' like this."

"It's new, all right," Jones said. "Your standard .45 caliber revolver, but it's stronger and lighter than the poor weapons folks are making now. And maybe better than the ones from ancient times."

The gun was fine-looking, but Howie doubted that. "You mind me asking where you get a gun like this? If you don't want to say . . ."

"California," Jones said. He showed Howie a broad grin. "And I don't mind saying, because it's my Order makes 'em, and I'm proud to tell you that."

Jones caught Howie's look. "I can tell what you're thinking. That men of God don't have any business making instruments of death. Some might see it that way, folks that won't think a thing through. A rock or a branch off a tree can kill a man as well as a gun, and those are God's creations, not the devil's. A man with a weapon might do foul murder, or defend his wife and child—it's his heart tells him which he's going to do. The heart and the mind perform good or evil deeds, not the weapon you hold in your hand."

"Yes, sir. I guess so," Howie said. If you asked Jones which way was east, Howie thought, you'd likely get some preaching in return. He studied the etched design on the gun. There were oak leaves and acorns, and even flying birds. Just above the grip, he found a picture different from the rest, a thick-boled tree, its roots growing out of a stylized heart.

"Does this mean something?" Howie asked, pointing at the curious design.

"Why, it surely does," Jones said. He took the pistol from Howie. "That's the symbol of our Order and what it is. The Tree of Life ascends straight up from the heart of Man, where God Himself dwells. And that, son, is the meaning of life itself; the whole story's right there. At High Sequoia there's a verse we like to quote that makes it clear. 'If a man's heart is—' " Jones stopped, and looked at Howie with concern. "Something troubling you? The color's plain gone from your face."

"Nothing," Howie said. He tried to look somewhere else. "I—guess my foot's actin' up."

"No, sir. That's not it at all." The preacher leaned in close, and squeezed one eye nearly shut. "I don't think I've got to ask. I figure I can tell you what it is. You're thinking that you've heard some bad things about this High Sequoia place. That's it for sure. I've seen that look of yours once or twice before."

Howie looked at his hands. "I guess I might've heard a couple of things."

"You know anybody who's ever *been* to High Sequoia?"

"No," Howie lied. "I just heard, that's all."

Ritcher Jones straightened up with a sigh. "Well, you heard right, then. And likely all you heard was true."

Howie looked surprised.

"*Was,*" Jones said, and held up a finger to make his point. "Satan prevailed at High Sequoia, that's a fact. It wasn't a Holy Order then at all. Far from it, I'd say. It was a place where evil men of all sorts practiced thievery and lust. A den of larceny and greed. That was all before Lawrence came along."

"Who's that?"

Jones smiled and half closed his eyes, as if his thoughts were off somewhere else. "Lawrence is Lawrence," he said.

Howie frowned. "That don't say a whole lot."

"Son, I don't mean to hide my words behind mystery and that kind of thing, the way some of your religions are wont to do. But there's nothing I can say to help you see. Lawrence is Lawrence, and High Sequoia's where God-fearing people work to see peace restored to this sorely troubled country of ours. Brothers and Sisters who follow the Light."

Jones tapped the long-barreled gun. "It isn't this weapon keeps me safe in this wilderness of sin. Yes, sir, I know you've been thinking on that. It's the Light that watches over Ritcher Jones. The same Light that watches over you."

Jones laid the weapon on his pack. "If you don't mind, boy, I'm accustomed to taking a little rest at this time. You might do the same. Sleep heals a man's wounds and mends his troubled soul." He smiled and gave Howie a wink. "I reckon you've heard me say *that* before."

Ritcher Jones turned over and settled into the grass. In a moment, Howie knew he was asleep. He kept looking at the preacher's sleeping form, at the bright silver gun. Lord God, Jones bringing up High Sequoia had taken him by surprise. A man would be a fool if he didn't see that, and whatever Jones was, he sure wasn't any fool.

High Sequoia . . . The name brought a vivid, painful picture to Howie's mind. Kari Ann, tall and lean as a sapling, skin fine as silk, and perfect little breasts tipped with amber. He could see her sitting right there now, cross-legged on his bed, filing a piece of metal, working in quick short strokes. The prettiest girl he'd ever seen, and she likely knew more about guns than anyone alive. She could take a weapon apart, fix it, and put it back together again. Why, she might've made the weapon he was looking at now.

Howie realized he'd been holding his breath and let it out. Just thinking about Kari did that. He had ached so much to have her he'd wanted to die, but there wasn't a man alive could touch Kari. Something had happened—and whatever that was, it had happened at High Sequoia. That's where Kari had been before he knew her. They had taken something away from Kari there, something that left her cold and empty inside. She was everything a man could dream about, but dreaming was all you'd ever do.

Howie looked at Ritcher Jones again. The man had to be a preacher like he said. Nobody else would leave a gun and a horse and a pack of good food out loose and go to sleep. Howie leaned back and looked at the sky through the trees. Whoever this Lawrence fellow was, he must've worked a fair-sized miracle out West. High Sequoia sure didn't sound like the place Kari was. Not anything like it at all.

CHAPTER SIX

HOWIE TRIED TO FOLLOW JONES'S ADVICE, BUT SLEEP wouldn't come. His foot was aching bad, and there was too much going through his head. Kari was part of that; his memories of her now were both as vivid and as elusive as Kari herself. It pained him to remember how she was, to think of her at all, yet she wouldn't go away. She was there, all mixed up with things he liked to recall, and a lot more he'd just as soon forget.

There were sounds in the forest, but nothing that didn't belong. Birds flew overhead now and then, and a light swept through the trees. Still, Howie found it hard to rest easy. Shots brought trouble; as sure as something dead brought buzzards to the scene, men would come too if they heard. Someone had to win every fight, and someone else had to lose. There might be good pickings left, you couldn't tell—a hat or a fine pair of boots. Or if a man was quiet and smart, he might trail the winner and take away his prize.

None of this seemed to bother Ritcher Jones, but Howie couldn't get it off his mind. They'd left the river far behind, but that wouldn't stop a good tracker—not if he knew there was a horse up ahead. A man would follow *that* trail till hell froze over.

Ritcher Jones woke, sat up and scratched. "Well now, that was a fine nap indeed," he told Howie. "It's God Himself grants a man rest, and watches over him while he sleeps. That's a fact."

"I reckon so," Howie muttered to himself.

Damn, the man was a pure aggravation! Howie was worn to a nub, and Jones looked fresh as new grass. Howie couldn't say how God had been spending the afternoon, but *he'd* been awake keeping watch, for sure. Jones hadn't bothered to mention that.

The preacher stood and ran his hands through his thinning hair, squinted at the woods as if he weren't sure they'd been there before, then bent down again and started gathering up his things.

"Still some good afternoon light," Jones said, folding up his pack. "Time to make a few miles before dark." He turned and looked at Howie. "Which way you headed, son?"

"Uh, north," Howie said, the first direction that came into his head. "I got a bunch of things to do." He hadn't thought about where he'd go next, or what exactly lay ahead. All he was doing was going away from where he'd been.

"I sure wish you well," Jones said. "I'll pray that you walk in the Light." Something seemed to occur to the preacher, and he laughed. "We've known each other for a spell and I never got your name." He stuck his hand out to Howie. "I clean forgot to ask."

"Cory," Howie said, remembering the name of a friend who was dead.

"Well then, Cory," Jones grasped Howie's hand. "We didn't get to know each other well, but I figure men who've fought Satan's minions and shared a meal, why that's a good enough start to being friends."

"I guess it is," Howie said, and had to smile. "I'm sure grateful for what you done."

"No, no, just glad the Lord put me there to help."

"You going west or what?"

"California," Jones said. "I've been gone too long from the promised land. It'll be a pure blessing to return."

Howie thought about that. He had driven a meat herd west, and fought clear up against the high Rockies. That was one hell of a trek, but it still wasn't as far as California.

"You got some ride ahead," Howie said. "Even on a horse it's goin' to take you quite a spell."

The preacher looked puzzled, then laughed aloud. "Oh dear no, may the Lord spare me that. It's a boat for me, Cory. I do *not* intend to sit this beast through the heat and awful dangers of the West."

"You going on a *boat?*" Howie tried not to show his surprise.

"Out of Alabama Port," Jones said. "About—what? A hundred and fifty miles straight west. Got boats leaving all the time."

"Won't that take a while?"

"For certain it will. But it beats horseback, I'll say that. Ever been to Alabama Port, Cory?"

"I guess not."

"It is something to see. It surely is." Jones frowned and shook his head. "Sin's on a rampage there, that's a fact. They could use about two hundred preachers, and I doubt they got three."

As far as Howie was concerned, the whole thing didn't make a lot of sense. Geography was somewhat muddled in his head, but he recalled Mexico and a lot more than that was in the way. He thought about the boat he had rowed along the swampy coast and to the keys, and tried to picture Jones doing that all the way to California.

Howie followed Jones into the woods, helping carry all his packs. The trees marched down a steep slope, and the horse was there peacefully chewing grass.

Howie had kept the thought at the edge of his mind. It had been there since the two men had attacked him on the river, since Jones had showed up to save his hide. He was thankful for what Jones had done. It was clear the man meant him no harm—hell, he had saved his life, then fed him a fine meal, and you couldn't ask a lot more than that. Still, the thought prayed on his mind, and even if Jones didn't like it, Howie had to ask.

"I got to say this," he said, before he could change his mind. "Maybe you'll figure that I ain't got the right. But I got to know, mister. You showing up like that, I mean—them fellows ridin' down on me by the river, and you there right on hand to help . . ." Howie felt his face color. Jones sat his horse, and his expression didn't change. "Damn it all, it's a peculiar thing to happen. You got to say it is."

For a moment, the preacher's eyes clouded. Then the slight touch of anger Howie saw turned to sorrow and regret.

"Son, have I transgressed upon you in any way? Have I now? Answer me that."

"No, sir, you sure haven't. I just—"

Jones held up a hand. "Walk along with me a ways," he said gently, and slowly turned his mount down the draw.

Howie followed, more puzzled than ever now. The preacher hadn't answered his question, but he had managed to make Howie feel ashamed. He figured he was in for a sermon. If he was, why he'd just have to sit still and listen. There wasn't any way he could—

Howie stared. The trees ahead thinned, and opened

into a small clearing. There was a high stand of grass and a patch of bright sun—and there were three more horses, beautiful mounts with strong backs and shiny flanks.

"God A'mighty!" Howie said aloud. He gazed at the fine beasts in wonder, then looked up at Jones.

"You never asked why those other two were there," the preacher said solemnly. "Appears that you wondered about *me* and not them." He nodded toward the mounts. "That's what they were after, Cory. They weren't looking for you. You just happened along and got in the way. That pair tailed me all the way from Tallahassee. 'Course, we were all on foot at the time. I knew they were there but I couldn't shake 'em off. So I kept cutting back, trying to lose them before I picked up the mounts where I'd hid them." Jones showed Howie a weary smile. "I know once they saw what I had, they'd track me till I had to smite 'em down. I surely didn't want to do that."

Howie looked at his hands. "I—reckon I owe you regrets."

"Yes, sir. I expect that you do."

"Well, you got it." Howie hesitated, then looked at the horses again. "I don't know why a man'd be real surprised he didn't have every thief in the South on his trail. Mister, that's a damn fool trick, leadin' four horses around in bad times like these!"

"You might be right at that," Jones said. "Yes sir, I expect you've got a point." He studied Howie a long time, then suddenly smiled, as if he were greatly pleased with himself. "Cory, you bound and determined to go north? If you're not, I'd be obliged if you'd ride along with me for a spell. Two guns are better than one, if you happen on sinners again. I can offer three good meals a day, and it wouldn't take a lot of your time. Give you a chance to rest up that foot."

Howie gazed at the preacher. "You want me around? After what I went and said?"

Jones waved him off. "A man's entitled to his suspicions, Cory. Even if he turns out wrong. Like you said, these are hard times."

Howie glanced at the fine-looking mounts. "I—guess I could put off my business. Isn't nothing that won't wait.'' The idea of riding instead of walking sounded good. And maybe he owed Jones the help.

''Well, fine,'' the preacher said. He tossed the rifle he had taken from one of the thieves to Howie. ''I suggest you take the black mare. She's fast, and isn't near as dumb as the rest. Which isn't saying much, I'll grant you that. It's clear to me the Lord intended horses for riding. He sure didn't bother to give 'em brains.''

Ritcher Jones led them south, out of the heavily wooded country, to the flat coastal lands near the Gulf. At first, Howie didn't feel this was a good idea; anyone who was near could spot them a mile away. Still, he could see what the preacher was thinking. You didn't have to worry about the water, so there was only one direction to watch. And they could see someone approaching as quick as that someone could see them. You couldn't say that about the woods—if trouble found you there, you had about half a second to face it, and maybe not that.

The riding was easy, and they made good time. Howie hadn't seen this part of the coast before. Walking back from Mexico, he had traveled farther north after crossing the Big Muddy. He thought he likely knew the river that flowed into Alabama Port, but he didn't tell Ritcher Jones that.

And that was a curious thing. When he left Tallahassee going south, he was gone a long time. Jones never asked him where he'd been. Maybe he didn't think it was any of his concern, and Howie was grateful for that. On the other hand, the preacher was not at all reluctant to talk about himself. He explained how Lawrence sent the Brothers and Sisters of High Sequoia across the land, to gather in souls for the Lord. No easy task these days, Jones said. Still, there were true believers everywhere, and this is how the horses had come into his hands. One of the faithful who lived a few days north of Tallahassee had hidden his mounts from the army. He simply refused to give them up. If the army had found him out, they would have hung him on the spot. When the man knew he was dying, he gave the horses to Ritcher Jones. ''To do with as the Lord sees fit,'' as Jones said.

''I guess the Lord knows what He's doing,'' Jones said.

He sighed. "I surely don't question that, though these poor beasts have near cost me my life."

"I think I'd've let 'em go," Howie said. "Take one and leave the rest of them behind."

Jones seemed surprised at that. "Cory, you don't shun God's gifts. That's a sin in itself."

"Well, so its gettin' yourself killed."

"You have a point," Jones admitted. "Yes, you surely do." He squinted at the sun. "I would have taken leave of Tallahassee a lot sooner if I could. I assure you of that. But after the trouble there, the countryside was swarming with men. It would not have been the wise thing to do."

"What kind of trouble's that?"

Jones looked curiously at Howie. "Ah, well, of course. You couldn't know. Happened just after you were gone. Terrible, terrible thing. They found a body buried in the woods. Throat cut from ear to ear. Anson Slade, the man's name." Jones nodded at Howie. "I believe you saw the man one night in the tavern, Cory. Of course you did. Asked me who he was, as a fact."

"Yeah, I guess so," Howie said. He didn't dare look at Jones. He found a burr in the horse's mane, and busied himself with that.

"Uh, what happened to this—Slade?"

"Rebels, most likely," Jones said. He flicked the reins of his mount. A flock of gulls took flight, screaming as if in mortal pain. "The same bunch that struck Silver Island, no doubt. I expect Mason will be most relieved he went to California, when he hears."

"Who's that?"

Jones looked surprised. "Why, Harriver Mason. You haven't heard of him? He's the man who ran Silver Island. Sent there by the President himself."

Howie felt as if a hand had reached in and clutched his insides. "I—been fightin' in the war," he said, forcing out the words. "We don't hear a whole lot."

"Oh, well, certainly not." Jones shook his head. "Barely escaped with his life when the Rebels attacked. All those fine young boys and girls. What an awful thing. I met the man at some gathering. He's quite well thought of in California."

"And he's out there now?" Howie asked.

"He was. Five, six months ago. Be a good idea if he stayed there, too, I'd suppose."

Howie didn't look at Ritcher Jones. He didn't look at anything at all. He felt it start again, felt the rage begin to burn him inside; he knew, if he let it, it would rise up and take him, consume him then and there.

Carolee . . . Carolee—!

Howie took a deep breath and let the anger subside. It didn't go away. He didn't want that. It smoldered there, quietly and under control.

"Cory, you all right?"

Howie knew Jones had been talking, but didn't have the slightest idea what he'd said.

"I'm fine," Howie said. "I'm fine as I can be."

CHAPTER SEVEN

THE RIDING WAS EASY, AND HOWIE AND RITCHER JONES saw no one at all along the way. A summer storm followed their path down the coast, always staying just out to sea. The slate-blue clouds were swollen with rain, but not a drop reached the dry and thirsty land.

On the fifth day, late in the afternoon, small settlements began to appear along the Gulf, drab, makeshift towns of weathered wood and canvas haphazardly scattered along the beach. Men, women and children ventured out to gaze in wonder at the rare sight of horses. Jones picked up the pace, saying how it wasn't right to tempt these poor souls to sin, especially with the night coming on.

Several miles farther, the preacher reined in and pointed at the flat, brassy expanse of water ahead.

"That's Alabama Port," he told Howie, "there on the other side. Sodom and Gomorrah all rolled into one is what it is. You want to keep an eye on your immortal soul, boy. These folks'll skin it off your back 'fore you can blink."

"Sin costs money as I recall," Howie said. "I reckon I'll be pretty safe."

Jones gave him a sober look. "I wouldn't jest about sin if I was you. That's just what Satan likes to see—a man grinning in the face of damnation is a man about to fall."

"Yes, sir, I reckon you're right about that," Howie said, certain this was the answer Ritcher Jones would like to hear.

The sun was low and directly in Howie's eye, turning the water blood red. There was land over there, six or seven miles away; too far to see a town, and way too far to spot sin. Still, if Ritcher Jones said it was there, Howie didn't doubt that it was so. The preacher had a nose for such things, and could sniff damnation a week away.

A ferry made of logs took Howie and Jones across. The horses didn't like the idea and kicked up a fuss. A man and his wife and two children were aboard. The children were young and hadn't see a horse before, and screamed all the way. The parents gave Jones hateful looks until the preacher gave each of the youngsters a copper coin. The children would never get to spend it, but Howie figured Jones knew that, too.

Howie tried to hold the horses still as he watched the silty water move by. The man who ran the ferry said the water stayed brown fifty miles out to sea, but Howie didn't much believe that. The bay was peppered with muddy islands; to the north, nearly out of sight, the river twisted through flat delta land. Great columns of man-made stone showed Howie where a bridge had spanned the river in the century before, or maybe some time before that. The columns were stained with rust, so the bridge that had been there was iron. He tried to imagine the enormous amount of metal that would take, and how the bridge must have looked when it was new.

The ferry had scarcely bumped against the shore before a crowd began to gather around the horses. Word had gone ahead somehow, or someone had spotted them coming across. Men shouted out numbers, stabbing their fingers in the air. Men in linen coats and fine boots, stout men in garments stained with grease, gaunt, hollow-eyed men who carried the sour smell of sweat.

Howie felt a quick sense of panic, smothered by the sudden crush of bodies all around him. For a moment, he was back in the choking pall of battle, men dying and horses screaming everywhere. He shook off the fear and struggled to hold the mounts.

The men parted abruptly as a wedge of Loyalist troopers shoved their way up to the front. An angry murmur swept through the crowd at the soldiers' appearance.

"Come on, give the rest of us a chance," a man shouted.

"Hell, an honest man can't do no business without the army buttin' in!"

"Gentlemen, *please!*" An officer with bright captain's tabs held up his hands. He was a large, dark-bearded man with a barrel-thick chest and scarcely any neck at all.

"Now you know well as I do the army's got to have mounts," the captain said. "I can't allow no open sale; that's the law, and I didn't make it." He grinned and shook his head, as if to say that he was on their side, and didn't want to do this at all. "Now you can believe this or not, but *I* didn't start this goddam war we got, either."

The men met his words with a groan, but there was more bitter laughter now than anger in the crowd. Howie saw how the officer had disarmed them, as surely as if he'd had them drop their weapons in a sack. He had done it with his manner, and not with his size, shown them all that he was a victim too, helpless to change the way things had come to be.

Some of the men wandered off; a few cursed the army and laughed at themselves. They had known all along that no one would get to buy a horse. Others stayed around, simply for the chance to admire the fine mounts, and compare them to horses they'd seen before.

The captain stepped up and grasped the preacher's hand. "Well now, Mr. Jones, for a man left here on foot, I'd say you done right well."

"The Lord provides," Jones said. "He that asks, so shall he receive."

The captain threw back his head and laughed, a harsh, booming sound that came from deep within his chest. "If that ain't the truth. Yes sir, you sure been provided, all right." His smile faded slightly and he squinted at the mounts, rolling his tongue thoughtfully in his cheek.

"We're payin' eighteen silver," he said. "To be honest, that's for anything that can stand. What I'd like to do is give you twenty-four each for these here. They're extra-fine, I don't have to tell you that. I figure that's better'n fair. You're welcome to check the going rate."

"Oh, now I don't have a need to do that," Jones said. "No need at all."

"Well then. The deal's done." The captain took off his hat and wiped sweat from his brow with a blue bandanna. "I'll have the funds drawn up and brought over to you personal. You staying at the Lansdale, I reckon."

The officer spoke to Jones, but he was looking right at Howie. All the time he'd been talking his eyes had flicked back and forth, taking Howie in, a quick smile and a nod between words, as if such attention might hold Howie there. The preacher caught the captain's interest and laid a hand on Howie's arm.

"Cory, like you to meet Captain Tom Ricks," Jones said. "Cory and me have been traveling together for a while."

"Is that a fact? Well, I'm pleased to meet you, Cory." He gripped Howie's hand, and held it while he studied Howie's eye. "I can tell a soldier when I see one, son. And a soldier's wound, as well. Where'd you lose that eye?"

"Caught a piece of iron from a Rebel cannon," Howie lied.

"And where was that?"

"Colorado."

The captain shook his head. "Lord, I hear that was some bad."

"I'd say it was."

"What outfit you with?"

"Illinois Volunteers," Howie said. He was stacking one lie on another, and that was a dangerous thing to do. Still, he had spotted Captain Ricks's Missouri patch, and he was sure that bunch hadn't ever been close to the mountains.

The captain seemed to lose interest at once. He dropped Howie's hand and turned back to Jones. "You have some time to spare, why I'd like to drop by and have a drink." He winked broadly at the preacher. "I hear the hotel got some real fine wines last week."

"That'd be a pleasure," Jones said, and shook the officer's hand again.

Captain Ricks walked off without another glance at Howie. Howie wondered if that was good or bad. He watched the troopers who'd come with Ricks take the horses down the street. Jones waved at a young boy standing about and hired him to take their packs.

"We'll find some rooms and get cleaned up," Jones said. "Ah, a hot bath." He rubbed his hands in delight. "Cleanliness is a habit that I sorely miss upon the trail, but God's work doesn't always take you where a tub of hot water's close by. No sir, it surely does not."

Howie stopped and shook his head. "Listen, I got a little money, but I don't reckon I can spend it on no hotel. I'll find me another place."

"No, no, no." Jones held up a hand. "I simply won't hear of that. The rooms are paid for, Cory, you might as well use 'em. The Lansdale holds a place for me all the time."

"I appreciate the offer," Howie said. "It ain't that. I just don't want nobody havin' to pay my way."

"The hotel's got a fine cook to boot. Well, *reasonably* fine, I have to say. The man knows little about the proper way to season good food."

"I appreciate your kindness," Howie said. "But I guess I better go my own way."

"A man can go his own way in a town like this," Jones said, "and he might be fine, that's true. On the other hand—on the other hand, now—a man might soon find himself among ungodly folk. That's a fact. It's an easy thing to do."

Howie wasn't listening too close. He was thinking about Ricks. All the questions he'd asked, and the way he kept looking, trying to see right through his head. A wagon went by, loaded down with crates, six men straining at the ropes. Howie and the preacher jumped aside.

"You know that army feller?" Howie asked. "Seemed as if he knows you."

"Met him once or twice. It's not that big a town."

"He give you a fair price for them mounts?"

The preacher's face split in a broad grin. "You've a keen eye, Cory. Fair, that's what you want to know? Well, *fair* is a word you have to study on some. The law says the army's got first pick of mounts. So *fair* you might say is what the army wants to pay. You can't keep a horse yourself, not if they want to buy it, so the answer would have to be—yes, I got a fair price for sure."

"How much you figure they're really worth?"

"Exactly two and a half times what I got," Jones said.

Howie had to laugh. "I don't guess the army's changed a lot. *Fair's* just the way it used to be."

The farther they walked from the bridge, the more the town seemed to grow. The wide, dusty streets were bordered on every side by clapboard buildings with high false fronts that made them look much bigger than they were. There were stores of all kinds—clothiers, butcher shops, hardware stores, and even a store that sold nothing but pastries and sweets. There was a place that sold vegetables and fruits indoors, instead of out in market stalls, and Howie had never seen one before. Walking on south, he saw signs with words he didn't recognize. Ritcher Jones told him these were merchants who dealt with ships—sailmakers, chandlers, and the like. Long wooden sheds lined the street, buildings that held cargo coming in and going out. And past one of these streets Howie caught a glimpse of tall masts and furled sails, a crisscross pattern sketched against the darkening sky.

"Glory be," Howie said beneath his breath, "if that isn't something!"

"You ever seen a ship before?" Jones said.

"No, sir. Heard about 'em, though."

"We'll walk down in the morning for a look."

"Is one of them the ship you'll take to California?"

"I expect so. That's where most every ship's going these days."

Howie watched the sight a long moment. "I expect I'd like to see one close. They let you do that?"

"We'll sure work something out," Jones said. He smiled at Howie. "Don't blame you at all. A ship's a mighty exciting thing to see."

The streets were lit with lanterns, more than Howie had ever seen at one time. There were buildings made of brick and stone, some of them four and five stories high. The structures themselves were fairly new, he could see, but the bricks and stones were worn, and had clearly been used in the past.

"A city was here before," Jones explained. "Name of Mobile, I believe. Built Alabama Port right on it."

Howie was appalled. "On top of an *old* city?"

"They're doing that a lot now, Cory. You just haven't seen 'em. In California, they've brought a great many of the old places back. Not anything like they were before, of course."

"It don't seem right to me," Howie said.

The Lansdale Hotel was a four-story building of man-made stone; each great block was patterned in intricate squares. No one could have carved them that smooth, Howie knew, but he couldn't tell how it was done. The place inside where you stopped to get a room had a couch and two chairs where people could sit and talk if they liked. Howie tried to act as if he saw hotels every day, but it was hard not to stare. A large room nearby was brightly lit, and he could see men and women dressed up, sitting around tables with white cloths. Shiny plates and glasses caught the light. Everyone seemed to be laughing and talking, and Howie could smell the tantalizing aroma of good food. He thought about the dried-up farms on his way to Tallahassee, the hungry faces he'd seen. Eating hard corn and glad to get it, drinking from muddy creeks. Walking east, he had crossed the rivers north of here that emptied into Alabama Port. That wasn't likely thirty miles away, but it seemed like a whole different world.

Howie protested again and said he didn't want to take Jones's offer, but this time his heart wasn't in it. The truth was, he knew he wanted to stay; the thought of a real bath and hot food was too good to pass up. And anyway, he reasoned, he had turned the preacher down several times, and Jones had kept on asking. When a person did that, it meant he wasn't just being polite.

Jones flipped a coin to the boy who had carried their packs. Another boy who worked for the hotel took their belongings upstairs. The rooms were four flights up, and Jones breathed hard all the way and complained about the walk.

Howie was surprised when Jones told him he had a room all to himself.

"Why, a man needs his privacy," the preacher said. "It's a God-given right. You just make yourself at home."

Howie found that wasn't hard to do. The room had a bed with real sheets. A chair and a table with a pitcher of water and a bowl. A chest where you could put your things away, though Howie didn't have enough belongings to concern himself with that.

As he was peering out the window at the brightly lit streets, a boy knocked and rolled in a great white tub on wheels. Another boy carried pails of steaming hot water, and kept going back out for more. There was soap and clean towels—enough towels, Howie figured, to dry off a couple of hundred times.

As he sank down into the tub, he tried to recall when he'd had a real honest-to-God hot bath before. He tried, but he couldn't remember when that might have been. And that seemed a sorrowful thing indeed.

The dining room was only half as full as it had been an hour before, when Howie peeked in from the lobby. That was some relief, but not a lot. Even in a fairly clean shirt and decent pants from his pack, he felt uncomfortable and out of place. Ritcher Jones seemed to know everyone in town, and they all dropped by the table to say hello. Men wearing white shirts and jackets, trousers pressed with a crease in the front. Officers in fine uniforms with polished sabers at their sides, men with their hair slicked back who smelled like some kind of flower.

Howie had never seen so many blue officer tabs and silver braids in his life. Not a one wore the small heart cut from purple cloth to show he'd been wounded in the war. And not a one had a badge to show he'd fought in some important campaign. More than that, they were all too fat—you didn't get that way in a war.

A waiter handed Howie a card that listed all kinds of food. Howie asked for baked fish, and Ritcher Jones raised a brow at that.

"They've got some fine steak here," he told Howie. "You ought to try one of those."

"I ain't much on meat," Howie said.

"Not a bad idea," Jones said. "The price has sure gone out of sight."

There was wine, which Howie didn't like, and a soup of some kind that tasted good. When the main course arrived, he tried to ignore the preacher's steak. The dark crust sizzled and the plate ran bright red with juice. The smell made his stomach turn over; for a moment he was sure he'd be sick. He concentrated on the fish, forced himself to eat. He didn't want anything now, but hunger overcame the other sickness inside.

Jones was too busy with his meal to notice Howie's discomfort. When the meat was all gone, he mopped up the juice with his bread, then asked for peach pie for them both. Howie ate a little, and the preacher finished off what he left.

"Well now," Jones said, leaning back with a sigh, "to my way of thinking, this is somewhat better than camping out beneath a tree. Praise God for the comforts of civilization—though of course there is much to be said for the glories of the outdoor natural sort of life."

"It don't seem right," Howie said. "Not to me it don't."

"What doesn't, boy?" Jones tapped both sides of his mouth with a white napkin.

Howie felt his face grow hot. He hadn't meant to voice his thoughts aloud.

"The—the food, and this here place," Howie said, trying to put the words together. "Everyone eatin' all they want. And most of the country flat starving. I've seen it. I've been one of 'em, too. That's what I'm saying. It don't seem right."

"It is *not* right, Cory." The preacher's eyes grew solemn. "It is not right at all. The Lord wants all of His

Then the girl leaned down and pecked Ritcher Jones on the cheek.

Howie blinked. He sure hadn't expected that.

Jones looked up in surprise. A broad grin creased his features. "Sister Lorene! God be praised!" He stood and took her hands, held her out from him, and looked her up and down. "My, it's been some time. And you're still as pretty as a picture. Come now, sit down here, girl. Tell me how you've been."

The girl blushed shyly and slipped into a chair. Jones looked at Howie, apparently puzzled to find him there.

"Good heavens, now where are my manners?" The preacher laughed at himself. "Sister Lorene, this is Cory. A fine traveling companion and a friend."

"I'm pleased," Lorene said gently.

"Yes, ma'am," Howie said, trying to find his tongue. "I'm—I'm pleased, too."

Howie bounced up quickly, then sat down at once. He realized how foolish he looked, but the girl simply smiled, setting him at ease. Lord, that voice! It sounded like someone pouring honey. *Sister* Lorene? Howie was a lot more interested in the Light than he'd been a few moments before.

"We were *so* concerned about you," Lorene said. She touched a hand to her throat and sighed. "You were gone so long, Brother Jones. I'm afraid we feared for the worst."

"Now God watches over His children," Jones chided. "You know that's so." He winked broadly at Howie. "Though I *will* say the journey had its moments. Cory here will vouch for that."

"Yes, sir." Howie cleared his throat. "You could sure say it did."

Lorene showed him a curious smile, then turned at once to Jones. She had news for the preacher, word about people that Howie didn't know. Brother Earnest and Sister Amelia had a small chapel going in Alabama Port. It seemed to be doing rather well, considering the rowdy nature of the local townsfolk. Lorene had trained Brother Lew to handle local administrative matters for High Sequoia. There was rather bad news concerning Brother Emil. He had been brutally attacked on the waterfront by a drunken band, felled while doing the Lord's work. His injuries were quite serious, and Lorene had sent him back to California the week before.

Ritcher Jones's face clouded at the news. "Such is the fate of those who love the Lord, I greatly fear. A fine boy, too. I shall remember him in my prayers."

Howie couldn't take his eye off Lorene. All the time the pair talked he studied her face, the high cheeks and flawless skin, the little curl at the corner of her mouth when she spoke. She sat straight and proper, and her dress was as modest as could be. Still, there was a woman underneath all that, Howie knew, and his mouth went dry at the thoughts that were forming in his head.

"Cory, is this your first time in Alabama Port?"

"What? Yeah, I guess so." Howie came to his senses. "I mean, it sure is. I never been here before."

"Yes. I see." Lorene smiled faintly and looked at her hands. Howie felt the color rise to his face. Oh Lord, he'd ruined it all now. The girl had caught him straight out; she knew exactly what was going through his mind.

Lorene stood, and said goodbye to Ritcher Jones.

"Cory, it was very nice meeting you," she said politely, scarcely looking in his direction. Gathering her skirts, she moved gracefully across the room.

"A very lovely young lady," said Ritcher Jones.

"Yes, sir," Howie said. "She seems real nice."

"A truly fine person." Jones sighed, and brought the tips of his fingers together. "Dedicated, too, I'll say that. She walks in the Light of the Lord."

Howie muttered an answer. He didn't want to risk a look at Jones. Not now. The way Lorene walked had impressed him, too, but a totally different image had come to mind.

Sleep wouldn't come. For a long time he sat on his bed and stared out the window. The night was sultry and oppressive; there was not enough breeze to stir the thin curtains. Howie wished his window faced the east. He could see the bay then, and the ships.

In spite of the late hour, Alabama Port was still very much alive. From his perch on the fourth floor, he could see a great deal of the town. Lanterns winked in the night.

There were lights in taverns, in homes, and in the streets. He followed a line of streetlights west until they came to an end. Past that was the dark, the beginning of open country again. There might be a few farmers out there, but they wouldn't be burning any light. Fuel for a lamp cost money; a farmer did what he needed to do by the sun, and when he was done he went to bed.

There weren't any campfires, either, Howie saw. Only a man who didn't value his life would call attention to himself these days. It wasn't smart to let everyone know where you were.

The idea of that struck Howie and brought him quickly out of his thoughts. Lord, he was doing the very same thing. He surely was. Not out in the woods, but it wasn't much different—worse, if you thought about it some. The town was full of troopers and folks from all over. And a man with one eye brought attention to himself. Why, he could walk outside in the morning and run smack into someone who knew who he was. Someone who knew his name, and how he'd lost his eye. Take that Captain Ricks. He'd asked a bunch of questions for no good reason at all. And looked at him funny to boot.

Howie was filled with sudden anger at himself. "What the *hell* am I doin' in this place?" he said aloud. He stood abruptly and walked to the far end of the room. He pressed his hands against the walls and closed his eyes. Turned and went back, grasped the window sill, and stared restlessly out into the night.

The truth was, he didn't have any business here at all. He had followed Jones to Alabama Port simply because he didn't have anywhere else to go. And that was a damn fool reason—less than *no* reason, for a fact.

He thought about the girl. She hadn't been much off his mind since supper. Lord, but she was pretty. She made Howie hurt all over—the kind of hurt he'd put aside for some time. There hadn't been room for pleasure in his life. But maybe that could change. Of course it wouldn't be Lorene—you could *think* about a girl like that, but that's as far as it would go. There were other girls, though. Plenty of 'em in Alabama Port. And the way Jones talked, they weren't against a little sin now and then. . . .

Howie swept the thoughts aside. Damn it all, there wasn't any time for that now. He had to get *out* of this place! Go somewhere. *Any*where there weren't a bunch of people thick as flies.

He remembered he had mentioned to Jones he had business in the north. Fine. In the morning, he'd tell the preacher that's what he had to do. Thank him for the room and the meal and get on his way.

Howie peeled off his clothes and stretched out on the bed. He felt better already, knowing this was the right thing to do. And there were girls most everywhere you went. Maybe not girls with blue eyes and yellow hair, but in a while he might forget about that.

By the end of spring he had left the foothills of the high range behind. One day he turned and saw the distant peaks were only thin blue shadows on the horizon. Ahead, the land stretched flat and hard, and he knew he had reached the edge of the great southern desert of Mexico. . . .

He couldn't remember when he had seen another person. He followed a dry riverbed and lost count of the days. Each one ended and began much the same as the one before. Until the morning when he awoke, sat up, and saw the man. . . .

He was walking east to west, trailing a small herd of stock. Howie counted eight—hardly enough to count it as a herd. The man was black, just as black and shiny as pitch. Howie had never seen a black man before—except the one they had stuffed at the Bluevale Fair.

"How'd you lose the eye?" the man said.

"A feller cut it out with a knife."

"You fight him back?"

"There wasn't much way I could."

After supper, the man took what was left of the beans and the bread and carried it out of camp into the brush. Howie was horrified. The man was giving the food to his stock! The meat jumped right in and dipped the beans out of the pot with their hands.

"Mister," Howie said, "it ain't none of my busi-

ness, but I never seen a man feed good beans and bread to his stock.''

''They ain't exactly stock,'' the man said. ''They just kinda 'pear to be.''

''That don't make sense,'' Howie said.

''I'm just telling you,'' the man said. ''They was wandering around half starved. Picking up leaves and bugs. Got all this far, though. Halfway 'cross the country.''

Howie thought about that. It didn't strike him right. ''Now how do you know that? Where they come from and all.''

''One of 'em told me, is how. Rest has got their tongues cut, but this one of 'em talks.''

Howie stared. ''Meat—you heard meat talking? Mister, I ain't arguing with a man that's feeding me breakfast. But if something talked to you, then it sure ain't meat.''

The man showed him a humorless grin. ''Well, that's what I'm saying, now ain't it?''

''It don't make sense,'' Howie said. ''It don't make any sense at all.''

Then Howie looked up from the campfire, and there was Ritcher Jones, sitting at a table with a fine white cloth. Howie thought this was a peculiar thing to see, a man in the desert all dressed up nice, a table with a cloth and shiny plates and tall glasses that caught the light. Jones winked at Howie and jabbed his fork into a steak, and Howie saw the meat was still raw, that it wasn't cooked at all. The preacher sliced deep with his knife and blood squirted in his eye. Jones laughed aloud and sliced again. Blood splattered in his face and pocked his clean white shirt. Howie yelled for Jones to stop, but he didn't seem to hear. The preacher cut and sliced and the red pulsed out until Howie couldn't see the man's face or his arms or hardly anything at all. Howie screamed and—

—sat up straight, clutching at the sheet and staring wildly at the dark. He heard the tail end of his fear, the awful sound that came with him from the dream.

Howie groaned and put his feet on the floor. He could taste his own sweat. He stumbled to the dresser and splashed water in the bowl and drenched his shoulders and his face. He left the bed alone and got a straightback chair and pulled it up to the window. A slight breeze touched his skin, but it was too hot to do any good.

I'm not sleeping anymore, Howie thought. I ain't going through that.

He wondered how long you could really stay up. Probably a pretty long time. The only thing was, you did that and things started getting spooky anyway. People talking in your head. Sparks of light that weren't there.

He thought about Lorene. The way she looked, what she said. Everything he could recall. He thought about Kari. Had Kari ever known Lorene? Likely not. Lorene might have been too young. She was maybe close to his age, Kari a little older than them both. He hadn't seen Kari in, what? Somewhere over a year. Hell, how long had she been gone from High Sequoia before that?

Howie's eyes grew heavy and closed. He shook himself awake. Knew he couldn't keep that up. That he'd fall asleep again. Go right back where he'd been.

"Well by God you'll have to come and get me," Howie said between his teeth. "I sure ain't goin' on my own."

Heat lightning blossomed in the west, and Howie counted till the thunder reached his ear. Pa had taught him that. You could tell how far the lightning was, and whether it was coming or going away. Heat lightning was all it was, just noise and no rain, and the day when it came would be dry as the one before.

CHAPTER NINE

IT WAS NEARLY TEN O'CLOCK WHEN HOWIE FOUND HIS way to the hotel dining room. The waiter seemed to disapprove; he led Howie to a table at the far end of the room, though the place was almost empty. Howie asked for two orders of pancakes and syrup. The waiter raised a brow at that, but Howie stared him down.

Sunlight blazed through the large windows. The awful brightness stabbed at Howie's head. He couldn't recall when he'd slept so late before. He knew it had been very close to dawn when he'd finally dozed off, sitting in his chair. At least the dreams had left him alone for the night, and he was grateful for that.

The first order of pancakes were gone and he was wolfing down the second when Lorene walked into the room. Howie spotted her at once, and lowered his fork to the plate. Oh Lord, she looked fine! Her eyes were bright and cornflower-blue, and the sun made burnished copper lights in her hair. Her gown was plain and simple, white with no frills. A broad blue sunhat framed her face.

"Well, good *morning*," Lorene said cheerily, and slipped into a chair. "Now, you just keep on eating, don't bother gettin' up. My heavens, you are certainly a sleepyhead, I'll say that." The smile behind her little scold said she meant no harm at all.

"I guess I am," Howie said. "Didn't sleep too good."

"Oh, I'm sorry to hear that." Lorene cocked her head and brushed hair off her brow. The light caught the bones of her cheeks and the soft pale curve of her lips. "Coming into a place you haven't been and all. That'll upset a person some."

"I reckon that's it. You, uh—seen Mr. Jones anywhere?"

"For a minute, that's all," Lorene said. "He's in one of those *meetings*—likely be tied up all day." She sighed and rolled her eyes. "That poor man. There is always something, you can bet. I try to take what burdens I can, but you *cannot* make him stop. Listen now, you have anything important you have to do? If you do, why you just say. I thought you might like to walk around the town."

"Why, I don't have a thing in mind," Howie said, trying to keep from leaping out of his chair. "That'd be real fine."

Did he have something *important* to do? Lord God, not unless war struck Alabama Port!

"Well, that is just delightful," Lorene said. "Now you just finish up your breakfast."

"Oh, I'm all done," Howie said, pushing a full plate of pancakes aside. "I couldn't eat another bite."

Alabama Port seemed far less inviting than it had the night before. Darkness had masked the town's permanent coat of grime, the drift of odorous litter in the streets. Howie didn't care. He wasn't interested in scenery at all—not with Lorene by his side. It was clear that every other man in town was aware of her beauty as well. Merchants and troopers turned to stare. Howie gave them all fierce looks and swelled with pride.

If Lorene thought he'd looked her over far too boldly the night before, she gave no indication of it now. She was obviously pleased that he was there, and linked her arm in Howie's as if they'd known each other some time. Her smile and open manner set Howie at ease. She pointed out buildings of note, the courthouse and the square, and, with a shudder of distaste, a famous hanging tree.

At last she led him down to the water, telling him with a sly little smile that she had saved this for the last, that Jones had told her this was what he wanted to see.

Howie marveled at the crowded levee, the maze of boxes and kegs, the dockside mixture of smells—the clean odor of new, stacked lumber, the dry scent of fat sacks of grain. There were smells he'd never known before, as well—coils of tarred rope, tattered canvas left to mold in the flats.

"If this ain't something," Howie said. "I didn't even know there was that many ships in the world."

"Oh, there are a *lot* more than that," Lorene teased. "You ought to see the docks in California. Ships from as far as China and the Japans come in there."

Howie looked puzzled. "Where's that?"

"Way across the Pacific. And the ships that come from there have chimneys. The sails are all different colors instead of white."

Howie shook his head in wonder. "I never heard of any such thing. Chimneys on a boat. Why they want to do that?"

Lorene shrugged off the question with a sigh. "Goodness, I wouldn't know. They just *do*. I've seen it lots of times."

Howie didn't care. If that's what they did in California, then they did. He looked at the tangled forest of masts, the clean wooden hulls. He couldn't imagine how anything could be more exciting than that. He wished there were some way to stand on one—just for a minute. Jones had said he might manage that, but Howie wasn't about to tell Lorene.

Lorene pointed out in the bay, and Howie thrilled at the sight of a schooner underway, its white sails swollen with the wind. It seemed to fair race across the waves.

The girl gripped his arm then, and leaned in close to his side. "I'll be heading that very same direction 'fore long," she said. "I guess I shouldn't feel this way, 'cause there's God's work to do everywhere, but I won't be sorry to leave. I've just got to say that."

Howie looked at her, startled by her words. "You're leaving? On a ship?"

"Oh, yes. Real soon."

"Where are you going?"

"Back home, Cory. Back to California and High Sequoia. Brother Jones is going back, and I'm bound to go, too. I follow where my vows take me next. And of course I'll be awful glad to get back home."

Howie's heart sank. He hardly knew this girl, but he didn't want to think of her gone. "Yeah, well, I reckon it's always good to get back. That's a natural thing to feel."

Lorene seemed to catch something in his words. She looked up at him with a gentle, almost sorrowful smile. "I'm real glad I'm getting this chance to talk to you some 'fore I go. Brother Jones has a lot of fine things to say about you, Cory. He says you're—kind of a special person. That the Lord's clearly favored you with His Light."

"Uh, I don't know nothing about that." Howie turned quickly to the bay. Talk like that made him feel awful funny inside. The thoughts in his head right then didn't have much to do with God's Light, or even anything close.

"It's true, you know," Lorene said earnestly. "If Brother Jones says it, you can sure believe it's so." She held his arm tightly, and Howie was surprised to see tears fill her eyes. "Oh, I wish you could just *see* High Sequoia. The kind of things we're doing there. New ways to make life better. Things nobody's dreamed about before, or not in a real long time. And peace—that's the most important thing of all. This whole country's full of sin and privation, men fightin' and killin' one another, everyone going without food. And Cory, Lawrence is *doing* something about that. He truly is. Nobody ever thought it could happen, but it's so. He's bringing Rebels and Loyalists together. Asking them to sit down beside one another and work things out. It's going to happen, too. The Lord's put His hand on Lawrence, and there's going to be peace in the land. You wait and see."

"If he can do that, it'll sure be something," Howie said. "Yes, sir, it sure will."

Lorene was looking right at him; she caught his expression and the doubt in his voice. She stopped, and firmly took both his hands in hers.

"I don't blame you for feeling the way you do," she said evenly. "I know what you've been through, Cory. I don't know exactly, but I can tell by how you talk, the look that comes over you now and then." She paused, and seemed to come to some decision. "You mind me asking? About your eye? What happened to you?"

Howie tried to recall what he'd told Captain Ricks. It seemed like a good idea to keep telling the same thing.

"A shot from a cannon hit our bunch real close. I got a piece of hot iron."

"Oh, how *awful* for you." Lorene closed her eyes and took a breath. "I'm so sorry, Cory."

"I got off alive." Howie shrugged. "A lot of the boys with me weren't all that lucky."

"I pray for *all* this nation's soldiers," Lorene said. "Whatever side they're fighting for. I thing they're both wrong. Killing is an evil thing to do, and it doesn't matter which flag an army flies if that banner's dipped in blood."

"I don't guess I can argue much with that," Howie said. The girl made a lot of sense, he decided. More than she guessed, most likely. The things he had seen in the West made it plain enough that greed played a bigger part in the war than the slogans people shouted back home. Hell, you could see the truth of that right here. In Alabama Port. The way goods were pouring in and out and not a lot getting close to the troopers in the field or the folks starving out on the farms.

"Cory?"

Lorene cut through his thoughts. Howie saw a curious expression on her face. "I'm sorry, you say something?"

"You might—think this is a peculiar thing to say, I mean, seeing what I am," Lorene said. "But I guess I got to say it anyway. Have you got a weapon on you? Right now?"

Howie was startled. "Well, yeah. I sure do."

"Good." Lorene set her chin in a firm, determined manner. "*Keep* it with you, then. All the time you're in Alabama Port. I just hate weapons of every sort, but this is an awful place to be. Brother Jones says it's right to go armed if your heart's with the Lord. Especially in times such as these."

"Thanks," Howie said solemnly, trying to hide a smile. "That's real sound advice."

And especially if you happen to be a dead shot like Brother Jones, Howie thought. A man who felt bad if he didn't hit a man between the eyes. He wondered if the preacher had told Lorene about their encounter in the woods. Likely not. It wasn't the kind of thing he'd want this girl to hear.

* * *

Lorene led Howie past the docks and back west. Only a few short blocks from the center of town, the surroundings suddenly changed. Buildings and storefronts gave way to quiet streets, small frame homes set back among sycamore and oak. Lorene stopped before a narrow two-story house covered with green trumpet vines and fiery orange blooms.

"I hope you don't mind walking me home," she told Howie. "Especially since I didn't even ask. Brother Jones doesn't like us out alone. Even in the broad light of day."

"I'm more'n glad to do it," Howie said. He looked at the house with some surprise. "You live here? I kinda thought—"

"That I'd be at the hotel?" Lorene tossed her head and laughed. "Oh, my heavens no. Brother Jones would *never* allow that. Sister Amelia and I board here with Miz Laintree. She's one of the faithful and awful nice. Come on, you've seen me this far, might as well take me all the way."

Howie started for the front gate, but Lorene took his hand and led him past the house to a line of trees and shrubs along the side. Farther on, a door and a shaded porch appeared, and Lorene slipped a key in the door and walked in. Howie hesitated.

"Don't stand out there," Lorene said, stifling a laugh with her hand. "Just be *real* quiet. Miz Laintree stays up front and doesn't hear real well, but she likely wouldn't approve."

"If you're sure it's all right," Howie said. He peeked cautiously inside, then stepped past the door. The room was quite small; the wooden floor was scrubbed clean and there was a window with pale blue curtains. A cane chair that had seen better days, and a table with a lamp. One corner of the room held a bed; the other was partially curtained off, and Howie saw dishes and plates and a pantry for food.

"It's not a whole lot," Lorene said. "But it's just right for me and Sister Amelia."

"And where's she?" Howie asked.

"Over at the chapel, I imagine." Lorene took off her sunhat and fluffed up her hair. "Where *I'm* supposed to be, for a fact.'' She grinned shyly at Howie. ''Only really, there simply isn't all that much to do. You know? We've got a few believers, praise God, but not as many as we'd like. Now you just sit right down and I'll make us up some tea.''

Howie sat. Lorene busied herself with kindling at a little iron stove. She hummed to herself while she worked. Howie watched, taking in her every move. He couldn't believe he was here, right in Lorene's very room. Not that it made any difference, but he was.

He suddenly recalled he'd gotten up that morning determined to tell Jones he was leaving town at once. Well, there was plenty of time for that, Howie reasoned. A man who didn't know where he was going didn't need to hurry off.

Lord, she was a beauty! Every time he looked at Lorene he wanted to cry. And he was certain that she didn't even know, didn't have the slightest idea how she looked, what she did to a man. By God, his luck was running true. Alabama Port was plain full of girls raised on sin—and he had to find the only one in town likely pure as new snow!

''There now.'' Lorene set cups on the table, found a straight chair by the wall, and placed it across from Howie.

''I hope the tea's all right. I've got a little bit of sugar if you want.''

''No, this is just fine.'' Howie took a sip and burned his mouth. He quickly set the cup down.

Lorene didn't seem to notice. ''You haven't told me where you're from. All right if I ask?''

''Up north of here and east,'' Howie said. ''Arkansas Territory.'' It wasn't much of a lie; Tennessee was just a border away from Arkansas. Still, he felt bad about deceiving Lorene.

''You live in a town?''

''No, we was out on a farm.''

''Oh, now how about that?'' Lorene brightened. ''I come from a farm too, Cory. Up in the Dakotas.''

''Is that a fact?''

''Your folks still there?''

"They—they both passed on," Howie said. "A few years back."

Lorene looked pained. "I'm awful sorry 'bout that." She reached out to touch his hand. "A person's kin are 'bout the most important thing a— Oh, *Lord!*"

Lorene's hand hit Howie's cup and tipped it right into her lap. The cup hit the floor and shattered; Lorene jumped up, wiping frantically at her skirt.

"You—hey, you all right?" Howie backed off in alarm. He wasn't sure what to do. "You burned bad?"

"Just—just a little." Lorene looked shaken. She kept patting at her skirt, as if this action might make the problem simply go away.

"Cory, I—I'm going to have to get out of this—garment, I'm afraid." Her face colored just saying the words aloud.

"I'll step out back," Howie said quickly, moving toward the door. "You call me when you—"

"No, no, wait." Lorene nervously chewed her lip. She ran a hand across her cheek. "You better not do that. Miz Laintree, if she was to go out in the garden or anything . . ." She blew out a breath. "Oh, what am I *thinking* about? Just turn around, Cory. I won't be a minute getting into something else."

Howie looked alarmed.

"Cory, it's all right," Lorene said. "Just *do* it."

Howie looked at the wall. He could hear the dry rustle of clothing at his back. He could hear Lorene moving about. He tried not to think about sounds. The room seemed a great deal warmer than he recalled. He wondered if humming might help. If he did it loud enough he couldn't hear. Oh Lord, that wouldn't work at all. The girl would think he was a fool.

"Cory . . ."

"Uh-huh?"

"Cory . . ." Lorene's voice sounded funny. As if something was caught in her throat. "Cory, you're going to think I'm just awful. I—I can't help it. I don't know what to do."

"What's wrong, Lorene?"

"*Me*. That's what's wrong." Her voice broke again.

"Cory, something terrible is happening in my head. I think I'm caught up in sin."

"Huh?" Howie swallowed hard. "Well—how caught up do you think you are, Lorene?"

"I guess a whole lot. I never felt anything like this before. Cory, what's in my head is I want you to—turn around. I shouldn't and I know it's wrong. God forgive my weakness but that's what I think I got to do."

Howie drew in a breath. "Are you sure, Lorene?"

"I'm real sure, Cory. Just turn around. *Please.* This is something that can't be stopped. It's just got to happen is all."

Howie turned. Lorene stood halfway across the room. The white dress was on the floor. She wore a thin cotton garment Howie figured was underwear. He knew she was naked underneath. The garment started just above the swell of her breasts and ended right above her knees. Her legs were longer than he'd imagined; it looked as if they went on forever and didn't stop. She held her hands behind her back, like a little girl caught being bad. Her hair fell over one eye. She wouldn't look right at him; tears rolled down her cheeks, and she looked all frightened and shy, and something else besides that.

"Oh, God," Howie said. "You're pretty as you can be, Lorene."

"I'm shameful is what I am," Lorene said. "But I can't help that, 'cause Satan's flat got me in his grip. Come over here, Cory."

It seemed a long way across the room. His legs didn't want to work right. Lorene looked at him then and raised her hands up high, and Howie thought sure she was going to pray. Instead, she found his shoulders and slid her hands around his neck and drew him close. A sob started in her throat and her whole body trembled in his arms. Howie held her cheeks and kissed her. He was dizzy with the smell of her skin, the heady perfume of her hair. His hand found the curve of her back. He knew he had to be dreaming all this; it couldn't be happening for real.

"Lorene," Howie said, "you don't know what you're doin' to me.'

"Oh, Cory, yes I do," Lorene moaned, "I can't help it but I do!"

Howie dropped his hands to her hips. His fingers burned at the touch. He found the bottom of the shift and slid it up across her waist. Lorene gripped his hands and helped, slipping the garment swiftly over her head, shaking her hair free.

Howie's mouth was dust-dry. He marveled at the way the sun filtered through the curtains and kissed her skin a dusty shade of gold. Her hard little breasts were set high and wide apart. He reached up and touched them with his hands.

Lorene gasped and closed her eyes. "Cory," she said calmly, "I reckon we're going to sin a little more. I don't see how we can stop."

"I don't rightly see how we can," Howie said. "That'd be awful hard to do."

Lorene sighed. "Well, if we are we might as well get to it. Thinking about it's just as bad as the wicked act itself. . . ."

CHAPTER TEN

AS THE DAY BEGAN TO FADE, SHADOWS LAZED ACROSS the dirt street to climb broken board fences and unpainted walls. Harsh points of sunlight flashed through the foliage overhead. Locusts chattered in the trees, in the overgrown yards and the gardens gone to seed. Little else stirred in the sultry afternoon.

Howie was fairly sure he hadn't come this way before. He had no idea where he was and didn't care. His head was full of Lorene. The sweet taste of her flesh was in his mouth. He could smell the scent of her hair, feel the delicious pressure of her legs across his back, see her lips stretched tight in the joy of release.

He stopped abruptly in the street, stunned by the pictures in his head. God A'mighty, he wanted to turn right around and go back to her again! Start all over and love her till he flat passed out or maybe died. Hell, dying wouldn't be bad at all. Not if he could feel her jerk against him once more, hear her ragged cries of delight.

Howie grew hard as a rock at the thought. Lorene hadn't wanted him to go. Her eyes had filled with tears and she'd said she didn't want him to stop. Not ever. She had looked right at him and said the words aloud, and Howie had stared at her naked in the afternoon light and taken her again. And that was the best time of all, both of them laughing and crying and loving each other hard and fast in the thrill of desperation, Lorene saying Sister Amelia might walk right in and all the time drawing Howie deeper inside.

Finally, she had helped him to find his clothes and said they'd made enough noise to give poor Miz Laintree a stroke, and Howie had stumbled out the door.

Lord, the girl had drained him dry and left him limp, but he knew he couldn't ever get enough. There wasn't any way to do that. Not with Lorene. And there wasn't nothing *wrong* with it, either. He didn't feel bad about it happening the way it did, and Lorene said she knew they'd done right. That they'd started out in sin, but it hadn't ended up that way at all. Somewhere after about an hour and a half, she knew plain lust had turned to something fine and good and the Lord must have meant it that way. She said she felt it in her heart, and Howie said he did too.

He knew this was true. Still, walking back toward town he had a sudden, sobering thought, and an image of Ritcher Jones. He stopped for a minute and felt his throat grow dry. How could he face the preacher now? Jones would see clear through him. He'd know right off what they'd done. Howie was certain of that. You couldn't hide sin from Ritcher Jones. Even if it likely wasn't sin anymore. Jones would see them tangled naked in the bed and he wouldn't see love pure and fine, he'd see dark violation and corruption of the flesh. And he'd sure as hell figure it was all Howie's fault. He wouldn't understand that a Sister of the Church could feel stirrings inside like any other girl. That if the right man came into her life, even a girl as clean and refined as Lorene would have to follow where her heart said to go.

What Ritcher Jones would do, Howie knew, was pray for Howie's soul and forgive him on the spot—then draw that long silver gun from his belt and put a sanctified hole in Howie's head. Amen.

Maybe, Howie reasoned, if he avoided the hotel for a while, the pictures in his mind might fade just a little, and Jones wouldn't see them real good. It was sure worth a try. He thought about the ships and how they'd look with the sun going down. That would be a good thing to see.

The day was nearly gone when he found his way back to the docks, but there was still enough light to see the tall masts sketched against a purple eastern sky. How fine it would be, sailing off across the sea. Ritcher Jones said most of the time you couldn't even see the land. That was kind of scary, but a person could get used to that. Why, you'd have to if you were a sailor, or someone like Jones who rode ships all the time.

How fast did they go? Howie hadn't asked Jones about that. The ships he'd seen in the bay under sail didn't look to be faster than a horse. But that was sure fast enough. And of course you didn't have to stop and rest. As long as there was a wind you could sail all day and all night.

And in his head right then, Howie saw a picture of himself and Lorene, off on a ship going somewhere no one had ever been before. The ship would stop and let them off; the sailors were good and honest men, and they would promise not to tell anyone where they were.

Howie had to laugh at himself. Hell, there weren't any places like that. And if there were, the sailors would cut his throat and take Lorene for themselves the first day out to sea. There wasn't a man alive who could keep from doing that.

The place was a few minutes' walk from the pier and on a street that had lights. Inside, the walls were freshly whitewashed wood. A bar was set along one side, and there were tables in the back where you could sit and order food. Howie asked for potatoes and fried fish. It was still early yet, and there weren't a lot of drinkers at the bar—a few sailors and workers from the docks. They acted as if they'd been there all day and intended to stay the night.

Past the dining tables at the far end of the bar, four troopers sat around a table playing cards. Howie wished they weren't there, but there was no use worrying about that. The army was in Alabama Port and meant to stay. At any rate, the soldiers were intent on their game and didn't notice he was there. An overweight bargirl kept the players supplied with ale. Each time she passed by a skinny trooper pinched her rear; the girl shrieked with delight and seemed constantly surprised.

The potatoes weren't done but the fish was the best he'd ever had. Howie mopped up his plate with a thick slice of bread and grinned at a secret thought. By God, it was true as it could be. Lovin' sure made a man hungry. He was starved right down to the bone. If a fella was to wrestle with Lorene every day, he'd have to spend all his coppers on food—just to keep from getting weak and falling down. He laughed aloud at that, and two stout merchants at a table close by looked up and frowned. Howie grinned back and the men turned quickly away, likely thinking he was crazy or a fool. Well, they could by damn think what they liked.

Howie ordered a cup of ale and another after that. The more he thought about food and Lorene, the funnier the joke seemed to be. After a while, the merchants got up and found a table near the door.

As it had the night before, dry heat lightning raced across the summer sky. Howie had felt fine in the tavern, his head full of fanciful thoughts. He'd find Lorene and steal a horse. Ride west and then south to Mexico. They'd be long gone before Ritcher Jones guessed they were even out of Alabama Port.

At the time, it had all seemed easy enough. There wasn't much he couldn't do. Now, on the street again, the stifling night air seemed to wilt all his dreams. His head felt full of nails and the ale had gone sour in his belly.

Goddamm it, isn't none of that ever going to be. Lor-

ene's going off to California. And I'm not going anywhere at all.

Howie kicked savagely at an empty whiskey jug and sent it shattering against a wall. A pair of drunken sailors cursed him from the far end of the alley, then laughed at what they had done.

It wasn't right at all, Howie thought. He didn't want to let her go. And Lorene didn't want to leave *him,* he knew that. Lord, he didn't have to wonder about Lorene, not with the thought of her bare-ass naked astride his thighs, her eyes rolled back in her head. She liked lovin' as much as he did, and there wasn't any doubt about that.

Howie saw the man coming toward him, cutting a dizzy path down the street. He was singing to himself, taking slow, exaggerated steps, as if that might do the trick.

Howie had to grin. At least he wasn't near as drunk as that. The way the poor fellow was going, he'd take half a week to get home.

"Wunnerful night," the man muttered as he passed. "Goddam wunnerful night."

"Sure is," Howie said, giving the drunk a wide berth. The man lost his footing, reached out, and caught himself against a wall, muttering and trying to find his feet.

"Might be a good idea to stop and take it easy, friend," Howie said. "Seems to me y—"

Howie felt a chill clutch his spine. He was staring right into the barrel of a pistol, and the man's eyes were sober as his own.

"Raise 'em." The man grinned. "Just back up slow against the wall. Move and I'll blow your damn brains all over the street."

"Mister, I got a few coppers, that's all," Howie said carefully. "You're sure welcome to 'em. I ain't looking for any trouble."

"And I'm not looking for any coppers, Howie Ryder. What I'm looking for is you."

Howie's heart nearly stopped. Too late, he recognized the skinny trooper from the tavern, the one who liked to pinch barmaids on the sly. Howie cursed himself for a fool. He'd never caught the man looking at him at all; he had never once given himself away.

"Guess you got the wrong man," Howie said, forcing an easy grin. "Name's Cory, and I—"

The barrel of the weapon was a blur. Howie tried to jerk away and the iron struck him hard across the brow. The pain was like a cannon going off in his head. He went to his knees and retched. Something far off in a place that didn't hurt said, *Get the damn pistol from your belt—do it now!* He reached feebly for his waist. The man kicked him in the ribs. Howie groaned and brought his knees up under his chin. A boot found his back, then a hand snaked down and found the pistol under his coat. Howie heard it hit dirt, and knew the man had tossed it away.

"Sit up," the man said harshly. "I ain't goin' to kill you lyin' down."

"Why the hell not?" Howie spat blood on the ground.

"Boy, you want some more kickin', that's purely up to you."

The tone was convincing. Howie struggled to his feet, sliding his hands up the rough brick wall. The man was no fool. He stayed well away in case Howie had something more to give. Howie knew he didn't. Nothing worth wasting on a man who had a gun aimed right between his eyes.

"You got a blade or anything on you, drop it on the ground right now," the man said.

Howie laughed. It hurt like hell. "You should've thought of that when you had me on the ground. You ain't thinkin' too clear."

The man didn't care for that at all. His eyes turned hard.

Howie grinned. "Go ahead and shoot. Then you can look for that blade."

The man's anger began to fade. He studied Howie a long moment as if there was something he needed to find. "Don't reckon you recall knowin' me," he said finally. "But I sure remember you, Ryder. I knew you right off. The minute I seen you back there." The man's eyes caught the light. "I remember when we all rode into the city, every one of us wearin' new jackets with white wooden buttons, and fine feathers in our caps. Wasn't a man there didn't know we'd likely never ride out, but didn't any of us care. I was right beside Colonel Jacob when we come into town. And I was there later on when they come and said that you'd been taken, that you were right there, too. Lord, you should have seen the colonel smile. It was something fine to see."

"I reckon I seen it once or twice," Howie said calmly. "The man just *thought* about hurtin', he got to feeling good inside."

"You goddam traitor!" The trooper's gun hand trembled. Howie read the fury in his eyes and was sure he'd pull the trigger right then.

"Anything happened to you, Colonel Jacob had the right. I seen what you carved on his chest, Ryder. We all saw that. I seen his blind eyes and the ruin you left between his legs. The man had a *right!*"

"I reckon you'll think what you want," Howie said.

"Isn't any thinking to it. God's truth is what it is." The man grinned at Howie with sudden pleasure. "I'm right glad the colonel didn't have time to take out your other eye. I'll consider it an honor to do it for him. But that isn't right now. You're goin' to get it down *there* first off." He waved the gun at Howie's groin. "You're going to get what you gave Colonel Jacob 'fore I—"

Howie went for him. The instant the gun barrel moved he threw himself hard at the trooper's legs. The weapon exploded; Howie felt its heat sear the top of his head. Reaching out blindly, he grasped the trooper below the knees and sent him sprawling. The man yelled and fired wildly in the air, kicking out at Howie's face. Howie took a blow to the shoulder, caught one boot and held on, twisting as hard as he could. Howie felt bone give way; the trooper screamed and jerked over on his belly. The pistol fell from the man's hand; he came up on his good knee and tried to find it. Howie kicked him in the face and slid the gun aside. The trooper cursed and clasped his hands to his nose.

Howie searched about for his own pistol and spotted it against a dark wall. He picked it up and walked back to the trooper. The man wiped blood from his face. Howie saw the fright in his eyes.

"Listen, I ain't goin' to tell no one who you are," the trooper said. "I swear. Goddam, just don't kill me."

Howie looked at him. "I got your word on that?"

"Oh God, yes!" The man looked relieved. "I ain't no fool."

Howie shot him in the face. The trooper's head snapped back and he lay down flat, as if he'd suddenly grown tired of the day.

Howie squatted down and went quickly through his pockets. A few coppers, nothing to show who he was. Not that it made a lot of difference. He'd either told his cardplaying friends what he planned to do or he hadn't. Howie figured the man had kept it to himself or the others would have been there too. That made sense.

Howie stood and took a breath. If no one else knew, it would work out fine. Only that wasn't so. There were plenty of other soldiers in town. The same thing could happen again.

Howie gingerly touched the back of his head. His hand came away wet. Staying in Alabama Port was no good. The place was too big. There were too many people, too many troopers. He thought about the few belongings in his room. There was nothing there he needed, nothing he couldn't do without.

And what would Lorene think? Would she understand what he had to do, would she go off with him, just like that? The kind of life she'd have to live wasn't anything like what she had in California. Things would be hard, and a girl like that . . .

He swept his doubts aside. Hell, she'd go, all right. Lorene cared for him, needed him the same as he needed her. She'd do it. She *had* to.

With a last look at the dead trooper, Howie started walking quickly back east. It was late, and Lorene would be asleep. Still, she could—

Howie froze at the sudden sound of voices nearby. Around the corner, somewhere just ahead. He turned and ran back the way he'd come, saw the lanterns bobbing in the dark. A man shouted, pointed in his direction. Howie stopped, turned, and saw the others clearly now. A rifle shot whined above his head, then another. Angry voices split the dark. Ahead and behind. Howie looked desperately for a street, a door, anything at all, and suddenly there was no place else to go.

CHAPTER ELEVEN

After the terrible battles out West against the Rebels, many troopers had been sent back to rest up and lick their wounds.

"They're hungry, and most of 'em hurt," a visitor to the farm told Papa. "They got no will to fight Lathan anymore, but there's plenty of mean in them still."

And mean, he told Papa, meant brawling and burning, and a rape or two thrown in. It wasn't so bad in the countryside yet—but it would be, as soon as the towns got too tough for the troopers.

If that wasn't enough, news came soon about the War Tax. The Rebels had stripped the land out West, and there was nothing but stubble on the ground. Every farmer had to give the government a portion of his stock and his crops, whether he wanted to or not. Papa was fit to be tied about that.

"When you figure they'll come?" Howie asked.

"I'm thinking maybe tomorrow," Papa said.

"And Colonel Jacob? He'll be with the soldiers?"

"Stands that he will, son."

The soldiers didn't come the next day. Or the day after that. When they finally arrived, Howie was on the porch, looking right at them. They rode silently over the far swell of land, moving down the furrowed hill against a gray smudge of dawn. Twelve mounted troopers and a wagon trailing behind. Closer, Howie could see these were nothing like the parade soldiers he'd seen at the Bluevale Fair, nearly four years before. They were gaunt, shadow men—hollow faces under grizzled beards. There was no fat about them, only hard planes pulling flesh at awkward angles.

Their clothes seemed all alike and had no color at all.

"Milo, it's been a long time," Colonel Jacob said.

"It has," said Howie's father, and there was something in his voice Howie hadn't heard before. Colonel Jacob sensed it too, Howie knew. The colonel was darker and thinner than Howie remembered. His face was gone to leather, and his body was hard as stone. The eyes, though, the eyes were the same, and Howie hadn't forgotten how Colonel Jacob had looked at his mother at the fair, and what the look had said. His mother had gone pale with sudden fear, as if the colonel's look held her and she couldn't get away. And even being twelve at the time and not knowing much at all, Howie had seen right then there was something real bad that had happened in the past. He had seen it in his mother at the time, and the bad thing was back there again, between Papa and Colonel Jacob.

"You got a right fine boy," Colonel Jacob said, looking right at Howie. "And the girl, she doing all right?"

"Carolee's gone," Papa said. "They picked her at the Choosing."

"Well, now that's fine, Milo."

"I guess it is," Papa said.

Howie's mother didn't come downstairs until the troopers had taken the War Tax goods and gone. Howie wanted to cry, just looking at her. She seemed so frightened, as if all the life had gone out of her, just knowing Colonel Jacob had been there in the yard. Later, Howie heard her crying, and Papa's deep voice trying to soothe her, tell her everything would be fine.

And some time after that, when Howie woke deep in the night, he went to the window and saw Papa outside, a dark figure listening to the silence, watching the hills where the troopers had disappeared.

Howie didn't even try to sleep. The cell had a plain dirt floor, packed hard as stone. Men had thrown up where they lay, sweated and relieved themselves against the walls, and some had likely died. The floor held every foul smell that had ever come along, and daily added each new odor to the overwhelming stench of the years.

There was one narrow window, barred, and too high to reach. Howie sat against a far wall and watched the square of darkness outside and waited for the night to go away. He felt somehow that the day would make things all right. And of course that was wrong as it could be, any damn fool could see that. In the morning, they'd come and get him out and take him up before a judge, and the judge would tell him when he had to hang. They wouldn't waste a whole lot of time, Howie was sure of that.

"Don't make no plans for after breakfast," one of the jailers said with a grin, which told Howie more than he really cared to know.

He thought a lot about Lorene. He wondered why something like this had to be, and there wasn't any answer to that. The window turned a dirty shade of gray, the color of army soup. What if it finally rained? Howie wondered. Would they hang somebody in the rain?

The street outside had scarcely begun to stir when he heard a door open down the hall, a heavy, solid sound that drew the air with it, and he recalled coming in that way, and the big door itself, solid oak half a foot thick and bound with iron.

Two men talked, and one seemed angry with the other. He didn't know the angry voice, but the other seemed familiar, and when he looked up again, Ritcher Jones was standing there just outside his cell, a jailer at his side.

Howie had to smile. "You lookin' for a funeral to preach, I reckon I can help."

"Cory, shut up," Jones said. He looked at the jailer. "Open the door. We're wasting time."

The jailer glanced nervously down the hall, fumbling with his keys. "Mister, I don't like this business. Don't like it none at all."

"Brother, you don't have to like it," Jones said. "Just do it."

The key clicked in the lock. The sound echoed down the hall and made the jailer cringe. Jones grabbed Howie's arm and led him quickly down the darkened hall. Two drunks were in another cell. One looked up and muttered as Howie passed.

The jailer opened the heavy oak door; Howie started off to the right.

"No. This way." Jones guided him to the left. Howie knew this wasn't the way he'd come. The corridor was nearly dark. A single lantern hung from a nail on the wall. Howie realized then that the jailer had disappeared.

The hall smelled dusty and dry, as if no one came this way at all. Two shadows appeared, and Howie stopped. Jones muttered under his breath and pulled him quickly past. Howie looked at the two men standing in the dark. One was a local lawman he'd seen when they brought him in. The other was Captain Ricks, the officer who had purchased Jones's horses. The lawman looked down at his feet. Captain Ricks looked straight at Howie.

Jones stooped before a door. The door didn't fit like it should, and daylight filtered in from the street. Jones opened the door and peered cautiously outside, then ushered Howie out. Howie squinted against the bright morning. A closed carriage stood by the door. A driver was perched on top. A spotted horse was in the harness; the horse turned to look at Howie and Jones. The street was narrow, covered with back-alley debris.

"Boy, don't stand there gawking," Jones said. "Get in!"

The preacher gave Howie a shove; Howie stumbled, grabbed for a hold, and pulled himself in. Jones climbed in behind and closed the door. The carriage jerked off to a start.

"If this ain't something," Howie said. "I never been in a carriage before. Only seen one twice."

"Lord, thy servant is doing the best he can," Jones said. He leaned back and closed his eyes. "I pray you'll free the day from any further tribulation."

Howie couldn't believe his luck. He was free—whatever Jones had done, he was free, and he wasn't going to hang.

"I don't know how to thank you," Howie said. "But I want you to know I'm sure grateful. I don't guess I can say more than that."

"Tell me exactly what happened," Jones said. He didn't look at Howie. "*Exactly.* All of it."

Howie looked curiously at Jones. "You mad at me or something?"

"*Cory . . .*"

"Yeah, all right. Isn't a whole lot to it. A feller tried to rob me's what happened. Followed me from a place I ate supper. I saw him in there."

"The law says different," Jones said.

"Don't give a damn what they said," Howie protested. "The bastard tried to kill me. You think I just shot the man for nothing?"

"It is reported that you were going through his pockets."

"I guess I was."

"What for?"

"Well, hell. He was dead."

"So you decided to rob *him.*"

"I *decided* to get my own money back. There isn't nothing wrong with that."

Jones looked thoughtfully at the top of the carriage. "You saw this man in a tavern. He followed you and drew a gun. Demanded your belongings."

"That's right. That's the way it happened."

"And you took his gun away. How did you manage that?"

"He was talkin' when he should've been looking."

"Talking about what?"

"How he was going to—shoot me in the gut. Make me die real slow."

Jones raised a brow. "Now why would he want to do that?"

"How the hell do I know? He was a mean son of a bitch, I reckon. Maybe he was crazy. Ain't you ever seen a crazy man before!"

"Cory, there is no need to shout," Jones said. "I can hear you quite well."

"I don't see why you got to ask a bunch of questions. I can't tell you what another man's thinking."

"So you got his gun away," Jones persisted. "Then you shot him with your own weapon. Why did you have to kill him, Cory? I do not entirely understand that. The lawman I spoke to said his weapon was some twenty feet away."

"Maybe 'cause I'm meaner'n he was," Howie said between his teeth. "Hell, I don't know. I wasn't doing much thinking at the time." He wanted Jones to believe him, wanted him to think it had happened that way. He didn't want him sitting there thinking something else. "I was mad and I was scared. It's like in the war. You don't stop and think, you just do it."

"All right," Jones said. "I guess I can understand that."

"Good. I'm sure glad to hear it."

"And what did you do before that? Before you went to the tavern?"

The question took Howie unaware. *Careful, careful* . . . "I walked. Just walked around some."

"Walked where?"

"I haven't got any idea. I never been to Alabama Port before. What difference does it make?"

"None at all, Cory."

"None at all, huh?" Howie sat up on the edge of his seat. He looked at Jones until the preacher was forced to meet his eyes. Jones was clearly tired and irritated, a man who hadn't planned on getting up and out of bed before dawn.

"Listen, just say it," Howie said. "You think I flat murdered that man, why'd you bother to get me out?"

"Because the Lord has a weakness for fools," Jones said. "Don't ask me why. There is a great deal about His ways I don't pretend to understand."

Howie laughed aloud. "I should've guessed it was something to do with God. Is that how you got 'em to let me out? You tell them how favored I am, that I'm shining real bright in God's Light?"

Howie caught the sudden anger in Jones's eyes; he thought for a moment the preacher might go right at him, right there in the carriage. Then, Jones abruptly turned away, lifted a curtain and peered out.

"What I did," Jones said, still studying the streets, "was offer several very large bribes. Money for Captain Ricks, and four of his officers and men. More for the lawmen who brought you in, three jailers, and a judge and various court officials whom you were fortunate not to meet.'' He looked right at Howie. ''We did the devil's work today, Cory. Not the Lord's. I pray He'll understand that I felt you were destined for better things. As I believe you put it, God has seen fit to favor you with His Light.''

Howie was startled for a moment, then wondered why he should even be surprised. Money was what Alabama Port was all about. Not the war or getting people fed. Getting plenty for yourself, and eating in a fine hotel. Still, he was embarrassed by what Jones had done, and didn't know what to say.

''Listen, you got my thanks, you know that,'' Howie said. ''I'm sorry if you're mad or anything, but I didn't start nothing with that trooper. It was his doing, not mine. And I didn't mean to cause you no trouble.''

Jones let out a breath. ''No, I don't believe you did, Cory. And I was not truly angry. Disappointed, perhaps.'' He waved the words away. ''Well, that is not entirely correct. I *was* somewhat irritated, I cannot deny that. But on the whole, my overall feeling was one of concern. All right?'' He gave Howie a weary smile and placed a hand on his arm. ''I suggest we forget this incident for the moment. There is other business at hand.'' He leaned forward and raised the curtain again. ''I believe we have arrived. There will be time for us to talk again later.''

Howie was intent on the preacher's words, and hadn't realized the carriage wasn't moving anymore. Jones opened the door and stepped down, and Howie followed. The sight hit him like a physical blow. A *ship!* They were pulled right up to the dock and the ship was no more than a dozen steps away. Tall masts towered overhead; a maze of rigging was webbed against the sky.

Howie knew. He didn't have to ask. They hadn't come here just to *look* at a ship.

Ritcher Jones grinned. ''We leave on the tide for California, Cory. 'Less of course you want to stay here.'' He cleared his throat and studied the masts. ''I think I'd choose to go, if I were you. Reason tells me if you are still in Alabama Port when we sail, the good folks of this town will hang you sometime this afternoon. Yes, I would give that some thought."

Howie laughed. "I don't guess I'll think too long."

"Wise choice," Jones said. "You might show some promise yet, boy."

CHAPTER TWELVE

HOWIE COULD HARDLY BELIEVE HE WAS REALLY ABOARD a ship. He had longed simply to look at one close—now he would actually ride in this magnificent vessel, all the way to California. He wanted to see everything. Talk to the sailors and ask them what every rope was for, how the big sheets of canvas caught and held the wind. Instead, Ritcher Jones hurried him belowdecks at once, and he scarcely saw anything at all.

Howie protested, but the preacher wouldn't listen. "I want you out of sight till we get to sea. You've got a knack for attracting trouble, and I sure don't need the aggravation."

The cabin was no bigger than a closet, and stifling hot. The ceiling was so low Howie couldn't stand up straight. A bed with a six-inch rim was bolted to the wall. Howie wondered what the rim was for. It made the bed look like a box. There was a lantern on the wall. Below that, a small shelf with another rim. A slop jar sat on the floor by the bed. Again, the jar was wedged tight in a wooden rim. Apparently, Howie thought, sailors like to wall things in. There was nothing in the cabin that moved.

A small glass porthole was set in the wall above his bunk. Howie looked out and saw the dock. He tried to pry the window open and let in some air, but the thing wouldn't budge.

To hell with it then. Howie stretched out on his bunk. The mattress was nothing more than a pad filled with straw, but he didn't mind that. He had slept on worse. His clothes were already drenched, and he pulled off his shirt and wiped his face. The rim around the bunk made him edgy. He felt as if he were lying in a coffin, waiting for someone to close the lid.

When would they sail? Howie wondered. Jones hadn't said, but Howie figured it couldn't be long. He sure didn't intend to stay down here and sweat all day. By God, a man couldn't live without air. Jones ought to know that.

Besides, if Jones was going back to California, Lorene was aboard the ship too. He hadn't forgotten that. Howie couldn't wait to see her. Of course he'd have to be careful when he did, or Jones would know right off what had happened between them. It might be a good idea to start practicing a look of some kind. A look that he could get when Lorene was around that wouldn't give them both away. He thought about that. It might be hard to do. Jones wasn't any fool. He hoped Lorene had maybe thought of this too, and was working on a look of her own.

Howie wondered if they'd get to make love on the ship, and didn't see how they could. And that would be bad, having her there close all the time and not being able to do it when they liked.

A spider was working on a fly overhead, and he watched it awhile until the sweat started stinging his eye. It was likely that spider had made a lot of trips to California and back, and didn't even know it.

When Howie woke, the cabin was even hotter than before. The room was in shadow, except for a band of orange light against the wall. The light was peculiar, as if something somewhere was on fire. He realized then, coming fully out of sleep, that the light was the afternoon sun. Which meant he'd slept the whole day. He shook his head and sat up. Hell, how could he have gone and done that? Then he remembered that he had sat up the whole night before in his cell.

Howie felt hungry and weak. His head hurt, and his skin was slick with sweat. The smell of his own body was overpowering in the confines of the small room. He pulled himself awkwardly over the rim of the bunk. The floor swayed beneath his feet; the sudden motion surprised him, and he grabbed at the bunk to hold on. Hot light burned through the porthole window. The floor dipped again, and for an instant the sun disappeared.

"God A'mighty, look at that!" Howie stared at the sight. There was nothing there but water. No land or anything else, just a flat expanse of blue. Somehow he hadn't expected that. Jones had told him they'd be on the open sea, but he had expected something else. He didn't know exactly what.

The air felt good on deck. Howie stood at the railing and breathed in the smell of the sea. It wasn't like land air at all; it was a smell he couldn't define, the salt and the water and maybe the ship itself. Everything was fresh and new, like nothing had touched it before. He watched the sailors as they swarmed through the rigging overhead. Now and then they called out to one another, or someone shouted from the deck. The words meant nothing at all to Howie, but he liked the way they sounded.

The ship was never even for a moment. It was hard to get used to that. The deck swayed from left to right, forward and aft, as the bow plunged down through the waves of foam and up again. The sailors didn't seem to notice this at all, but Howie found he had to hold on.

The sun burned down behind clouds and turned the sea copper-red. Almost at once, a cool breeze rose from the water. Howie's stomach felt funny, like something was rolling around in there and didn't want to sit still. He wondered where he could get something to eat. The sailors would know, but they never stopped long enough to ask.

He knew he was going to be sick. It happened so fast he hardly had time to stick his head over the railing. Bile spilled out of his mouth and caught the wind. In spite of the cooling breeze, his face was suddenly peppered with sweat. God, it was awful! There was nothing inside to come up, but his belly wouldn't stop. Just looking at the ocean made him sick. He closed his good eye, but that was worse.

"Well, you got your wish, boy," said Ritcher Jones. "You're on a ship at sea."

Howie groaned, and didn't look up at the preacher. "Dammit, I think I'm dying. That all you got to say?"

"You've got the seasickness," Jones said. "Dying doesn't feel that bad."

"I got what?" Howie gripped the rail and held on. "You mean it's goin' to be like this all the time?"

"Most likely not. Though some, I understand, never take to the sea. The Lord gives one man a burden and lightens another's load. There's a reason for this, but it's not for us to know. For myself, I was struck by the sickness my first week at sea. Of course this was some years back, but the event's still fresh in my mind. I prayed for release—begged the Lord to take me, same as you. Apparently, He felt my suffering was not too great to bear. He knew what He was doing, though I had strong doubts at the time."

"I ain't going to last no *week,*" Howie said. For the moment, his belly felt better, but the demon still lurked inside.

"What you need to do is eat," Jones said. "Get something down." Jones caught Howie's expression of horror and raised a hand. "I know it doesn't seem quite the thing, but take my word it's true." He sniffed the air and looked at Howie with some distaste. "Cory, you smell to high heaven. I brought your few belongings from your room at the hotel. I shall send a boy down with water and some soap. Clean yourself up. Change your clothes. I will have some soup and bread sent along. No matter how you feel, you *eat*. The sickness is taking all the room in your belly right now. Fill that cavity with food and it will drive the sickness out. Two things cannot occupy the same space. This is a simple physical fact. You'll be a new man before you know it."

Howie didn't believe a word the preacher said. He watched Jones stalk happily along the swaying deck, watched the sea rise and swell in the growing night, felt the sickness overcome him again, and wondered if he might find the strength to toss Jones in the sea.

The soup and bread helped. Howie had to force it down, but it helped. He realized he felt better than before. After scouring himself with soap and cold water, he put on clean clothes from his pack. The young boy who had brought the food and the pail of water had showed him how to open the port and let in some fresh air. Howie felt like a fool when he saw how it worked. The round window was secured by a large metal wing nut, a device Howie hadn't noticed at all. The boy warned him that the porthole must remain shut if the ship encountered heavy seas. Howie's stomach turned at the thought. *Heavy seas* didn't sound good at all. He couldn't stand up now without holding to the walls.

"How's the sea doing now?" he asked the boy.

"Why, smooth as glass, sir," the boy said. "It's a right fine night."

"And it might get heavier than this."

"Yes, sir. Quite a bit heavier than this."

"What do we do then?"

"We ride it out, sir."

"Oh." Howie considered that. "I thought maybe what they'd do is take the ship in to land. I mean—if the seas were some heavier than this."

The boy gave Howie a peculiar look. "If there's anything you need, sir, just ask for Jimmy."

The boy left. Howie wanted to sit, but the rim around the bed prevented that. He finally chose the floor, pressing his back against the wall and bracing his feet on the deck. He wondered how it was outside on the upper deck. A good breeze was going and the moon was half full. Of course the water was there, too. And things would be moving around, pitching back and forth. He had already learned that the higher you went on a ship, the sicker you got.

Howie cursed his own weakness. He listened to the sounds of the ship, heard the timbers creak and groan, felt the sea drum against the hull. A sudden picture appeared in his head. The trooper in the alley, the man he'd had to kill. If that hadn't happened, what would he be doing right now? He'd be doing something else, but he couldn't think what. Maybe running off with Lorene. Now that was worth dreaming about. He'd take her somewhere north. People said there weren't any folks in the Dakotas, and there wasn't any war up there because of that. And the Canadas were real close by, and there wasn't much of *any*thing there. He might've been doing that. You never could say where you'd be one day, or what might happen to you next.

Howie came quickly awake, unsure for a moment where he was. The cabin was filled with peculiar light, a pale luminescence that washed against the walls. He heard the faint night sounds of the ship, a rope stretched taut, the wind catching in the sails. That, and something else, a presence and a scent that had nothing to do with the sea. . . .

"Cory?"

Howie sat up straight. "*Lorene!* My God, you near scared the life out of me."

"Hush, Cory." Lorene came quickly to the side of his bed, a finger to her lips. She bent low to kiss him, and her long hair brushed against his chest. The touch burned right through him; he could feel it clear down to his toes.

"Voices carry something awful on a ship," Lorene warned him. "You're going to have to think about that."

"Lord, Lorene, you sure smell good." He reached out to hold her. Lorene suppressed a laugh behind her hand and slipped quickly away.

"My goodness, Cory, you just take a girl's breath away."

"Yeah, well, you're playin' hell with mine," Howie said. Just from looking at Lorene, his mouth was dry as sand. The girl was purely a vision. She wore something white, the same color as the light from the moon. The gown came down to her ankles, and that excited him all the more. He couldn't see a thing, but he knew what was there. Every lovely inch of Lorene was etched forever in his mind.

Lorene stood away from the bed, just out of reach, her hands clasped behind her back.

"Lorene, you want to come on back over here?" Howie said. "I can't hardly see you in the dark."

"The way you been looking, I reckon you can see me just fine."

"Lorene—"

Lorene looked at the floor. "You—kinda frighten me some, Cory. You know?"

"What are you talkin' about?'

"You. And me too, I guess. Cory, I never *did* anything like that. Not before you. I guess I *thought* about it sometimes. I know I wasn't supposed to, but I did." Lorene hesitated, then looked right at him. "I guess I'm trying to say I'm scared."

Howie was alarmed. "You saying you don't want to do it anymore?"

"No, now I'm not saying that." She came close again, placing her hands on the rim of the bed. "I got to tell you the truth, Cory. I want to do it something awful. That's the thing—I haven't thought about anything else. What I'm vowed to do for God and High Sequoia, how a Sister of the Church is supposed to act. I haven't thought about *any* of that. All I've thought about is you."

"Oh Lord, Lorene!" Howie ached to hold her, but he held himself back. He could see the confusion in her eyes, and the longing there too. He figured she was fighting things out, thinking on sin the way religious folks do.

"I was so worried about you," Lorene said. She laid a hand on his chest. "Brother Jones didn't tell me a thing. He just sent someone to get me and say we'd be leaving a day or two sooner than he'd planned. Said it had to do with you. He wouldn't say what till we got on board." Lorene looked away. "He said you—killed a man, Cory. That's why you'd be going on with us to California. Oh, Cory!" Tears filled her eyes. "I was so ashamed. I didn't even thing about you taking a human life. I was so relieved *you* were all right!"

"Lorene, I had to do it. I didn't have no choice. I couldn't do nothing else."

"I know. That's what Brother Jones said. He believes in you, too."

"I'm glad to hear it. I didn't much figure he did."

With Lorene so close, the smell of her skin nearly driving him crazy, Howie hadn't thought about Jones. He thought about him now.

"It's all right you bein' here, ain't it? I mean, I don't know how close the preacher's cabin is."

"It's not close at all," Lorene said. "But mine is, Cory. Just down the hall. And Brother Jones sleeps like a log. He says a man who's at peace with the Lord is a man who'll get a good night's sleep."

Amen to that, Howie thought.

"So you don't have to worry," Lorene assured him. " 'Course, we'll have to be careful. And when I see you during the day . . ."

"I already thought about that. I been workin' on a real polite look. Like I think you're a right fine person but nothing more than that."

Howie showed her his look, and Lorene had to bury another laugh.

"Don't overdo it. You look like you've flat passed out, Cory. I think you ought to work on something more natural, you know?"

"Acting natural with you's a real chore," Howie said.

"I guess I know that. You think I haven't been wondering what *I'm* going to do, nodding hello and eatin' supper and such? We're just going to have to try, that's all. Do the best— Oh, *Cory!*"

Lorene's eyes went wide and she jerked her hand away. She had started out absently stroking his chest, but as they talked, the hand had strayed south, reaching the only spot in that direction.

Howie grinned at Lorene. "You ought to not be real surprised. You done that to me before." He reached out gently and took her hand and brought it back. Lorene didn't resist, but he could see her blush even in the dark.

"Oh Lord, Cory!" Lorene closed her eyes tight. Howie felt her hand tremble, but she didn't let go.

"I can't get used to it, is all," Lorene said. "I mean, when we went ahead and did it, the first time, the way that was, and you gettin' like *that*—oh, I don't know *what* I mean!"

Lorene stepped away from the bed, grasped the gown below her waist and slipped it quickly over her head. Her skin was stark white from the moon; she tangled her legs on the rim of the bunk, sprawled on Howie, and laughed against his chest. The bunk was so narrow, barely made for sleeping and not meant for loving at all, that Howie was certain they'd both be battered and bruised before the dawn, and he didn't much care if they were.

CHAPTER THIRTEEN

"HOWIE . . ."

He woke up smelling first dawn, heavy with sleep, then suddenly awake, seeing his father there and feeling the strong hands on his shoulders.

"Howie, don't talk, boy, just listen," Papa said. "Get up and go in quick and get your mother. Get her downstairs and out back. Over the field, Howie, and don't make no noise at all."

"Papa—"

"Listen, boy." Papa gripped him hard. "I ain't got time to explain. I just know. Jacob let it show right there in his eyes. I know, Howie. I felt it. Son, for God's sake, you got to do it!"

Howie moved without thinking. For a moment, his father was behind him, then he was gone. When his mother saw him and what he meant to do, her eyes went wild and full of fear. He pulled her along through the dark, hurting her some, and not thinking about that, either. When they were halfway to the woods through the shallow ravine, he heard the sound behind him and turned and saw them. Two men on horses coming fast, gray against the first raw touch of the day. He heard his mother cry out and he stood to face the riders, saw the bright flash of fire and felt the darkness closing in. . . .

When he sat up straight he felt the pain, sharp and clear like a knife. He touched his head where the trooper's bullet had creased a furrow across his skull, and knew the men had figured he was dead.

He didn't want to go back, but he knew that's what he had to do. He could hear Papa telling him he had to be a man, and he didn't feel anywhere close to being that.

They had gone through the house, breaking things and tearing up whatever they could find. There was flour everywhere and broken glass. In the room upstairs where Papa and his mother slept he found her. Her clothes had been stripped away and her wrists and ankles were tied to the head and the foot of the bed with coarse wire. She had fought a whole lot. For a while, anyway. The blood made red bracelets around her wrists and ankles. There was blood in a lot of other places too, where they'd done things to her. He couldn't see all her face because her long black hair was tangled about her features, but he could see the small dark hole in her forehead, ringed with a faint aura of blue. He thought about cutting the wire loose and finding all the sheets and blankets that hadn't been torn too bad and covering her with that. Instead, he turned away and closed the door and went downstairs again.

Papa was halfway up the front steps. He still had on the heavy checkered shirt, but his trousers were gone, and Howie saw them out in the yard. He had crawled about ten yards over the hard ground, and Howie could look behind him and see the trail he'd made trying to get back to the house. He hadn't used his arms, because they were pressed real tight against his belly, where he had tried to hold everything in long enough to get back to the house. They had cut him up bad. One raw slice across the bowels, deep, from hipbone to hipbone. There were other cuts on his thighs and between his legs where they'd taken everything away.

In his room he reached up between the eaves and found his bow and quiver of arrows still there. He rolled up his extra pants and a shirt and his jacket. Downstairs, he picked through the wreckage and added half a loaf of bread to his pack and a clay jar of water. Then he walked outside to the grove of oaks where the War Tax goods had been stacked, squatted down, and studied the tracks of men and horses and the wagon. They'd gone west, across his father's land, toward the river road. He started walking, then, and never looked back at the house. . . .

Howie didn't feel sick in the morning, but the thought of the day before was still there, and he didn't want to do that again. Ritcher Jones was right—a full belly seemed to help, and Howie vowed not to ever let his stomach get empty till he stepped onto solid ground again.

The bed smelled pleasantly of Lorene, a musky scent of love that got him hard all over again. Lord, he'd have to wait till night to get her back in the bunk. That was an awful long time.

He stayed in bed another minute, savoring the smells and the memory of the night, then dressed quickly and made his way to the main deck. The sea was vibrant blue touched with green, a color he'd never seen before. White gulls squawked noisily about the masts. The boy named Jimmy who'd brought him bathwater and soup the night before told him how to get aft and then below. There was a place called a galley, and that's where everyone ate.

Howie found the place with little trouble, stumbling through a wrong door only once. The proper cabin was marked "galley" in gold-painted letters. When he stepped inside, several people were gathered about a wooden table. A man with a full gray beard sat at the head of the table, a younger man to his right. Both wore ship's uniforms. There was a well-dressed man and his wife, a boy about ten, a thin, balding man with bad skin. Howie didn't know anyone there except Jones and Lorene. When Howie stepped through the door, everyone stopped eating and looked up.

"Well now, Cory!" Jones offered his best preacher's smile, as if Howie's sudden appearance were the most important event of the day. "I am pleased to see you looking well," Jones said. "Thought we might lose you yesterday." He winked at the others. "My young friend here had a touch of the seasickness. I swear I never seen such a terrible shade of green on a man's face."

Everyone laughed politely. Howie took a seat, and Jones introduced him to Captain Finley and Mr. Adams, the captain's second-in-command. He met the Garveys and their boy, and Dr. Sloan.

"And of course you've met Sister Lorene," Jones said.

"Sure, real nice to see you," Howie said. He looked a good six inches past the girl, not anywhere close to her eyes.

"I am pleased to see you again, Cory," Lorene said primly.

Lorene seemed properly distant, and Howie approved. At any rate, it was clear the whole act between them was lost on Ritcher Jones, who was absorbed in other things. Jones didn't need a church to preach; the small breakfast crowd would do fine. When Howie joined the others, Jones simply thrust him into the sermon with little effort at all.

"You take young Cory here now," Jones said, taking up where he'd left off. "The boy bears the scars of this godless war, like many another lad. Taken from his home and rushed into bloody battle, likely in a place he never heard about before."

Jones raised his fork, jabbing it in the general direction of the heavens. "And for what, I ask you? Thousands of maimed and dead in this war, and not a one of those boys could tell you why."

"I'd say the answer's clear enough," said Garvey. "They fought to keep Lathan from taking over the country. That's the best reason I can see."

Ritcher Jones seemed delighted with this remark. "Ah, yes indeed. Then the purpose of the war is to keep the Rebels from ruling the nation."

"Well, of course it is. What do you think, man?" Garvey's tone said he thought Ritcher Jones was a fool.

Garvey reminded Howie of one of the big swamp frogs he'd seen in the 'glades, creatures with large bulging eyes that seemed continually surprised and ill at ease. A frog in a fancy suit and tie. The man was flat ugly, Howie thought. There wasn't any other way to put it.

"And what would happen in this country," Jones said, one eye nearly closed in thought, "what would happen if Lathan's army should win?"

Garvey made a noise in his throat. "I don't care for that kind of talk, sir. Smacks of treason, it does to me."

"No offense," Jones said. "For the sake of argument, my friend."

"The country'd be in ruin, that's what."

"But Lathan has said from the start that he feels his cause is just. That he merely wants to bring about needed reforms."

"He's a liar," Garvey said bluntly. "What do you expect him to say? He wants to take over is what he wants to do."

"There, now." Jones let his eyes sweep the table. "I believe Mr. Garvey has come up with the proper answer to our question. The Loyalists—that is, those in power now—wish to retain that power. Lathan and his followers wish to take it from them. Not a particularly *new* story at all. The government is in power and Lathan's not. Lathan says he can do a better job. He does *not* say he, ah—wishes to change the names of the states, make everyone wear a blue hat—" Jones winked at Garvey's young son—"paint little boys green, or make any other outlandish gesture."

Garvey's son giggled, and earned a frown from his father.

"What Lathan wants, simply, is exactly what the present government *has*. He wants to be *in*. He doesn't want to be out." Jones spread his hands. "And that is why young men are dying, why people are going hungry, and—no offense, sir, for I attach no blame to you—why merchants like yourself are presently making a great deal of money. I contend, ladies and sirs, that if you were to leave this nation for, say, a year, and return to find Lathan in control, you would be sorely pressed to find one small inkling of change. I contend that things would neither be better nor worse. That there would merely be a new face at the head of state."

"That is—preposterous!" Garvey slammed his fist on the table, rattling cups and plates. Howie thought the man's eyes might spit right out of his head.

"We have established a method of gaining political power in this country," said Captain Finley. "If Lathan wants the job, let him get himself elected."

"Hear, hear!" Garvey said.

"I couldn't agree more," Jones said. "But Lathan's

not a fool. He's from the West, and he knows the majority of our population's in the East. He knows he isn't ever going to win an election. That the only way he'll ever come to power's through a war."

"And your—*church*, they're going to stop this war, is that right?" Garvey's expression told everyone there what he thought about that. Both his manner and his words were contrived to rile Jones, but the preacher refused to take the bait.

"We are surely going to try," Jones said solemnly. "Satan is the only winner in a conflict as terrible as this one, sir."

Garvey smiled and shook his head. "I don't give this peace talk of yours any more chance than a fly in a pail of tar." He leaned forward and tapped a heavy thumb on the table. "Lathan's got no *reason* to stop, preacher. He is bleedin' us dry and he knows it."

"Lathan's people are suffering as well," Jones said. "I think the proof of that is the fact that he has pledged himself to send men to the peace table in High Sequoia. General Corrigan himself will be there. And Bruchner and Leeds. They will sit down across from Shiner and Henry Cord. Harriver Mason and General Crewes. That says something to me."

Garvey was quick with an answer, but Howie didn't hear it. He stared at Ritcher Jones, and something ice-cold touched his spine. *Harriver Mason.* There was the name again. The man who had run Silver Island. Jones had mentioned Mason only once, on the trail, telling Howie what he already knew, that Anson Slade had been murdered in Tallahassee. Only once, but Howie hadn't forgotten.

Howie looked down at his plate to hide the anger he knew was there. Looked at the crumbs of good cornbread he had quickly finished off, the slab of breakfast meat he hadn't touched. Fat and charred flesh. The cabin boy brought a fresh platter through the door, and Howie tried not to breathe.

When he glanced up again, he found Dr. Sloan studying him intently from across the table. Howie met his stare, and the man turned away.

Now what the hell's that all about? Howie wondered.

Sloan was a gaunt and balding man with a face like a bird. As far as Howie knew, he hadn't said a word during the talk between Garvey and Ritcher Jones. Seated between the overwhelming bulks of Garvey and Captain Finley, he hardly seemed present at all.

Howie listened with half an ear as Ritcher Jones praised the marvels of High Sequoia, the wonders of California. A new generation of peace was on the way. A new beginning for the land. Lawrence himself said it was so. Things would be better, even better than they'd been before the Great War of the past, when marvelous devices had made life easy, and shining roads linked the towering cities of America. All this would be once again, because the Lord had told Lawrence that the Light would bring long years of plenty to the nation, and that he, Lawrence, would make brothers out of warriors and plows out of swords.

The Lord's sure got a hell of a lot of work to do yet, Howie thought, before all that comes to pass.

He risked a look at Lorene. She was prettier than he'd ever seen her before, blue eyes shining with light and color in her cheeks. Mr. Adams, the ship's officer, seemed to think she was worth a look, too. The way he flat swallowed her whole with his eyes didn't sit well with Howie at all. And Lorene was *enjoying* it. Hell, just taking it all in. Adams whispered something in her ear, and she smiled and looked shyly at her hands. Howie felt his face heat up. Damm it, you can leave her alone! he thought. He gripped the sides of his chair and thought about pounding that fancied-up fellow in the face. Bloody that shiny blue uniform some, and see how you grin then.

"Mister, what happened to your eye?"

"What?" For an instant, Howie wasn't sure who had spoken. Then he saw Garvey's young son to his left.

"Hush, boy," his mother scolded. "The man lost his eye in the *war.*"

"That's all right, ma'am," Howie said.

"You're scary," the boy said. "I don't like you."

Mrs. Garvey slapped the child hard, and he started to bawl. Howie felt sorry for the boy. It was plain he was going to grow up looking just like his daddy.

The sea was running smooth, and Howie liked being up on deck. The ship still leaned and pitched about all the time, but he was getting used to that. A sailor named Jack told him he was getting his sea legs. That's what you called it when you didn't fall down all the time and get sick.

There wasn't so much for the sailors to do when the sea was slick as glass, and Jack told Howie how the ship could use the wind even when it wasn't coming up from right behind. He explained what the compass was for, and how you didn't need that if you could read from the sun and the stars. Papa had told him that. How to watch the North Star and the way the constellations moved about.

There were dolphin that followed the ship, and even fish that seemed to fly. Now and then, enormous white sea birds arrived in flocks to eat the garbage that was tossed off the ship. Jack said the birds could fly a long way from land, but that they weren't that far from shore now. The place where Mexico curled around and thrust a big bulge into the Gulf wasn't fifty miles off the starboard bow. Jack had been there once, and said it was a terrible thing to see. Nothing but bugs and heat, forests that choked on themselves and people that weren't friendly at all. Howie thought about that. Forests didn't sound like the Mexico he knew, which was desert where nothing but spiny things grew. He guessed that was because he'd only seen a little part up north.

He saw Lorene once or twice, but didn't try to say hello. Adams was taking her on a tour, likely showing off, since he knew everything about ships. Well, to hell with *him.* And he wasn't too pleased with Lorene. Of course, they couldn't be together during the day, he knew that, and Lorene had to act as if they didn't know each other real well. But she didn't have to act like she was *enjoying* that bastard so much. She didn't have to do that. She could look a little sad instead of smiling all the time.

His belly felt empty at noon, right on time. Still, he stayed on deck and didn't join the others in the galley. It seemed like a fool thing to do, going hungry out of spite. He'd have to eat with the others the rest of the trip, there wasn't any way out of that. Only skipping one meal wouldn't hurt. He would miss Captain Finley dropping food down his shirt, miss another sermon from Ritcher Jones. Miss that goddam Adams making eyes at Lorene. Hell, that was worth going hungry half a day.

Howie paused at the railing to watch the flying fish. He never seemed to tire of seeing the graceful creatures perform their acrobatics in the sea. They didn't really fly, Jack said, and Howie could see this was true. They leaped out of the water and glided across the waves, then plunged back under again. Flying or not, it was surely a wondrous thing.

Something rolled far off to starboard, a brief flash of silver in the sea. From the splash it made it had to be big. Howie walked quickly aft, keeping his eye on the water. Whatever it was, it might just do it again.

Searching the water intently, he scarcely heard the sound at first. The noise came again, louder this time, and he turned. The sight turned his legs to water; he felt as if someone had struck him in the belly, and he gripped the railing to keep himself up.

The sound came from the stern, just to his right. Two geldings and a mare squatted together on the deck. Each had a short length of rope about its leg, the other end tied to the far railing. It was the mare who was making all the noise. Like the geldings, she was no more than six years old, the age when stock was best for eating, though it was rare these days to see meat slaughtered anywhere near that young. All three were plump and fat, brought up to feed for the trip. Finley, or the owners of the ship, must be charging a great deal for passage, Howie thought, if they could afford to offer prime tender meat.

The mare was frightened, and this was the reason she was making awful sounds in her throat. Usually, stock didn't have the sense to know what was about to happen next, but sometimes they did. The mare knew. Her features were contorted and her blue eyes opened wide in fear. She stared at the ship's butcher, sharpening his tools, as if she guessed exactly what they were for.

The butcher glanced at the mare in irritation, motioned impatiently to his helper, and pointed at the mare. The message was clear: Take the one making trouble first. The helper, a young cabin boy, loosed the mare's rope from the railing and jerked her roughly toward the square chopping block near the stern. The mare screamed, dragged her chubby legs, and flailed out with her hands. The boy caught a handful of dirty yellow hair and tossed the mare roughly to the deck. The butcher took a step away from his block, drew a wooden club from his belt, and struck the mare at the base of the skull. The mare collapsed at once. It was over and done in an instant. The boy hoisted the mare upon the block and the butcher went to work, making the proper cuts swiftly with practiced ease. The two geldings didn't move. One idly picked his nose. They both looked at nothing at all with dull and vacant eyes.

Howie tried to turn away from the horror. His body refused to work, refused to let him go. He had seen all this before, nearly all his life, growing up on Papa's farm. Killing and dressing stock was something every boy learned about young. Only it wasn't the same anymore. Not now. Not with what he knew. Now it was a scene that struck him with an awful, unreasoning fear. Coming on the pens outside of Tallahassee, he had fled into the woods and gotten sick. Now that scene was repeating itself again. He felt the churning in his belly, felt everything rising to his throat, and barely had time to turn and lean across the railing.

Breakfast came up in a single gush, racking his body with one painful spasm after another. He could feel the tears coming too, scalding his good eye and running down his cheek. Each new convulsion seared his gut. He wanted to scream, just like the young mare, but the sickness choked off his cries.

Howie felt a hand on his shoulder, felt another bring a cold wet rag to his face.

"It's all right, boy. It's all right now."

Howie nodded dumbly. The spasms slowly ran their course. The man stayed with him until they passed.

"Here," the man said, "you hang on to the rag. Soon as you're able, go on down and get some rest."

Howie muttered his thanks. When he looked over his shoulder the man was gone, walking quickly forward, and he recognized the skinny form and balding head of Dr. Sloan.

CHAPTER FOURTEEN

HOWIE LAY JUST ON THE SKIRT OF THE CAMP, BELLY *flat against the damp forest floor, hardly daring to breathe, his eyes taking in every trifle—how the grass bent, and where the dim moonlight touched the ground. There was a guard between him and Colonel Jacob. He stood just outside the small clearing where the other troopers slept; he was quiet and almost invisible against a broad oak.*

Howie knew he had to go for the head or no place at all. Anything less and the man would cry out. He didn't let himself think about missing.

The bowstring sang and the shadow dropped silently to the base of the tree. . . .

He'd thought about how to do it. Even a grown man used to moving fast couldn't stop a quick knife across the throat. Only that wasn't the way it was supposed to be. It had to be the other way or it wouldn't be right. . . .

Colonel Jacob slept with his mouth open, one hand across his chest. Howie slipped the bone knife from his belt. He had already wrapped the butt with layers of cloth from his extra shirt. Grasping Jacob's hair with one hand, he brought the padded hilt down solidly, just above the ear. Jacob stiffened slightly, but made no sound at all. . . .

It took nearly an hour to make the thirty yards to the river. There was a clump of scrub oak masking the far shore and a sand wash behind that. He stripped Jacob, leaned him against a tree, and wired him securely to the trunk, pulling his feet straight out and wiring them as well. Then he stuffed the man's socks in his mouth and used his shirt to make a tight gag knotted behind his neck.

When Jacob came awake, he gazed curiously at Howie for a moment before his eyes went wide with understanding. Then he jerked frantically against his bonds, moaning behind the gag.

Howie ignored him. He straddled Jacob's legs, drew the bone knife from his belt, and started working on the colonel's chest. He went carefully and slowly, making the letters neat, like his mother had taught him. It was hard to see in the dim light and he had to keep wiping the blood away to tell what he was doing. Jacob's eyes bulged and sweat beaded his face, and Howie could hear the noises he was making but nothing came through the gag.

When he was through he went to work on the eyes, being careful to do just what needed to be done. He didn't want Jacob to pass out and miss anything, or lose more blood than he had to. He was still conscious, Howie knew, but near out of his head, and that was good. That was the way it was supposed to be.

When he finished with the eyes he looked at Jacob and touched the blade lightly against the man's thighs. Jacob jerked uncontrollably, nearly pulling his arms out of the sockets. He knew pretty well what was coming. Howie did the best he could, but the fear and the pain were more than Jacob could handle. He quickly dropped into unconsciousness. That was all right, too, Howie decided. He'd wake up and have plenty of time to think about what had happened to him. . . .

By midafternoon he was far to the north, in the midst of deep woods ringed by high, rugged cliffs. He had no idea where he might be, only that he was far from the camp by the river. If the soldiers were after him he didn't know it, and at the moment he didn't much care.

He tied the stolen horse to a tree and stumbled through low brush until his legs gave way and he went shakily to his knees. The tears came then, and he remembered Papa and his mother and what they'd looked like at the house. He tried to think of nothing, but his mother was still there. And Papa, looking surprised at dying. He saw Colonel Jacob and what he'd done to him on the riverbank. The hollow eyes and the terrible empty place between his legs. And the bone-deep letters on his chest that would last as long as Jacob and wouldn't ever go away:

HOWIE SON OF
EV AND
MILO RYDER

He knew he couldn't stay there. He had to get back on the horse. And he remembered a whole day had gone by and it was April now, and tomorrow he'd be sixteen. . . .

"Cory, you all right?"

"Yeah, I'm all right, I'm just fine."

Howie could see her in the pale light, leaning over him, her eyes lost in shadow.

"You were moaning in your sleep. I figured you had a dream."

"I might have. If I did I don't recall," Howie lied. He reached up and touched her bare shoulders. "Come on back to sleep."

"I got to get up now, silly. It's real close to morning."

"It ain't that close."

"It is too," she said. Lorene brushed her hands past her cheeks, drawing back her hair. Howie cupped her breast in his hand. Lorene shuddered and closed her eyes.

"Lord, Cory, don't make it any harder on me than it is. I don't *want* to go, you know that."

"Thought maybe you was getting tired of me. Might be thinking about that fine-looking officer or something."

"Cory!" Lorene looked appalled. "Don't you even tease me 'bout something like that."

"Well, he sure does moon around you a lot," Howie said. "Hell, you're with him all the time."

Lorene sighed. "What do you figure I ought to do?

Maybe I just ought to say, 'I'm sure sorry, Dan. I can't walk around on the deck with anyone 'cause see I'm making love to this other fella every night.' "

"That's his name? Dan?" Howie made a face. "What kind of name is that?"

"It's just an ordinary name, that's all. Oh, Cory, you don't *really* think I care anything about him, now do you?"

"You better not."

"Well I don't. I just care about you. My heavens, a few days back I didn't know a thing about men, and now I'm—doing all *kinds* of things with you every night, things I never even thought about before, and you're worried about me and Dan Adams." Lorene laughed. "I sure have come a long way."

The laughter grated on Howie. "That ain't funny, Lorene."

"Honestly, *you're* the one that's funny. The way you're acting. You just— *oh, Cory!*"

Howie pulled her roughly to him, thrusting one hand between her thighs. Lorene drew in a breath, tried to squirm free and said she had to get up, that it was getting close to dawn, and then she cried out once and threw her arms around his neck and didn't say anything at all.

Howie woke at first light. He couldn't remember when Lorene had finally left. Lord, that last time was something! Like they'd never even touched each other before. And it was Lorene who'd come at *him* so hard at the end, loving him with a fierce desperation as if she'd gone right out of her head, and it was Howie himself who'd had to stop.

He leaned back and looked at the ceiling and grinned at the spider overhead. For the first time since he could remember, he felt as if everything in his life was going fine. He had Lorene, and he was headed for California. It was far away from any place he knew, far from anyone who'd ever heard of Howie Ryder, and what had happened between him and Colonel Jacob.

And Harriver Mason was there. Ever since Jones had brought his name up again, Howie had given the man a lot of thought. He couldn't find everyone who'd done those awful things to his sister, but he sure had to do what he could. Anson Slade was gone, and that was one. And Harriver Mason would be at High Sequoia. Ritcher Jones wouldn't like what Howie had in mind, and Howie felt bad about that. The preacher had sure treated him fine. But there were some things that just had to be. Carolee was dead, and Mason didn't have any right to be alive. He didn't have any right at all.

CHAPTER FIFTEEN

GOING BACK TO EAT WITH THE OTHERS WASN'T EASY. The scene he had witnessed on the stern had shaken Howie badly; feelings had rushed in that he'd tried to put away. He didn't think he could ever watch folks eat meat again without getting violently sick on the spot. Not after that.

For three days he avoided the galley. He told Lorene the seasickness was acting up again.

"Don't seem to be sapping your strength a whole lot," Lorene said, with that sly look she knew drove Howie up the wall.

Ritcher Jones accepted this story until word got to him somehow that Howie had made friends with the cook. It seemed he was dropping by four or five times every day for bread and jam, potatoes and soup, and was making quite a dent in the ship's small supply of fresh vegetables and fruit.

Finally, Jones took Howie aside. "I guess I know what's the matter," he said. "I should have guessed it before."

Howie felt his throat constrict, and tried to avoid Jones's penetrating eyes. 'Uh, I don't reckon I know what you mean."

Jones smiled his best preacher smile and laid a hand

on Howie's shoulder. "Now Cory, don't think I don't know what happened down there the other day. I might look like I'm jawing all the time, but there isn't a whole lot I don't see." He looked soberly at Howie. "It's the Garvey boy, isn't it?"

Howie looked genuinely confused. This was apparently the reaction Jones expected.

"It's all right," the preacher said. "I didn't know you were sensitive about your eye, Cory. I guess you just don't let it show. Children have a way of stepping on feelings sometimes. Here, I got you this."

With a broad smile, Jones drew something from his pocket and handed it to Howie.

"Well. I'm sure grateful." It was a tangle of black cloth and string, and Howie wasn't sure what it was for.

"It's a patch," Jones explained. "For your eye. Covers up the scar. Go on, try it on."

Jones gave him a hand, then stepped back and looked him over. "Well, now. That's just fine. Real nice, I'd say. Gives you a kind of—*dangerous* look, you know?" He showed Howie a wink. "The young ladies in California will go for that, my boy. You wait and see. Now, I'll expect you at supper tonight." He wagged a finger in Howie's face. "No more of this sneaking around to the cook."

Howie didn't like the patch at all, and the fact that it doomed him to the galley again. Still, there was little else he could do other than share his true feelings with Jones, and he sure wasn't about to do that.

Little had changed while he was gone. Ritcher Jones preached the glories of peace and High Sequoia, and Garvey argued with every point he made. It suddenly occurred to Howie that the two men thoroughly enjoyed these fiery exchanges, that each would be greatly disappointed if the other gave in and agreed.

Occasionally, Captain Finley managed a word here and there, continuing to spill food down his shirt. Howie did his best to ignore the awful sight and smell of meat. Young Garvey stared at his patch. Dr. Sloan never looked his way; it was as if the incident on the stern had never happened, and Howie was grateful for that.

Sometimes, at night, when Lorene slipped into his bed, Howie would berate her for mooning over Adams. The subject was always good for a fight, but since neither of the two dared quarrel above a whisper, one or the other would start to laugh at some point and they would end up in each other's arms. The lovemaking that followed these exchanges seemed even more heated than usual, and both Howie and Lorene began to look forward to the evening's accusations and denials. The outcome was clearly worth the effort.

The ship's progress was posted every morning, and passengers could learn how many miles they had traveled the day before, and what lay to starboard and port. There were latitudes and longitudes—which made no sense to Howie—and remarks about the temperature and wind.

Ritcher Jones had made the passage south many times before, and delighted in telling everything he knew. Once he pointed out a distant gray mass to the west and told Howie it was part of the Central Americas, lands that used to be nations right below Mexico.

"No one goes there anymore," Jones said grimly. "It's a place of desolation. They got hit hard in the Great War."

Howie asked why that was so, and Jones couldn't say. It was the same farther down, he knew that. He showed Howie a map of South America. Millions had starved down there in that same terrible war of the past. There might be people still alive, but no one knew for sure.

"America got hit bad enough," Jones said. "But I don't guess anywhere near like the rest of the world did. Asia came through like us, but there isn't anything in the Europes. A ship took a look over there about thirty years back. War's a horrible thing, Cory. Even a *small* war like the one back home can bring a people down for good. We can't let that keep happening—it's just got to stop."

Howie had seen ruined cities from the past; it was easy to tell how bad things must've been. But it was hard to imagine a whole world like that, places all over as big as America where nothing lived at all. He had never heard of Asia or the Europes, and didn't want to admit that to Jones.

* * *

Everyone knew that the ship would make land right at dawn, and all the passengers were up on deck for the big event. The sun rose to a bright and cloudless day, and a few moments later, Howie could see a shoreline topped with emerald green. Finley passed his spyglass around, and everyone got a close look. Young Garvey swore he could see people moving about, but Howie doubted that. When it came Howie's turn, he saw a tangle of thick foliage that reminded him of the 'glades. Waves of heat warped the view, and this confirmed what everybody said—that the tropics were about as close as you'd care to get to hell.

An hour later, the ship passed the green shore to starboard, and Jones said they were entering a saltwater passage that linked the Atlantic and the Pacific, that the land on both sides was called Panama Province. Before the Great War, only a few ships could go through this passage at a time, but terrible weapons had been used here as well, and now the way was forty or fifty miles wide, right through to the other side.

"Whatever did that must've been a sight to see," Howie said.

The remark earned Howie a stern preacher look. "Anybody saw *that*, boy, made a real quick trip to the devil or the Lord."

Howie could smell the port of Nueva Panama before he saw it. It was a mix of dead foliage, rotting fruit and stagnant water; that, and odors he couldn't name, all borne on stifling waves of heat. The steamy climate of this part of the earth was more evident now that the ship was barely making way. There was no breeze at all, and great swarms of insects from the shore discovered the vessel and its passengers at once. There was no escape from these hordes of mosquitoes and gnats. Mrs. Garvey fled with her son to their cabin, but discovered soon enough that the room had become an oven, and returned to face the army of bugs.

There were many other vessels in port. Howie counted over a dozen. As the ship made its way through the maze of hulls and masts, he spotted homes and buildings among the trees, one-and two-story structures in sun-faded tones of mustard and pink, lavender and blue. He could make out people on the dockfront now, men scurrying about, moving barrels and crates.

Something caught Howie's eye, and he strained for a closer look. He was startled by what he saw. God A'mighty, everybody's skin was dark as pitch. The people on shore were all black!

Jones, standing at the railing nearby, caught his expression at once.

"I take it you've never seen such folks before," the preacher said. "The first time can be a little scary, that's a fact."

"I seen a stuffed nigger once at a fair," Howie said. "When I was just a kid."

"I would not advise you to use that particular term around these people," Jones said. "They would take great offense."

"How come they're here?" Howie asked. "I thought they all died 'bout a hundred years ago."

"They mostly did. But some survived." Jones shook his head. "That was a terrible thing, Cory. A shameful thing at best. All men are the same in the eyes of the Lord—or nearly the same, I'd say. Lawrence had some thoughts on that which I'd be glad to discuss at some time. Suffice it to say, there are black persons here. Panama Province belongs to them, and the city here is quite important as a midpoint of trade. Many ships from California or Alabama Port stop here and off-load, trading cargo in Nueva Panama port instead of making the trip from one ocean to the other. It's quite convenient. And very profitable for the blacks, since they take a cut of every bit of business that's done, and charge docking fees, loading fees, and fees for most everything else. They do *business* with us, but they are not overly friendly to persons of white skin. This is simply their way, and there's little that can be done about it."

"I guess not," Howie said. He watched as the ship neared land, thinking of the black man he'd met in the desert of Mexico leading a handful of pitiful creatures south, people who looked like stock and weren't really stock at all. Jones didn't need to know about that. It was something Howie could never share with anyone, not even Lorene.

The black man had taken Howie in, and fed him by his fire. That didn't seem real hostile to Howie, but maybe the blacks down here weren't the same.

Once, after Howie had seen the stuffed black man at the Bluevale Fair, Howie had asked his father why people with that kind of skin weren't around anymore. Papa had kind of pushed the question aside, as he did sometimes, telling Howie there was "trouble" back then, before he himself was born, and anyway it was a lot of years ago. That was all he'd ever say, and Howie didn't ask anymore.

Now, Howie thought how if everyone had tried to kill them off, even before the Great War, the black people might have good reason not to care much for anyone else. Maybe the preacher couldn't see that; it didn't much appear like he did.

Jones raised all kinds of hell when Howie said he planned to go ashore and look around. The preacher ranted once again about the dangers of "mixing with folks who are different." And, besides that, he said, it was clear that a certain young man had a knack for getting himself in situations where other people had to come and bail him out.

The more Jones raved, the more determined Howie was to have his way. The ship would be in port until dawn the next day, and he wasn't going to just mope around in the heat. Finally, the preacher stomped off in a huff, muttering dire predictions of Howie's fate.

Jones had forbidden Lorene to go ashore, and Howie was secretly pleased about that. He knew Dan Adams had been itching for a chance to get Lorene off to himself. Lorene had casually mentioned the invitation the night before, mostly to see how he'd react, Howie guessed. Adams wanted to take her ashore to "see the sights," Lorene said, and Howie knew he had more in mind than that.

Mr. Garvey stashed his family below, in spite of the heat, warning them not even to come on deck while they were in this "evil clime."

Before Howie left the ship, he saw Dr. Sloan hurriedly stepping ashore with his meager baggage. That seemed odd, a white man getting off in the port of Nueva Panama, as if he meant to stay. But Dr. Sloan was a kind of peculiar fellow anyway.

Howie was delighted with the town. The narrow cobbled streets were lined with colorful adobe houses, one packed close against the next. Most of these dwellings were thatched with dried palms, but some of the large structures had steep roofs with orange tiles set in a wavy pattern.

The people didn't seem near as unfriendly as Jones had warned. For the most part, they simply ignored him and went about their business. Everyone seemed happy and busy at some task. Men, women and children were well dressed and clearly had enough to eat. Nueva Panama didn't look at all like the dreary towns of America. The people were doing well here, and Howie didn't blame them for keeping to themselves. They prospered from the trade that came their way, and had no reason to welcome further intrusion from that desolate country to the north.

Purely by accident, Howie stumbled into the busy marketplace, a street of crowded booths and stalls. It seemed as if everyone in town had converged on this colorful spot at once. Merchants shouted their wares, thrusting fresh fruits and vegetables in every customer's face. Howie marveled at the variety of foods for sale. There were melons of every kind, brilliant fruits of orange and yellow and green. Nearly everything there was something he'd never seen before. Most interesting of them all was a long fruit that looked for all the world like the enormous yellow pod of a pea. It hung in thick clusters from the stalls, and seemed to be a favored item of everyone who passed. Howie was determined to try one, and offered a merchant a coin. The man looked it over closely, one side and then the next, then handed Howie two of the strange fruits.

Howie studied the things, not sure what to do with them at all. A small black boy saw his dilemma and laughed. He took the fruit from Howie and peeled the yellow skin from one end, revealing the ivory-colored part inside. Howie took a bite. Lord, it was about the best thing he'd ever eaten in his life! He bought two more, and gave the boy one for his help. The boy grinned and ran away.

As Howie was moving through the marketplace, he glanced up through the crowd and spotted a familiar face. Dr. Sloan was less than ten feet away, standing before a booth that sold hats and other items made of straw. Sloan looked concerned, in heated conversation with a tall black man and a strikingly beautiful black woman. The man matched Sloan's agitation, but the woman seemed absolutely calm. Finally, the black man turned and left, and Sloan and the woman walked off quickly in Howie's direction.

Howie ducked out of sight; he couldn't say why, simply that it seemed the thing to do. If Sloan saw him, maybe he'd think Howie had followed him from the ship, and Howie didn't want that. Howie watched for a moment as the pair made their way through the crowded street, then followed at a safe distance behind.

He knew he had no business tailing Sloan and the fine-looking woman. Whatever they were up to was no concern of his. Still, he didn't let the two out of his sight. Sloan struck him as a man who didn't act like other men; he wasn't at all like Garvey or Ritcher Jones. He kept to himself and never said much at all. That wasn't much reason to follow a man through a strange town, Howie knew, but it seemed good enough at the time.

Maybe Ritcher Jones was right, he decided. Maybe he couldn't help being where he didn't belong.

CHAPTER SIXTEEN

For a while, it was no problem to keep Sloan and his lady friend in sight. Even after the crowded marketplace gave way to a quieter section of town, the close-set houses and narrow, twisting streets made it easy to follow the pair without risk of being seen. Then, with no warning at all, the town stopped abruptly, a last pale blue house giving way to a green tangle of foliage, a barrier as formidable as any fortress wall.

Howie stopped. Sloan and the lady couldn't have simply vanished. He was certain he hadn't lost them in the town—which meant there was a path or a road nearby. In spite of the heat, the place where he stood gave him a chill. He could almost see the jungle grow. If all the people left Nueva Panama today, Howie wondered how long it would take the green mass to advance and simply swallow up the town and drive right to the sea.

The best thing to do was turn around and go back. It was time to stop acting like a fool. A bird as big as a hawk took flight from a branch overhead. It had a big hooked beak and feathers of every color you could name. Howie jumped in spite of himself. Hell, now I'm scared of birds, he thought sourly. I better go back and hide down belowdecks with young Garvey.

He found the path a few yards to the left of the blue house. It was wide enough for a cart, and someone used it enough to hold back the growth on either side.

Howie heard the sounds of the place before he saw it. A woman called out; children laughed and played at some game. When the first sign of a building came into sight, he stepped off the trail and made his way a few feet through the foliage. It was a small settlement in a clearing. Five or six small houses, and one long building, all painted in the same pastels as the dwellings in the town. Howie couldn't spot Sloan or the lady. Several black men and women moved about, and there seemed to be plenty of children.

There was a thatched roof by the side of the long building. The clearing was so bright it was hard to see into the shade. As his eye grew accustomed to light and shadow, he could make out people on the porch. To his surprise, the people in the shade were all white. Young people, men and women near his own age. They didn't seem to be talking or doing much of anything at all. They just sat. Everyone was dressed the same: sandals, white trousers, and white shirts.

Howie felt uneasy at the sight. What were they doing here? Maybe the blacks were keeping them in this place for some reason. Only that didn't make a lot of sense, because Dr. Sloan was here and *he* was white, too. Unless he'd turned against his own kind. That was a thought. He sure was friendly with the pretty black woman.

Howie kept watching, wondering why in hell he was standing there with salty sweat stinging his good eye, while every bug in Panama Province ate supper on his face and his arms. He sure didn't intend to walk in and say hello, tell Sloan he was just passing by. Maybe, he thought, if he waited another minute, one of the white persons would get up and *do* something. He felt like he wanted to see that. One of them walking, or speaking to a friend. Anything but just sitting. Just sitting there bothered him a lot.

He felt a sharp jab and reached up to slap the back of his neck. The jab returned at once. Howie cursed under his breath, slapped at the spot again, and turned around. He saw a black man standing there two feet away, a blade in his hand that was as long as Howie's arm.

"You lose your way, mister?" the man said.

Howie tried a grin. "Yeah, now I guess maybe I did. You mind pointin' the way back to town?"

The black man didn't smile. Howie noticed he didn't seem to sweat, and wondered how he managed that.

"I think maybe you need a little drink 'fore you go

back to town,'' the man said easily. ''Maybe you sit down and rest.''

''I thank you, but I'm just fine,'' Howie said.

''No. I don't think this is so. You don't look so good to me.'' The man nodded toward the settlement. ''You go this way.''

Arguing with the man was a poor idea, Howie figured. The blade looked as if it was used to cut down small trees. He moved off back toward the path, keenly aware of the black man behind.

Howie's captor led him into the clearing. Two men spotted them approaching and started toward them at once. One of the men had a rifle.

''You wait,'' said the man with the blade, and walked toward the long low building.

Neither of the two men spoke. The rifle looked old, but that didn't mean it wouldn't work. The sun beat down without mercy on Howie's head. No one suggested that they go and sit down in the shade. The covered porch he'd watched from the trees was less than twenty feet away. He could see the white people clearly now. Four men and two women. They sat on a long wooden bench and didn't talk. Just watching them gave Howie the creeps. If he hadn't seen their eyes wide open, he would swear they were asleep.

A bird called out in the jungle. It sounded like the one he'd seen with all different colors. One of the men on the bench got to his feet. He stood very still for a moment, then turned his head and looked right at Howie. A big grin spread across his features. Howie's knees nearly gave way. There was nothing at all behind the smile, nothing in the blue vacant eyes.

The man turned and started walking out of the shade, still grinning from ear to ear. He walked real funny, his shoulders slumped down and his arms hanging loose by his sides.

''Michael, now you want to go on back and sit down,'' the man with the rifle said gently. ''Just go on back and sit. Louanne, she'll be out directly and see what you need.''

The young man cocked his head to listen. Howie could

imagine all the words taking shape somewhere inside his head, working up into a thought he could understand.

"Go back and sit," the man said again. "Go and sit down."

The white man's eyes seemed to brighten for an instant. He turned and walked back and sat on the bench, almost as if he'd never moved.

Howie found he'd been holding his breath. He let it out slowly, and felt another chill. He didn't want to look at the people on the bench, but couldn't bring himself to stop.

Dr. Sloan suddenly appeared in the doorway of the long building. He looked at Howie a long time—just looked, and didn't say anything at all. Finally, he motioned to the man with the rifle, and turned and walked back inside. The man nudged Howie toward the door and then on into the room.

"It's all right, William," said Dr. Sloan. "I'll call if I need you."

Sloan sat in a straw-backed chair. There were tables stacked with papers and books, and very little else in the room. The pretty black woman sat by the window. She looked curiously at Howie, and he was certain she started to smile.

"Cory, what are you doing here?" said Dr. Sloan. He looked bone-tired, as if the heat were sucking out all his strength.

"I don't guess I got any reason," Howie said.

Sloan didn't care much for that. "Did someone tell you to follow me, Cory? Who was it? I want you to tell me who it was."

"Sir, no one done that," Howie said. "That's the truth. I saw you and—you and her in the market. You and her and another man. Then I just—started following after you here. I don't know why." Howie tried to smile. "I guess I didn't have nothing better to do."

"Sit down, Cory." The woman spoke for the first time. Her voice was soft and nice, as beautiful as the woman herself. A real fine easy voice, yet it clearly belonged to a woman who was sure of herself, a woman who knew what she was doing. You *wanted* to listen to her when she talked, and hear what she had to say.

"My name's Elena," the woman said. "Pour yourself some lemonade if you like, Cory. I'm sure you could use a drink. The body loses liquids quickly in the tropics."

"Thank you," Howie said. He poured himself a drink from a clay pitcher. Whatever lemonade was, it tasted sour and sweet at the same time.

Elena turned to Sloan. "I think Cory here is telling you the truth, doctor. I don't believe anyone sent him here. That *is* the truth, isn't it, Cory? You didn't have any reason to follow us here."

"Yes, ma'am. That's the God's truth."

"Well, you had no business doing it, boy," Sloan said. "No damn business at all."

"I guess I know that," Howie said.

Sloan was clearly making an effort to control his anger. He leaned forward and gripped the arms of his chair. "You saw the people outside. The white people." It was a statement and not a question.

"Yes sir, I did."

"And what did you think about them?"

Howie shifted uncomfortably in his chair. "I don't guess I thought anything at all."

Sloan glanced sharply at Elena. "You see, he's lying straight out. You saw something, boy. And you *thought* something, too. Don't tell me that you didn't." Sloan slammed a fist on the table. "Dammit, you'd better be truthful with me. This place is no concern of yours at all. You're here, and I can't help that. But if you won't *talk* to me, Cory, I can—"

"Doctor . . ." Elena smiled and stood. She seemed to keep unfolding, like some kind of flower coming up. "Cory, why don't you come with me," she said. "Let's just walk for a while."

Sloan started to protest. Then he sank back in his chair and ran a handkerchief over his brow. He seemed too weary to do anything else. He didn't look at Howie again.

"It isn't always easy to let ourselves see things we don't want to see," Elena said. "That's simply the way people are. We want to push things aside that make us feel real bad."

"I guess that's so," Howie said. He wasn't sure what

Elena was saying, but it was fine to watch her talk. She was so tall and slender he had to look up while they walked. That had never happened to him with a woman before, but it didn't seem awkward at all. Not with Elena. Elena was just the way she was supposed to be. Dark hair hung down to her shoulders, braided like he'd never seen hair done before, hundreds of tight little strands, each end decorated with bright beads. Her eyes were velvet brown, and seemed to tilt slightly at the corners, and her skin was as slick as dark glass. She walked with her back held straight, and though the clearing was covered with small stones, he never heard her steps.

"Dr. Sloan talked to me some," Elena said. "Before he called you in. He told me about you."

Howie gave her a wary look. "There isn't much to say about me."

"Oh, I think there is, Cory." She stopped for a moment and smiled, laying her hand lightly on his arm. Her touch made Howie feel funny inside, like when Lorene touched him, only different.

Elena began walking again, keeping to the shade of the trees past the clearing. "Dr. Sloan told me what happened on the ship. How awfully sick you got when you saw that slaughtering going on. He also told me that you don't eat meat. You likely didn't notice, but the doctor doesn't eat meat, either. None of us do, Cory. Nobody here."

Elena paused. "I do not believe anyone sent you here. I know you are traveling with a preacher from High Sequoia, and such men can be quite curious sometimes when it comes to other people's affairs. But I believe what you say is the truth. That you came here on your own." Her eyes found Howie and held him. "I also believe you were *not* telling the truth when you said you saw nothing . . . *unusual* about the young white people here. That's not exactly so, is it, Cory?"

"No. I guess it isn't." For some reason, he found it hard to lie to Elena. It didn't seem to hurt too much to tell the truth.

"Something happened to you, Cory," Elena said gently. "I don't know what it was, but something made you get sick there on the ship. I believe that happened because there is something you don't like to think about. Something very deep inside. You *know* this thing, but it is so painful to you, you don't want to look at it again."

Elena took his hand. "Come with me, Cory. I want you to meet someone. I'll just be a moment."

Elena left him under the covered porch and slipped through a narrow door. The white people sat in exactly the same positions in which Howie had seen them last. He tried to look at something else. Elena returned, a young man at her side. He was stockily built, with neatly trimmed brown hair. He was white, but his face and arms were deeply tanned. He looked at Howie with a pleasant, easygoing smile.

"Cory," Elena said, "I'd like you to meet Tom. Tom and I are great friends. Isn't that so, Tom?"

"Yes ma'am, Miss Elena," Tom said. He looked at Elena with pride, and open adoration. Turning to Howie, he thrust out his hand. "I'm real pleased to meet you, Cory."

"Same here," Howie said.

"Tom goes to school here," Elena said. "Tom, Cory might be interested in hearing what you're learning."

"I can read," Tom said. "And write some, too. I'm not real good at sums, but Miss Elena says everyone doesn't have to be good at everything they do."

"That's right," Elena said. She tousled Tom's hair. "Thank you so much for coming out. You can go back and help Louanne now if you like."

"Pleased to see you," Tom said. "Maybe we can talk again sometime."

"That'd be fine." Howie said.

Tom disappeared. Elena led Howie to cane chairs at the far corner of the building. "Now," she said, sitting across from Howie and taking both his hands in hers, "I want to tell you some things about Tom, but first I'd like to talk a little more about you. I want to know what happened to you, Cory. That might not be real easy, but I'll try to make it all right. I'm going to trust you, and I would like you to trust me as well."

Elena squeezed his hands and leaned in very close, so close he could smell the fine spice of her skin. "Tell me about yourself, Cory. Tell me who you are. Tell me about *you.*''

Elena's dark eyes seemed to peer right through him. It seemed as if a strange kind of strength and understanding were flowing directly from her hands into his. He felt her kindness and her love, a love that was so different from anything he'd known that the tears began to scald his good eye. The intensity of her presence was almost more than he could bear; yet, he wanted to tell her everything, every hurt and every pain, every bad thing that had happened in his life.

The words spilled out in a rush. He told her about the Bluevale Fair when he was twelve, about the way the farm looked, the way the fields turned colors in the spring. He told her how Carolee had been picked for Silver Island, and what a fine thing everybody thought that was. With the tears coming hard, he told her what Colonel Jacob had done to his mother and father, and what he, Howie, had done to Colonel Jacob after that. He told her about joining the big meat herd heading west to feed the army, how he'd never really been in the army at all, but everyone figured that he had, and it was easier not to tell them any different. He told her how he'd come to get mixed up in the war for Colorado, where Colonel Jacob caught him and took his eye, and would have done a lot more if the Rebel artillery hadn't blown the town apart when it did. He told her about the girl, Kari, how they'd gotten away together, and how Kari had stolen his horse after that and left him dry.

How he'd walked forever then, and wound up in Mexico, and seen the black man in the desert with the survivors from Silver Island. He told her about Tallahassee, and even about killing Anson Slade. About going to Silver Island to look for Carolee, though he knew he'd never find her alive. Finally, he told her about the survivors he'd found in the 'glades, how there were still people there, people who'd gotten away.

And when it was over, and all the words were gone, Elena took him in her arms for a while and told him how the hurt would go away.

''I know you can't believe that now,'' Elena said, ''but

it will. It will someday. I promise you, Cory, that time is going to come."

She held him away from her then, and a lovely smile touched her face. "Somehow, when I saw you, I thought it might be you. I know about your meeting in the desert. I knew about that before you told me. I knew about the boy with one eye."

Howie stared at her. "Why, you couldn't know that. There isn't any way that could be!"

"The man you met, Cory. His name was Earl Seevers, and he was my father. He was bringing those people down here. All the way through Mexico, and the awful desolation below that. He brought them right here to this settlement."

Howie shook his head in wonder. "He came here? Well—is he here right now? Can I see him?"

"No, Cory." Elena looked away for a moment. "He died, shortly after he got back home. But he brought the people here. Two are still with us, but the others are at another settlement farther down the coast."

Elena ran a hand across her throat. "The people Father brought back told us what happened at Silver Island, the horrors that your government has seen to do. You are not alone in your pain, you see. There are others who know, and understand the terrible things that have been done."

For an instant, Howie could almost smell the smoke of the evening fire in Mexico, see the old man's face.

"I couldn't stop thinkin' about that bunch he had with him. They looked like stock, but he kept hinting maybe they wasn't. Fed 'em *people* food from the fire, and said one of 'em could *talk.*" Howie looked down at his hands. "That's when I found out. I went and talked to the boy who could speak. I didn't know. I didn't ever guess how such a thing could be. . . ."

Whatever you're thinking, it ain't that," the boy said. "You couldn't know it. Not 'less you been there, you couldn't. Hadn't anyone ever got out of that place before us. What they did there is use you like they want. You ain't meat, but you're by God close enough to it."

Howie felt something give way inside. "Use you how? What are you talking about?"

"They do it 'cause stock gets weak and don't breed good anymore. Meat don't care if it's humpin' its sister or its ma, and that makes the blood go bad. You can't stop 'em doing that, so they put good blood back in the herds. Only it ain't meat blood. It's people's. The boys got to serve the best mares. The girls are put in with healthy bucks—"

"Goddam, you're lying!" Howie exploded. "No one'd do a thing like that! No one!"

"They can do whatever they want," the boy said.

Howie was shaken. "Someone . . . someone'd find out. They couldn't do that without someone findin' out."

"Isn't anyone going to do that," the boy said. There was no feeling at all in his voice. "It's down in the old keys and you don't get close unless you belong. It's a lie, the whole thing. Silver Island and kids gettin' picked at a Choosing, going to live in some fine place where everything's pretty and nice. That ain't what it's for. That ain't what it's for at all. . . ."

"Oh Lord, Cory!" Elena laid a hand on Howie's cheek. "I was right in thinking what I saw in you. You've been through a whole lot of hurt, a whole lot of awful hurt."

"I didn't know his name," Howie said. "Didn't even ask. He told me—that he'd known Carolee. That they didn't always cut your tongue right, and she could talk. She told the boy about me and our folks sometimes, and how it was back home. And then the people in the 'glades, they knew her, too."

He looked up at Elena. "It's awful what they done. They didn't have no cause to do that!"

"No, they didn't, Cory," Elena said.

Howie looked at Elena, squinting his good eye. "That boy you had me meet. The one named Tom, who said he was going to school. That's what you do here, isn't it? You and Dr. Sloan and the rest. You take care of folks who got away from Silver Island." He nodded at the people on the bench. "There was folks like them in the 'glades. Some of 'em just like that. They couldn't say nothin' because the men at Silver Island had cut their tongues. You can make 'em talk again, can't you? You can make them get better, like Tom."

Elena looked at the ground and ran a hand across her cheek. She turned to Howie then and studied him a long time, not saying anything at all, just bringing up her hands to Howie's face, touching the corners of his mouth with the tips of her fingers, then finally bringing her hands flat together, as if she might be starting to pray.

"Cory, you understand some of what I said. Now you've got to understand the rest. We had people here from Silver Island—but no more than the ones my father brought back. The ones you saw in Mexico. There aren't any others here. That's all."

Elena nodded toward the bench. "Those folks, and Tom, they're people too, but that's not what everybody calls them. We don't use the words here, but I'll say them so you'll know. Tom and the others here with us are stock. *Meat,* Cory. That's who we're trying to help."

Howie felt cold all over. He stared at Elena in disbelief. "No, now that can't be. Meat's meat, and—"

Elena brought a finger to his lips. "Listen. Listen to me," she said. "You know the truth the same as I do, Cory. You *know.* That's part of the pain you've got bottled inside. The thing you don't want to see. The hurt isn't just about your sister, or what they did at Silver Island. You know the truth, Cory. It's a terrible truth to know, but it's there and it won't go away. *Stock and people are just the same.* There isn't any difference at all. It's the most horrible lie there ever was. The Great War killed most of the animals people ate, and the rest got slaughtered real fast. They had to believe that awful lie. That some folks were meat and some weren't. That made it all right. They told themselves stock were different, that they didn't have a soul. If they told themselves that, they could eat and they wouldn't have to starve. A lie that goes on a long time starts to look like the truth, but that doesn't change a thing. This lie's had a long time to grow, but it's still a lie, Cory. It won't ever be anything else."

Howie's throat felt dry. Every muscle in his body

wanted to tear itself apart; it was only the calm, soothing voice of Elena that kept him silent in his chair, that, and the touch of Elena's hands.

"But stock can't talk," Howie said. "Hell, they ain't hardly got a brain. You ain't going to make 'em say a thing—"

"Cory . . ." Elena looked off into the dense green wall past the clearing. "Cory, if I took you away from your mother when you were born, and put you in a room with a lot of other children, just like you—if I put you there and no one ever spoke to you at all, just fed you and kept you locked up, what do you think you'd grow up to be? You wouldn't know a thing, now would you? You couldn't talk, you wouldn't know about clothes, or what anything was for. You'd grunt and defecate on the floor. You'd eat and sleep and stalk around, and mate with whatever was close by. No one could tell you from stock. You'd be just the same. And that's the difference between people and meat. The only difference there is. One child is brought up in a pen, the other in a house."

Elena looked at the people on the bench, and a terrible sadness filled her eyes. "The real little ones work out pretty well. They're not as smart as regular children, because it isn't *important* to be smart in a herd. The young we have here are bigger, stockier, than children raised in a home—because that *is* important. Big males get the females first, when they're breeding in the herd. And ranchers breed for size, too. So the children we get aren't smart, but they're larger than other children. The only thing is, they're weaker, in a way, because inbreeding makes them that way. Stockmen know that," Elena said grimly. "And the men at Silver Island knew it, too. They could see the herds' blood getting thin, and they knew just what to do about that."

Elena glanced once more at the bench. "Even if you're healthy as can be, and smart as anyone you know, something happens if you don't start using your brain real early. We don't know why, but it's so. That bunch is in their twenties. They aren't going to get much better than they are right now. We've had Tom since he was five, and he's nineteen now. He's doing real good—but he's always going to be a little slow. There's no fixing that. Five's just too late to start."

The enormity of what Elena was saying, what she and the others were trying to undo, struck Howie like a blow. "But what *good's* it going to do?" he blurted out. "You take a handful of those—those whatever you want to call 'em right there, dress 'em up and maybe teach them to read and say, 'Morning, nice to meet you.' They're me—*meat*—I can't think of any other word, 'cause that's what they are now. Lord, there's meat everywhere—thousands of 'em, maybe millions, I don't know. You can't do a thing about helping all of them. Not a damn thing."

"I know," Elena said. She kept looking past him, past the thick barrier of trees, and somewhere beyond that. "We're trying, though, Cory. I *know* we can't do much, but we've simply got to—*try!*"

Elena looked at Howie then, and Howie saw all the terrible sadness in the world. "Don't you see? Things have got to change. That has to be. *It just has to be. . . .*"

PART TWO

West by Southwest . . .

CHAPTER SEVENTEEN

THREE DAYS NORTH INTO THE PACIFIC, BLACK CLOUDS appeared in the west without warning, suddenly turning the clear, bright day into night. The temperature dropped in an instant, leaving an ominous chill in the air. Captain Finley turned the ship about at once, fleeing to the south, but the storm moved in with such intensity and speed there was no time to escape its awful wrath.

Seamen scurried about the decks, and Finley ordered passengers below, reminding them to fasten the portholes in their cabins securely. Howie was scarcely in his quarters before the first gusts of wind and driving rain struck the vessel. The ship creaked and pitched, but it didn't seem all that bad, no worse than a heavy thunderstorm on land. Bracing himself against his bunk, Howie pressed his face to the small circle of glass. It was an exciting thing to see, but not frightening at all, and he wondered why the captain had made such a fuss.

Rain pelted against the porthole, but he could still make out the sea, peppered now with rain, against an ever-darkening sky. He wondered what birds did in a storm. There wasn't any place to land, so he figured they just flew real fast out of the way. The fish wouldn't likely even care; a storm was all right with them. All they had to do was swim deep and not worry about a thing.

As Howie watched, the sky to the west began to change. The color didn't seem quite as dark anymore; it was almost the color of the sea, a deep blue-green webbed with filaments of white. The sky sucked the white strands high, and higher still, until they all coalesced into a horizontal band that stretched out as far as the eye could see.

Howie was fascinated by this peculiar event. It was a

strange, unworldly sight, something he'd never imagined and couldn't begin to comprehend.

Then, in an instant, his vision seemed to unlock the puzzle outside, shift into sudden understanding. At once, he saw what he hadn't seen before—it wasn't the sky changing color, it was the sea, the sea rising up in a wave nearly as high as the ship, a monstrous wall of water topped with angry white foam.

Howie cried out in alarm, a cry he never heard as the great wave exploded against the hull. Timbers snapped and a blast of thunderous sound engulfed the world. Howie grabbed blindly for the edge of his bunk. The force of the wave tore him free and slammed him hard against the far wall. Before he could get his bearings, the ship lurched again, tossing him back against his bunk. He felt as if he'd broken every bone in his body. Clinging feebly to the rim of his bunk, he hauled himself in, buried his head against the mattress, and held on for dear life. Glass exploded somewhere in the passage beyond his door. Something rolled heavily across the deck overhead. Howie thought he heard a cry in the wind. He wondered what Ritcher Jones's God was up to at the moment. He wasn't helping much around here.

The wind shrieked, and one wall of water after another picked the ship up like a cork and slammed it into the sea. Howie didn't wonder anymore why everything aboard was bolted down.

"How's the sea doing now?" he asked the boy.

"Why, smooth as glass, sir," the boy said. "It's a right fine night."

"And it might get heavier than this?"

"Yes, sir. Quite a bit heavier than this."

"What do we do then?"

"We ride it out, sir. . . ."

By god, the boy had clearly lied, Howie thought dismally. We ain't going to *ride* nothing out. We're all going to *die,* that's what we're going to do.

Jack, Howie's sailor friend, said the storm had lasted nearly four hours. Howie didn't believe that at all. Four days was more like it.

"Weren't too bad," Jack said. "We got her into the wind. I seen a lot worse."

Howie didn't ask when, or how much worse it could get. He'd learned sailors seldom thought anything was an average or typical event. They could always recall something better, bigger, smaller, or worse.

The scene topside told Howie much more than he wanted to know. It looked as if a battery of Rebel cannon had raked the decks. Canvas was tattered in shreds, and lines flapped uselessly in the wind. Deck cargo had come loose, smashing the rails in half a dozen places. A foremast had snapped clean off. One seaman had broken a leg, and nearly every man was badly bruised. Mrs. Garvey had a nick about a quarter inch long on her chin; Howie could hear her howling down below. Her husband stomped around on deck, demanding medical attention. Captain Finley was in no mood for that. He told Garvey in a very courteous tone that he should get below at once, if he didn't want several able seamen to toss him off the stern.

Ritcher Jones looked none the worse for wear. Lorene was pale as death, the fright still vivid in her eyes.

"Quite a little blow," Jones said, stretching as if he'd just had a fine day's nap. "You fare all right, did you, Cory?"

"I ain't dead," Howie said flatly. "I reckon that's what you call all right."

Jones threw back his head with a hearty laugh. "The Lord's hand is terrible and swift, gentle and kind, depending on the deeds He performs. He can churn up the sea in great fury, or draw a tender seedling from the earth into the light. The wise man won't try to fathom His ways."

"Yes, sir," Howie said, not at all surprised that the storm had inspired another sermon. It didn't take near that much to set the preacher off on a spree.

"I hope you didn't get too shaken up, Sister Lorene," Howie said politely.

"Why, I was pure scared out of my wits," Lorene said. "I knew, though, the Lord would prevail. I just prayed He would save me to serve in some further way."

"Well, I'm certain He's got some fine things planned for you to do," Howie said. "Some *real* fine things."

His face betrayed no expression at all, but Lorene nearly burst out laughing on the spot. She clamped her lips tight and her cheeks turned red with the strain. Howie was grateful the preacher was behind her, and couldn't see her face. If he had, the game would have been up right there. Instead, Jones beamed with delight at the conversation between them.

Lorene's eyes darted at Howie, and he knew he'd catch hell later on. It was worth it, though, he decided. Lorene had like to tore a couple of vessels, knowing exactly the sort of "fine things to do" he had in mind.

On the voyage through the Gulf, toward Panama Province, the ship had struck out boldly across open water, seldom coming in sight of the land. The trip up the Pacific coast was different; now there was always a shadowy mass to the east, five or six miles away. Jack told Howie this was the practice during the stormy time of the year.

"Sometimes they come up fast, as I reckon you already know," Jack said. "If you get any warnin' at all, and it looks like you can't ride her out, then you head toward shore and hope there's an inlet somewhere, a piece of land to hide behind awhile."

"Sounds like a good idea," Howie said, relieved to hear they might not have to go through such a harrowing experience again.

Jack frowned thoughtfully and shook his head. "Yeah, except there ain't a whole lot of safe places 'round here. And truth to tell, friend, I'd rather face the sea than take my chances over there."

Jack glanced warily to shore. "There's folks where the old Central Americas used to be, and likely on the coast of Mexico, I wouldn't care to run into at all. No sir, I'd a sight rather get drowned at sea."

Howie didn't like the sound of that at all. Ritcher Jones had alluded to the dangers of that region, and now his friend Jack had brought the subject up as well. When Howie tried to question him further, Jack suddenly found other things he had to do. Standing by the newly repaired railing, looking at the gray and distant shore, Howie decided the sea wasn't all he'd imagined it to be. It was fine when everything went right, and there were dolphins and flying fish to see, and nights in his cabin with Lorene. But he and Lorene could get tangled up fine in a bed on shore—and you could do without watching fish fly.

"There it is," Captain Finley said. He pointed to the east. " 'Bout four miles off the starboard bow. New Los Angeles and port." He shared a rare smile with Howie. "Can't say as I'll mind putting this voyage behind me. I'm damned if I'll sail again this time of year. One storm's bad enough—we're lucky we didn't get two." He spat over the side and retrieved his spyglass from Howie. "Did you ever, uh—lose a ship, sir?" Howie asked.

Finley's heavy brows masked his eyes. "Now that's not a question you put to a ship's captain, boy."

Howie felt his cheeks color. "I'm real sorry, sir."

"Huh," Finley grunted. "Three." He held up his fingers. "I lost three. All of 'em in the goddam ocean we're sailing now." He looked Howie up and down. "Don't know what you plan to do with yourself, Cory. But you might think hard on a life at sea. It's about the finest thing a man can do. I might take you on myself."

Howie forced a smile. "Thank you, Captain Finley. I sure will think about that."

Captain Finley nodded and stalked off, shouting orders to his crew.

"Well, I thought on it some," Howie muttered at Finley's back. "I don't guess I'll have to think about it again."

He stood and watched the sea. Late on the afternoon before, Jones had pointed far to starboard at the hundreds of small islands off the shore. The gray points of land looked peculiar; most were no more than stubs, ragged mounds of stone that seldom rose more than twenty feet above the sea.

"Don't appear real natural, do they?" Jones had said. "That's because they aren't, Cory. What you're looking at now is Old Los Angeles town. There's a whole city there on the bottom. Right about *there* is where the shore used to be." He waved his hand vaguely to the right.

"The War did that?" Howie couldn't imagine such devastation, or what might have caused it.

"Partly the War," Jones said. "Folks say it was more than that, though. That the unholy weapons of the time loosed something in the earth. The land just heaved up and cracked in two, and drowned the whole coast in the sea. Forty, fifty miles inland, and a hundred miles wide. No one can say if it happened that way—but the city's down there, and that's a fact."

Howie could think of nothing to say. Long after Jones left, he stood and watched the dreary islands, until they vanished far astern.

New Los Angeles was a hundred miles or more up the coast from the sunken older city. Howie remembered Tällahassee, and once again questioned the wisdom of naming new towns the same as places that had suffered a terrible fate. It didn't seem like a good idea, but people didn't appear to mind.

When the harbor came into view, Howie forgot all thoughts of ancient disaster and desolation. The port was a wondrous thing to see. Mountains marched right down to blue water, and hundreds of white structures sparkled in the sun. Everything seemed white and clean. The city sprawled along the bay—a bay which hadn't been there before the Great War, Jones explained—and fine houses climbed the side of the green, forested slopes behind.

There was too much to see all at once. The harbor itself was full of vessels of all kinds. Howie was amazed to see some ships with canted, brightly colored sails. These great planes of canvas pictured strange and frightening beasts, lizards with batlike wings and open maws that breathed fire, other creatures with long sharp teeth and eyes like pumpkin seeds. More astonishing than the vividly colored sails were the tall black cylinders that sprouted amidships on these vessels. Often there were three or four cylinders in a row. At first, Howie thought the ships were simply on fire. Then, as they passed a ship close to port, he saw the tall columns were chimneys that belched forth clouds of gray smoke. Lorene had told him there were ships that had chimneys, but he hadn't much believed her at the time.

Jones said the vessels came from Asia, and that mechanical devices inside produced steam, which turned ingenious paddles on the side.

"Why?" Howie asked, and Jones said they would discuss this matter another time. The question seemed to irritate the preacher, and Howie decided that he didn't know the answer himself.

It was close to noon when the ship found a berth and all the lines were secured. Two men came aboard to greet Jones, and it was clear at once they'd come from High Sequoia. They treated Ritcher Jones with great respect, gathering up his baggage, and Lorene's, and listening to every word that Jones said.

Both men wore white robes that came down to their knees; the robes had light green piping around the edges and on the sleeves. And on each breast was sewn the symbol of High Sequoia Howie had seen on the preacher's gun—a thick-boled tree, growing right out of a heart.

Jones introduced him to the men, who were named Brother this, and Brother something else. Howie couldn't keep them straight. Captain Finley and Adams shook hands with everyone as they left, and Howie didn't much like the way Adams held Lorene in his grip too long, or the sweet smile Lorene gave in return. He didn't see the Garveys anywhere, and didn't care if he ever did again.

It seemed strange to be standing on solid ground again. Nothing moved beneath his feet, but Howie found himself walking as he had on board, waiting for a pitch of the deck that never came.

Lorene glanced at him out of the corner of her eye and grinned at his awkward walk, though Howie saw she was doing the same.

The dock was alive with activity; the air was thick with harbor smells, and there was the usual noise and clamor. Howie noticed many of the men had peculiar tilted eyes, blunt features, and skin a shade he'd never seen before.

"They're *Asians,*" Lorene whispered, shaking her head in a frown. "Don't stare. It's not nice."

"I ain't staring," Howie said.

"You are so."

Well, he'd learned something new already. He knew

what an Asian was now. They were short, and had coal-black hair, and chattered in a tongue no one could possibly understand.

"Anyway, I already know what they are," Howie said. "I don't need you to tell me that."

"You didn't know any such thing," Lorene said. "You never even saw one before."

Ritcher Jones walked ahead with the two Brothers. He turned and raised a brow at Howie and Lorene.

"You two coming or not? I'm half starved, and determined to find a meal that doesn't slide off the table 'fore I get a chance to eat it."

The Brothers from High Sequoia glanced at each other and grinned. Howie decided this pair would be getting on his nerves before long. They thought everything Ritcher Jones said was either wise, inspiring, downright hilarious, or maybe all three.

CHAPTER EIGHTEEN

PAST THE DOCKING AREA, AN OPEN CARRIAGE WAS WAITING for Ritcher Jones and his party. The carriage stood beyond an open gate and a high wooden fence, and it was clear the fence was there for a reason—no one entered or left the pier without permission. At a small wooden shed by the gate, a sober-faced official gave Howie a blue card. His name and a number were carefully penned on the card with ink, and also noted on a list maintained by the official. The card was stamped with an ornate seal of California. This whole procedure went quickly, but Howie sensed this was due to the presence of Ritcher Jones.

All the others in the party showed their cards at the gate, though the other cards were green, indicating that Jones and his friends were residents of the state. Howie asked the preacher what the cards were for, and Jones explained that California simply liked to keep track of its citizens and quests.

"If we had come by land," Jones said, "we would have stopped at one of numerous stations like this on our eastern borders. The laws of California are quite generous and fair, but they are strict as well, Cory, and any crime or misdeed is dealt with swiftly and severely." He smiled broadly at Howie. "Only officers of the law carry weapons here. You simply don't *need* one, you see. There is very little crime, and it's quite safe to walk the streets."

Howie was astonished. "They don't let you carry a *gun?*"

"As I said, you don't need it. There's no reason for it. A person carries a weapon to either defend himself or commit some sort of offense. The police here are well suited to handle the latter. Thus there is nothing for the citizen to defend himself against."

It sounded like a real good law, the way Jones put it, but Howie wasn't sure he'd grow to like it. He had been without a weapon since they'd tossed him in jail in Alabama Port, and he still felt naked without something in his belt. What if somebody had a gun, and didn't *care* about the law? Why, he could walk up and laugh in your face, and put a bullet in your belly.

Howie didn't bother to ask Jones about that—or if he'd tossed his own long-barreled silver weapon overboard before they'd sailed into port. Howie had a picture of the preacher doing that.

The road twisted up a gentle slope from the pier. New Los Angeles sprawled among the foothills of the high green mountains at its back. Looking down the hills, Howie could see the docks, the unbelievably blue water, and more ships than he'd ever imagined in the bay. Only one thing marred this pleasant sight. To the south of the docks, a mile or so away, he could see the vast pens of stock. It was the largest operation he'd ever seen, acres and acres of meat. Howie felt something turn heavy in his belly, and he thought of the boy Tom, and the others sitting there on the bench, and the sadness in Elena's lovely eyes. He turned away at once, but the pens, and the image of Elena, refused to go away.

As he had noticed from the ship, the buildings and houses here were white and sparkling clean. Lush growth and clusters of bright flowers were everywhere. Howie sat on the edge of his seat, taking in everything they passed. He sat between the two Brothers, facing Jones and Lorene. Jones carried on a running conversation with the Brothers; Lorene sat primly at his side, hands folded in her lap, taking care to look at anything but Howie.

Howie was already concerned about Lorene, and the night to come. What kind of sleeping arrangements would they have at this High Sequoia place? The ship had worked out just fine, but that didn't mean they'd get that lucky again. He hadn't thought to talk it over with Lorene, and decided not to worry. *She* didn't want to stop either, so maybe everything was all right.

There were three- and four-story buildings set close together near the center of town. Tall trees shaded the hotels, clean open markets, and shops. And there were parks with ponds and gardens, right in the middle of the city. Everyone the carriage passed was well dressed. Howie noticed that at once. No gaunt and hungry faces, no veterans of the war with missing arms or legs. People *smiled,* and hurried here and there with cloth bags full of goods. The men looked hearty, and there were more than a few pretty women.

And horses—there was certainly no scarcity of horses in California. The broad, graveled streets were full of carriages and wagons and riders.

Howie shook his head in wonder at the sights. A war might be raging in the rest of the country, but you sure couldn't tell it here. Fighting and poverty seemed a million miles away. And the preacher was right—Howie didn't see anyone wearing a gun. Maybe these *laws* Jones talked about worked. Only that didn't account for everyone dressing nice, and clearly getting plenty to eat. There was some other reason for that.

Before the carriage left town and started up into the hills, Howie saw something he could hardly believe, even in California. There were Loyalist and Rebel officers in the streets, shopping, or simply walking around. Once the carriage passed a group of men from both sides, talking to one another on the steps of a hotel. Lord A'mighty, Howie thought, I guess I've seen everything now.

The foothills were comfortably cool, the streets shaded by tall, broad-leafed trees. Papa had taught him the name of every tree on the farm, but there were very few here that Howie recognized. The road, like the streets in town, was graded with white stone, and he had never seen that before, either.

Nearly an hour from the pier, the carriage came to a tall, white-painted gate. Two Brothers in robes were there to open the gate quickly, and the carriage passed through. Ahead, nearly lost among the trees, was the biggest house Howie had ever seen. It seemed to wander all about; one story would turn into two, and then the trees would reveal a high tower, or a wing that was three stories high, or a balcony or a porch. The house was white stucco, covered in places by vines, and the roof had curly orange tiles like the ones Howie had seen in Nueva Panama.

Richer Jones caught Howie's expression. "Well, what do you think of California, Cory? Does it look like you imagined it would be?"

"I never imagined nothing like this," Howie said.

The preacher's smile turned thoughtful, and he leaned forward and gripped Howie's knee. "I know what has to be going through your head, son. I've seen the rest of the country too, you'll recall. We're mightily blessed out here. Mightily blessed by the Lord."

Howie didn't need Jones to tell him that. "I knew High Sequoia would be something," he said. "But I never thought it'd be as big as this. How many people you got livin' in this place, if you don't mind me asking?"

For an instant, Jones looked bewildered. Then he leaned close to Howie again. "This house is sort of a . . . place to stay when the Brothers and Sisters are in town. It's a church, too, if you like. But it isn't High Sequoia, Cory. That's close to two hundred miles north and east."

Howie stared. "You mean you got another house, too?"

Jones shook his head. "High Sequoia's not a house, it's a *sanctuary,* so to speak. Lawrence likes to call it the Lord's quiet haven on earth. You'll see. There's nothing like it anywhere."

"I guess there's a whole lot of stuff I don't know 'bout California," Howie said.

One of the Brothers laughed softly at that, and Ritcher Jones silenced him with a look. "There is time to learn, son. Plenty of time for that."

Even after half a day in the big house, Howie was still completely lost. Jones had personally taken him on a quick tour, and Howie marveled at what he saw. The heavy, carved wooden furniture, the polished tile floors, and the plants everywhere—plants growing *inside* the house itself. There were living rooms and dining rooms and parlors, balconies and fountains, and even a room that was full of colorful birds. In the end, Howie managed to find his way from his room to the downstairs area and back again, and he was satisfied with that.

The room Jones gave him was bigger than the whole house where Howie had grown up. It had high glass doors leading to a balcony where you could sit and see way down the hill, and a patch of blue ocean beyond. He thought about his mother, and wished she could have seen something like this. The farmhouse had been fine enough for her, and Bluevale was likely the biggest town she'd ever seen. And Carolee and Papa, wouldn't they have marveled at a ship, and New Los Angeles and all?

Howie set these thoughts quickly aside. It wouldn't do any good to wonder what might have been. They were all three dead and he was here, in a place that likely cost more than Papa would have made if he'd lived a thousand years. The idea of that left a sour taste in his mouth, and the room and the fine glass windows and the view outside didn't seem quite as grand anymore.

From what Howie could tell, there were maybe twelve or fifteen people in the house, not nearly enough to fill it up. He couldn't imagine how many that would take. They didn't all appear at supper, so he figured they were eating in one of the three or four dining rooms he'd seen.

There were five, including Howie himself, on the brick patio outside. Besides Jones and Lorene, and one of the Brothers Howie had never met before, there was a Sister named Camille. The patio was lit by candles, and the meal was served by young men and women Howie learned were aspiring to be Brothers and Sisters. They wore pale yellow robes with no piping on the sleeves, instead of regular white garments like the others.

At first, Howie was surprised to find Jones and Lorene had changed into robes too, but this seemed the thing to do. He had never seen Lorene so lovely. Just looking at her—or trying *not* to—made him want her all the more. The candlelight softened her features and her hair, and it excited him a lot to imagine those incredibly long legs, the supple curves and secret places beneath the modest churchly attire. His face heated at the thoughts in his head, and he hoped Ritcher Jones wasn't looking his way.

The other girl, Camille, was pretty too, nearly as pretty as Lorene. She had hair black as night and olive skin, a thin, angular face, and enormous dark eyes. Howie made a point of not looking at her much; Lorene would sure notice if he did. He couldn't tell what Camille was like, because she seldom said a word during the meal. Lorene kept silent too, most of the time. Wearing robes seemed to have some effect, and Howie hoped this solemn, spiritual behavior wouldn't hamper the more earthly activities he and Lorene had come to share.

The other Brother at the table was called James, and he was somewhat older than the Brothers Howie had seen around the house. He was tall, and had very little flesh on his bones. He wasn't as old as he seemed; he just acted that way and it showed. He kept his face screwed up tight and never laughed. Even when Jones said something funny, James forced a smile, and looked as if it hurt to make the effort.

The talk was all of High Sequoia and what was going on there. James had just returned and had news about Lawrence and other people that Howie had no interest in at all. He perked up and listened when James discussed the upcoming peace talks between the Loyalists and the Rebels. James mentioned several names, but Harriver Mason wasn't one of them. That didn't mean he wasn't coming, of course, but it made Howie uneasy not to hear his name.

After supper, Lorene and Camille disappeared, and Jones excused himself, stating that he had to speak further with James. Howie was left on his own, and for a while he sat and looked at the growing dark.

Everything had happened so quickly—meeting Ritcher Jones and going to Alabama Port, then taking the ship to California. He had made up his mind what it was he had to do. Harriver Mason had run the horror of Silver Island. Mason would be at High Sequoia, so he, Howie, would be there, too. He would find Mason and kill him. He had no qualms about that, no more than squashing a mosquito on his arm. The man had done what he'd done. It was as simple as that.

Only now, with the prospect of High Sequoia very near, questions Howie had never thought about before began to worry at the edge of his mind. After he killed Mason—what would happen after that? Getting away was something he hadn't considered at all. Until today, he'd had no real image of California—he had known where it *was,* and that was it. That afternoon, he had discovered a finely drawn map, framed on one of the parlor walls, and he was appalled at the sheer *size* of California.

Hell, killing Mason was one thing, but he had never intended to get himself killed, too. After he saw the map, he stood and cursed himself for a fool. He found High Sequoia, but the names of the rivers and the mountains and the deserts meant nothing to him at all. California was a vast hunk of land, stretching every way there was—mountains, deserts, and the ocean. The Canadas were at the top, and Mexico way on the other end. The Canadas might be best, he decided; there weren't many settlements between High Sequoia and the border. And the deserts to the east looked deadly. Howie had seen enough of *that* kind of country in the north of Mexico, and wanted no part of it again.

Howie shook the troubling thoughts aside, stood, and looked out over the valley again. There were lights in the town, and farther out, a yellow glow upon the water. Were there other ports up to the north? He promised himself to study the map again. Of course, getting on a ship would be harder than taking off across the wild open country. In spite of the preacher's talk about men at border stations and having to show your card, the map had shown him the fallacy of that: There weren't enough people in California to watch even a small part of the state's borders. If you were *in*, they could catch you without a card and toss you out. But leaving was something else. If you stayed away from ports, there wasn't any way to stop a small army from leaving California.

"Well, a copper for your thoughts, Cory."

Howie started, turned, and saw Ritcher Jones.

The preacher smiled. "Didn't mean to sneak up like that. Guess you were off somewhere."

"I guess I was," Howie said. "Mostly I was thinking 'bout being out here. It's a pretty big place. All the stuff you told me about California, I still can't take it all in."

Jones poured himself a glass of wine from the table. He offered Howie a glass, and Howie shook his head.

"I think I can sort of make a guess on what's going through your head," Jones said. "I don't pretend to be a seer, you understand, but I've seen folks before when they first get a look at this place. They'll say, 'Now how can this be? How come it's so different out here?' "

"That's about what I was thinking," Howie said. He heard a girl humming somewhere, and wondered if it might be Lorene. "California don't seem to have a whole lot to do with the rest of the country. And what's going on there." Howie looked at Jones, trying to find the proper words. "I saw some government officers and some Rebels in town. They was talking to one another like they might be neighbors or something. You sure wouldn't see that anywhere but here."

"No, you certainly wouldn't," Jones agreed. "That's a fact. And I'd say it's a real fine thing."

"Yeah, I guess so. But it don't make any sense to me. It's like there isn't any war, and those fellas don't care if there is. Maybe bein' out here you just forget. California's got plenty of everything—but it ain't in the war. That's the thing. It don't seem right, and I can't figure how it came about. I don't guess you got an army, I don't know. I kinda got the idea that you don't.'

Howie paused and shook his head. "If I was Lathan,

now, I might get the idea that California rightly belonged to me. Seeing as how it's part of the West—'bout as west as you can get. Lathan says that part of the country belongs to him. And if he marched in here and took what California's got, why, it wouldn't be no problem at all to win the war. He'd turn right around and walk over the Loyalists in a month."

Jones nodded in thought and set down his glass. "You're thinking straight, Cory, and you've made a good point. We *don't* have an army, or nothing that you'd call one, anyhow, and Lathan—or anyone else for that matter—could march right in if he liked. But he won't. I'll tell you straight out that he won't."

"Why not?"

"Because it's easier to *buy* what you need than fight for it. It's as simple as that. California trades with whoever's got the price. Rebels and Loyalists alike. Asians, or anyone else." Jones rubbed his chin. "And let's say Lathan *did* decide to march on California. Even if we don't have an army, it's a mighty big state to have to cross, and it'd take every man that Lathan's got. And what would the Loyalists be doing while Lathan left his rear end exposed?"

Jones shook his head. "California's an island of plenty, son. The people here have worked long and hard to get what they've got. We've got everything everybody needs. And neither side in this war is fool enough to try and come and get it. They've got enough fight on their hands without starting something else."

Howie considered what the preacher had said. It made sense, but it brought another question to mind. "If California would quit selling to anyone, the war would have to come to a stop. You wouldn't need to have a peace talk, then."

"No, now that's not entirely true," Jones said. "I've talked to a great many high officers on both sides of this war, and they are all stubborn and dedicated men. They believe *their* cause is right, and I fear they are determined to fight to the last poor hungry trooper in their commands."

"I seen 'em do that, all right," Howie said.

"Yes. And I fear it won't stop, regardless of what California sells or doesn't sell.'' Jones filled his glass again. He looked suddenly weary, drained of his usual tireless drive.

''The thing is, Cory, you hit upon a sad bit of truth in this matter, I'm sorry to say. Merchants in California are getting rich off the war, there is no denying that. We abhor this in High Sequoia, but there's little we can do. We are, after all, only a religious settlement, and California is run by men who see profit in *this* life, and care very little for the glory of the next. Oh, we have some friends in high places, but not enough to count.'' Jones spread his hands. ''And if we *did* convince California to cut off supplies to the two forces, what then? As I just mentioned, it would not solve a thing. The fighting will go on until the bitter end. I wish I didn't believe this was so, but I do.

''No, cutting the armies off is not the answer,'' Jones went on. ''The answer lies in persuading both sides to stop, to settle their differences and bring the country together, save this nation before it crumbles into dust.''

''I don't reckon the rich men here in California will like that,'' Howie said.

Jones let out a long breath. ''I cannot tell you, my boy, how many hours I myself—and others as well—have spent trying to convince these 'rich men' you speak about that there is more money to be made in revitalizing a *peaceful* nation than there is helping to destroy it. I fear the human creature is very shortsighted, Cory. He tends to believe in what *is,* and is wary of what might be. I am afraid that's the way of the world. The Light of the Lord shines brightly in even the deepest corner, but a man has to open his eyes to see it. . . .''

Howie woke, and thought he was still dreaming. The glass doors to the balcony were open to the pleasant night air. Lorene stood just inside the room, bathed in the light of a half-moon.

''I'm sorry I took so long.'' Lorene sighed, dropping wearily to a chair. ''We had to do prayers, and *then* I had to climb all *kinds* of porches and balconies and stuff. Lord, Howie, I'm clear on the other side of this place where the Sisters have to stay.''

Howie sat up. "You couldn't just come through the house, Lorene?"

"You wouldn't say that if you tried to walk around this place at night," she said crossly. "There's always someone up and stompin' about."

Lorene patted a stray hair in place. "You know what I prayed about, Cory? What I asked for most of all?"

"I don't guess I got any idea."

"Us, Cory. I prayed about us. That the Lord would see fit to shine down on our union and bless us, and understand what we mean to each other, even if it looks like we're sinning and all. And I asked Him not to let us get caught."

"That's a right good prayer," Howie said.

"I feel like it was. I feel like it ought to do fine."

Lorene stood then, and slipped the gown over her head, and Howie caught his breath, and wondered if he'd ever get used to the glorious sight of pale flesh and tender limbs, revealed like a brand-new wonder every night, and he was certain he never would.

CHAPTER NINETEEN

RITCHER JONES DIDN'T APPEAR AT BREAKFAST, AND NEITHER did Brother James. Lorene and Camille were on hand, along with a Brother named Harmon, a dumpy young man built roughly in the shape of a gourd. Harmon's nose was too big, a chunk of pink putty carelessly applied to a perfectly round face. His cheeks puffed out as if someone had stuffed him with cotton, a condition that compressed his fleshy lips into a rosy pink wad and made Harmon look as if he were continually searching for a kiss.

Howie disliked the man at once, a feeling that had little to do with his appearance, though that didn't help. It was clear Harmon was taken with both Lorene and Camille. He grinned like a fool at the pair, found a reason to touch them when he could, and ate them up with his pallid blue eyes. This enraged Howie all the more because the girls didn't seem to mind at all. They listened intently to whatever Harmon said, which was nothing anyone cared to hear.

Harmon liked to tell jokes, and every story had something to do with farting, or people who had problems with their bowels. The girls laughed with delight at these efforts, and never complained when Harmon reached past them for a slice of fresh melon and happened to brush a young breast.

"You just got one eye," Harmon said, apparently just noticing that Howie was there.

"You're right about that," Howie said. He thought about young Garvey on the ship, and decided to pay no attention to Harmon.

"Cory was in the *war,*" Lorene explained. "He was hurt, Harmon, like a lot of soldiers were."

"Sure looks dumb," Harmon said. He peered curiously at Howie, stuffing a whole roll in his mouth. "Anybody fights in a war is real stupid, I'd say. God doesn't like us to fight."

Howie stared, forgetting his decision of the moment before. He wondered if it was worth getting up and throwing Harmon over the patio wall.

"Well now, Harmon," Camille said quickly, "that's as true as it can be. And I'm sure Cory didn't *want* to go to war. Isn't that so, Cory?"

"Why you wearing that black thing over it?" Harmon asked, paying no attention to Camille. He chewed as he talked, and crumbs flew out of his mouth.

" 'Cause it covers up the hole," Howie said. "I got a *hole* under there. You lose an eye you got a hole."

Harmon seemed interested in that. "Let me see it. Does it look real awful or what?"

"Listen, friend . . ." Howie braced his hands on the table.

Camille looked alarmed. Lorene shot Howie a warning look. Howie swallowed his irritation.

"I can't do that, Harmon," Howie said. "I'd sure like to, but I can't."

"Why not?"

"Because God said I couldn't. He said, 'Listen, you keep that hole of yours covered up good. Don't show it to no one at all.' "

Harmon looked bewildered. Then a frown began to grow between his eyes. "God didn't say nothing to you. You better take that back."

"Well, now maybe Cory *thought* that's what the Lord said," Lorene said sweetly, glancing sharply at Howie.

"I'll just bet that's it," Camille said. She laid a hand on Harmon's arm. Harmon shook her roughly off.

"He's makin' fun of me."

"Oh, no he's *not,* Harmon," Lorene said.

"I sure wouldn't do that," Howie said, wondering what the hell this conversation was all about.

"I don't like him." Harmon pouted. "He isn't even in the Church. So he doesn't talk to God, that's for sure. He's a liar and a blasphemer too."

"I got a lot of things to do," Howie said. He stood and tossed his napkin on the table. "It was sure nice talkin' and all. Hope we get to do it again."

Without looking at Harmon again, he stalked down the patio steps to the yard and the garden below. Behind him, he heard Harmon muttering how he'd like to get a look beneath that patch—there was a *demon* hidden there, you could bet on that.

Howie walked off through the garden and into the trees that shaded the west side of the house from the sun. He couldn't see the ocean, but he thought he could smell salt air in the strong onshore breeze.

He couldn't figure Harmon at all, or the way the two girls acted in his presence. The man was such a fool, Howie wasn't even mad anymore, just disgusted that he'd had to sit and listen, and watch the bastard eat. How could Lorene and Camille put up with all that? It didn't make a lick of sense—but not a whole lot else in the world did either.

There were paths winding all around the house, past flowering bushes and under different kinds of trees. Everything looked as natural as it could be, though Howie sensed someone had planned it that way, putting trees and rocks and pools just right, so every few feet you wandered into something new.

Past a bright stand of spiky yellow plants he couldn't name, Howie came upon a small clearing shaded by feathery trees. There was a wooden bench there, and he sat and wiped sweat from under his patch, and tried to recall how things looked with two eyes. Everything was flatter now, he knew that—not because he noticed it anymore, but he recalled how different it was when he first lost his eye. Nothing seemed far or near. Things didn't have an edge like they should. It was better when you or the thing you were looking at moved; you could see past it then, and it looked more real.

He heard the sound of running water somewhere, and guessed there was a pool close by. There were all kinds of ponds and small streams around the house, dripping over rocks. In some of the pools, there were bright orange fish. You could toss crumbs or any kind of food on the water and the fish would dart in and suck it up with their fat little mouths. Just like Harmon, Howie thought. Only the fish were real pretty, and didn't tell jokes about farts.

He heard someone on the path and looked up, and saw Lorene brushing through the yellow flowers. She stopped when she saw him and stuck her hands on her hips.

"Well, there you are," she said, blowing a strand of hair off her cheek. "I didn't know *where* you'd got off to."

"I got off to anywhere I could," Howie said. "I couldn't take no more of that."

"I didn't have any way to tell you." Lorene sighed. "I didn't know he was going to be there, Cory."

"Tell me what?"

"About Harmon."

"I don't think you got to tell me 'bout Harmon. I think I already saw near all there is to know."

"He's Lawrence's *son*, Cory."

Howie looked up at that. Lorene's face was screwed up so tight he had to laugh.

"It's not funny." Lorene flushed. "It's not funny at all."

"I guess not." Howie shook his head. "So Brother Harmon gets to do 'bout anything he wants. Tell awful jokes and feel the girls. And everybody smiles."

"He doesn't belong down here. He stays up at High Sequoia. He's just down here for—something special."

"Like what?"

"A ceremony. Something to do with the Church." Lorene waved the question aside.

"You and Camille, Lorene. Ol' Harmon wants to slip a fat hand under your robe, what then? You smile and say, 'Oh, Harmon, that's so sweet'!"

Lorene colored again, and glared at Howie's high-pitched imitation of a girl.

"Cory, how'd you like to—" She caught herself and lowered her voice. "How'd you like to *sleep* by yourself for a while? How'd that be? Just lie there an' think about the awful things you're saying to me?"

Howie wasn't sure if she meant it or not, but the threat in her eyes was enough to cause alarm.

"I was just joking, Lorene. Hell, I saw how he was pawing you two. I know it ain't your fault."

"It certainly is not," Lorene said. She looked away and sniffed the air. "Still, it might not be a bad idea. What I said. Stayin' away from you awhile. I mean, I'm there all the time. Whenever you want to *do* things to me."

"Oh. *Me* doin' things to *you.*"

Lorene bit her lip. "Well, we *both* do things. I didn't mean it exactly like that. Let's not talk about it. All right?"

"Wasn't me that brought it up."

Lorene grew silent a moment. She seemed to be searching for words. "Cory," she said finally, "this afternoon before supper, you might want to stay around your room. I mean, I think that's what you ought to do. Get you a book to read or something. You know?"

Howie looked at her. "I ain't much on reading, Lorene."

"Well, just *sit* there, then," Lorene said impatiently. "Think about something." She let out a breath. "What I'm saying, Cory, is that ceremony I was talking about.

It's this afternoon late in the chapel, and it's just for members and all.''

Howie studied her a moment, wondering why she was making such a fuss. ''Ritcher Jones ask you to tell me all this?''

''No. I mean, yes, he did. In a way. It's private, that's the thing. Everybody'll be there. All the Brothers and Sisters. I'm just saying you shouldn't wander around or anything. Not that you would, I don't mean that.''

Lorene was making an effort to be as casual as she could; Howie could see it was a strain, and again, he couldn't imagine why.

''Well, you don't have to worry,'' he said. ''All you got to do is tell me, Lorene. I'm not about to go and bust into church or anything.''

''Most of the time you'd be as welcome as could be.''

''Fine. I sure appreciate that.''

Lorene looked relieved. ''Well, then . . . I got things I have to do. I'll see you later on, Cory.''

''Tonight?''

''You are just *trying* to get me mad, now aren't you?''

Howie gave her a one-eyed grin. ''You ought to know what I'm trying to get.''

''Honestly, Cory!'' Lorene turned away and pranced off through the trees, but not before Howie caught the ghost of a grin on her lips.

He didn't mean it to happen, and didn't *plan* on doing it at all. He told himself all he meant to do was walk around some on the grounds instead of staying stuck up in his room. Lorene didn't actually say he had to stay there, just that it might be a good idea. There wasn't anything wrong with taking a walk.

Around the far side of the house, a wing of rough granite jutted out into a thick stand of tall, red-barked pines; the trees were so thick it was hard to even see the stone wall unless you came right up on it. Howie stood among the trees and looked up at the narrow, peaked windows of colored glass. He could hear the singing clearly; it wasn't really singing but more like people talking in one solemn note.

Well, they could do whatever they liked. It wasn't any

of his concern what religious folk did with their time. If they wanted to stand around and do church *ceremonies*, why they could.
He stood and listened for a while, just standing in the trees, seeing how one or two pines grew nearly flat against the wall, right next to a colored glass window that was open just a little to let in the fresh air from outside. The window was ten feet off the ground, and though the pines didn't have any branches that low, they wouldn't take much effort to climb.
If that's what a person wanted to do. Which he didn't. It'd be a real fool thing to even think about. If Ritcher Jones caught him doing that . . . And hell, what was there in there to see? A bunch of people in robes who couldn't sing.

Pressing close to the narrow opening in the glass, he could see the whole chapel, looking from the back to the front. There were rows of wooden seats, filled with Brothers and Sisters in robes. Howie was surprised to see so many, a lot more than lived in the house. Apparently they had begun drifting in during the day.
Up front, there were two or three steps and an altar. The altar was covered with a light green cloth, the emblem of High Sequoia sewn on in gold. On the high back wall, the heart-and-tree design was repeated in an immense, finely carved sculpture of polished redwood. The chapel was lit by hundreds of candles. They lined the stone walls and sat in stands behind the altar.
Ritcher Jones stood just before the altar, a gold heart and tree on a chain about his neck. Three others stood beside him, and they wore gold chains as well. One of the men was Harmon; Howie shook his head, but he wasn't real surprised. Ritcher Jones was high up in the church, but Harmon was Lawrence's son, and Jones likely had to be nice to him, too.
As Howie watched, the dull drone of voices seemed to change. Five robed figures walked slowly down the aisle. Howie knew who they were from the yellow robes—the young people who weren't full-fledged Brothers and Sisters.
The five stopped before the altar and knelt on the steps.

Ritcher Jones took a thin green taper from a holder by the altar; pausing before each of the five, he waved the candle past their heads and muttered something Howie couldn't hear. Then, spreading his arms, he raised his hands, a signal for the figures to stand.

Howie's legs were starting to ache. The coarse bark of the tree cut through his trousers to his skin. He tried to spot Lorene but couldn't find her in the crowd.

Again, the chanting below changed. Ritcher Jones nodded; one of the men beside him moved up behind the first of the novices and slipped the yellow robe over her head.

Howie's throat went dry. Lord A'mighty, the girl wasn't wearing a thing beneath her robe! He stared at the slim, naked figure. She couldn't be more than fifteen, but she looked real fine.

The Brother moved solemnly down the line. When he was through, all five of the novices were bare—two boys and three girls. They bowed to Ritcher Jones, turned as one, and bowed to the others in the chapel, then turned to the altar again. Jones walked down the line and gave each one a fatherly embrace. The other men at the altar followed Jones. Harmon was last. While the others had welcomed the five with a simple ceremonial greeting, Harmon took his time. He squeezed the girls and young boys alike close to his chest, putting his whole body into the act. Even from the distance of Howie's perch, it was hard to miss the sly, silly grin on Harmon's face.

The Brothers and Sisters in the chapel broke into song. Ritcher Jones handed each new initiate a neatly folded white robe. A gray-haired Brother slipped the robes over each young person's head. Harmon looked disappointed as each naked form disappeared.

Hell, that's what it was all about, Howie thought. The little son of a bitch had come down from High Sequoia for this, the chance to fondle some naked young kids. It was likely the biggest thrill the poor fool could imagine. And Ritcher Jones was probably fuming inside, because he couldn't do a damn thing about it. Lawrence's boy could do whatever he—

"I suggest you come down from that tree at once . . ."

Howie nearly lost his grip. Looking down, he saw the

grim features of Brother James peering back. Howie let out a breath and backed awkwardly down the trunk to the ground.

"Well now." Brother James didn't smile, but his eyes told Howie the man was delighted with his find. "I suppose you have some explanation for this, young man."

"What kind of explanation you figure that'd be?" Howie said. "You can see what I was doing."

"Yes. Oh, yes, I most certainly can." James shook his head. "This is a grave thing you have done. A most serious offense against the Church."

"I don't need no sermon," Howie said. "I didn't have any business being up there where I was. I did it. I got caught."

"And what did you think of what you saw?"

Howie decided he couldn't get in any more trouble than he was. "I saw what looked like a real nice occasion, those boys and girls getting their robes and all. I also saw that fat little bastard feelin' up some naked kids. That didn't look real religious to me. 'Course I ain't a *member* or nothing, so there's likely a lot of things I don't understand."

Brother James' expression didn't change, but a shadow crossed his face. "You know that I will have to report this matter to Brother Jones."

"I'm not surprised to hear that."

"And this, ah—causes you no concern?"

"I don't reckon I can do a hell of a lot about it."

James glanced at the chapel wall and back to Howie. "And what if I did not, young Cory? What if I decided to—keep this deplorable business to myself?"

Howie looked right at James. "I guess I'd be grateful for that."

"Yes. I'm certain that you would. How *grateful* do you think you would be?"

Howie let out a breath. "What are you gettin' at, mister? You want to just say it?"

The hard lines of the man's face nearly edged into a smile. "I was thinking, Cory, that a favor such as that—quite a generous favor, I would say—might well be returned in kind. Not now, of course. Perhaps at a later time."

"What kind of favor you got in mind?"

James actually grinned. Howie was certain the man's face would crack like a shattered stone and fall in small pieces to the ground.

"We shall simply have to wait and see," James said. "We shall simply have to see."

With that, James turned and vanished quickly through the trees.

CHAPTER TWENTY

BROTHER JAMES'S PROMISE DID LITTLE TO EASE HOWIE'S mind. If anything, it had just the opposite effect. The big house was filled with Brothers and Sisters, celebrating the initiates in their midst. Howie could hear their laughter from his room. Sitting on his bed, watching the growing dark, he imagined the gaiety coming to a halt, Ritcher Jones leading an angry horde of Churchers up the stairs.

It didn't happen, of course, but Howie's nerves were rubbed raw all the same. He cursed himself for pulling such a damn fool stunt—and worse than that, getting caught like a kid peeking in a bedroom window. His stomach was growling, but he knew he couldn't go downstairs. Not with everybody there. If they didn't already know what he'd done, they'd sure see it on his face.

Howie paced the room from end to end, stopping now and then to stare out the open balcony door. It was dark enough now to see the lights of the town through the trees. He imagined the streets and the stores; and beyond, the harbor full of ships.

The answer came to him at once. Hell, he didn't *have* to mope around in his room. No one could make him do that.

He flushed with sudden anger at the thought that touched his mind. He was so damn used to doing everything Ritcher Jones said, he'd near forgotten how to think for himself.

"California's a delight," the preacher had told him more than once. "But it offers quite subtle temptations to the stranger not used to our ways."

"What's that supposed to mean?" Howie had asked.

"It means the presence of plenty can blind a man to the true needs of his immortal soul, Cory. For neither all the fine goods in the marketplace nor all the pleasures of the flesh can fill the emptiness that comes with mortal sin."

Jones always answered questions with a sermon, Howie thought irritably. If a person had any sense at all, he'd quit bothering to ask.

It was a simple matter to drop from the balcony to the dark lawn below. The gate by the road was always closed, and a Brother or two were on duty night and day—but all the gate did was keep carriages and riders from going in or out.

Passing through a thick band of trees, Howie came out on the gravel road some fifty yards south of the gate. The lights of the town were far away, but he didn't greatly care. He was relieved to be out of the house, and the road was downhill.

Not ten minutes into his walk, a farmer stopped with a wagon full of onions and offered Howie a ride into town. Howie grinned as he perched beside the man, his good eye tearing from the pungent load behind. Now, if he could find someone going back *up* the hill he'd be fine. Take a look at the town and get back and go to bed. Lorene would almost certainly be celebrating late, and with any luck at all, he'd be lying there waiting when she arrived. He didn't have any doubts that she would. Her sly little grin as she'd left him in the garden told him that.

Even though he'd seen the town briefly on the way from the pier, being there and walking down the streets was something else. Howie was astonished at the goods in the stores, the way everything looked. There wasn't any garbage in the streets or any smells at all, except for lots of things that smelled real good.

And the lights—he couldn't get used to that. The streets were lit up with oil lamps on poles, lights behind glass that gave everything a soft yellow glow. They had done that some in Alabama Port, but not anything like this.

It was nearly nine o'clock and there were folks everywhere, well-dressed men and pretty girls, and soldiers from both sides of the war. The lights let people walk around, just like it was day. He wondered if folks in New Los Angeles ever went to bed. There were even a few Asians on the street, short men and women dressed in colorful jackets and funny pants.

Now and then, Howie spotted uniformed officers of the law. They wore blue suits with brass buttons and walked along in pairs, but there wasn't anything for them to do. No one was looking for trouble, everyone was just having fun.

There were fewer lights on the side streets, but plenty of things to see. There were open-air cafés, and fancy restaurants like the hotel dining room in Alabama Port. Howie figured that kind of place would cost a lot; some posted menus on the door, and he saw that he was right. Instead, he bought some hot fruit pies from a man who sold food from a cart. He couldn't tell what kind of fruit was inside, but they were hot, sweet, and delicious.

A narrow way wound downhill past the street full of places to eat. Here the streetlights were behind colored glass, casting pools of blue and green on cobbled brick. There were taverns on every side; Howie counted half a dozen before he'd walked a full block.

A drink seemed like a good idea; Ritcher Jones had all kinds of wine at the house, but there wasn't any ale. Howie had seen the preacher put down a few mugs in the Tallahassee tavern, but wine was clearly the drink he liked best. Either that, or he did things different when he was out of California.

Howie strolled into a blue-lit place called The Whale's Belly—and walked back out at once. The tavern was full of Loyalist soldiers. They had evidently taken this place as their own. Blundering into a nest of government troopers made him wary, and he was careful after that. Instead of going in just any place at all, he walked along and watched, seeing what kind of people went where.

The Blue Deep seemed inviting; the walls and the floors were made of decking and bulkheads from old ships. There were ship's lanterns and wheels, and a motheaten, poorly stuffed shark on the wall. In a moment, though, Howie saw the patrons were mostly old men, landlocked sailors who hadn't sobered up in some years. After one mug of ale, he was back on the street.

Laughter came from a tavern down the hill, a place with a most peculiar name, The Dirty Tub. Young men and women his own age strolled in and out of the swinging wooden doors; the girls were bright-eyed and slender, and Howie paused to watch. He made up his mind in half a minute, and followed a girl with red hair and awesome breasts inside.

At once, he was smothered in darkness. The place was as black as the inside of a barrel. Stubs of candles guttered at one end of the room, weak points of light that hardly helped at all. Howie stepped on a young man's foot, and got a muttered curse in return. He reached out and found a girl's waist. The girl laughed and glanced at him in the dark, and Howie smelled a sweet flower in her hair.

He moved along in the crowd, going where the press of bodies took him. The air was hot and stale with the smell of people, spilled drinks, and candle wax. By sheer luck, Howie bumped against a table, felt around and found a chair. Shadows told him that a boy and two girls had found the place before him, but they didn't seem to mind. One of the girls, a pale blur in the dark, leaned in and said something to Howie, but he didn't catch a word above the din.

An arm came from somewhere and set a mug of ale on the table. A voice asked for three coppers, which Howie thought was a lot. Ale was only one at The Blue Deep. Still, now that he was in, he wasn't about to try to leave against the tide.

Someone lit a lamp up front and turned the wick down low, then set the lamp on a box. The crowd began to still as if they knew what was going to happen next. In a moment, a girl in a plain white dress made her way through the crowd past Howie's table. As soon as the young people saw her, they began to clap and cheer. The girl found a three-legged stool and placed it by the lamp. Someone handed her a guitar.

There wasn't a sound in the room. The girl smiled and tried a few chords. Dark hair fell to her waist past a plain ordinary face with pale eyes and a pointed chin. The girl reminded Howie of Camille, if Camille hadn't been near as pretty as she was.

Then the girl began to sing. At once, Howie forgot how she looked. Her voice was high-pitched and clear, as sweet as any sound he'd ever heard. She sang, and her voice filled the room. The lantern by her feet made shadow and light dance in her face, and she didn't seem plain anymore.

"Oh, they came from the fields,
And the rivers and the plains,
Fine boys one and all, one and all.
Fine boys one and allllll. . . .
They left their girls behind
And took their guns and took their swords
When they heard the battle cryyyyy.
Fine boys one and all, one and all.
Fine boys one and allllll. . . ."

It seemed as if everyone in the room except Howie knew the words. They joined in at the chorus, and the girl looked pleased. Howie was surprised that the song was about the war. No one from New Los Angeles, or anywhere else in California, had fought on either side. Yet the young people clearly liked the song.

Howie's eyes were getting used to the dim interior, and now he could vaguely see several tattered banners on the wall, a few old rifles, and a sword. He felt a little sad at the sight. It was easy to listen to pretty words about war, if you didn't have to go out and fight.

The girl finished her tune with a flourish on the strings, and everyone in the room stood and cheered. The girl bowed shyly, and politely held her hands for them to stop. But no one wanted to quit applauding; they wanted to hold the girl right there.

Finally, the girl looked down at her guitar and fingered the beginnings of a tune. A collective sigh swept through the room and everyone found a chair. The girl smiled at the barely visible faces. She knew how to work this crowd, how to bring them to their feet and set them down, how to make them wait. After a while, she strummed the chords again, raised her head, and looked out across the room. Her eyes were on some distant place, somewhere past California far away.

"Oh, no one knew from where he came-oh,
No one even knew his name.
Born in sorrow and sadness,
No one knew from where he came-oh,
No one knew from where he came. . . .
Oh, the sun rose bright on the
Day the troopers came-oh,
The sun rose bright the day they came.
And the boy didn't know that the day would
Turn to dark, for the troopers had murder in their eyes-oh,
The troopers had murder in their eyes. . . .
They murdered his mother and his pa in cold blood,
For the troopers had murder in their eyes-oh,
Jacob's troopers had murder in their eyes. . . .

Howie felt as if someone had shot him in the gut. He was too stunned to move. *God A'mighty, she was talking about him! Him and Colonel Jacob!* He knew that couldn't be, but it was.

He wanted to stand and run, but his body wouldn't move. He wanted to die right there, but the girl kept on, telling how he'd carved his name in Colonel Jacob's chest, how he'd fought the gallant fight in Colorado, how Jacob had caught him and tortured him and cut out his eye, before Howie escaped to bravely lead the Rebels into the Loyalist keep and take the day. . . .

Howie couldn't breathe. He felt the cold sting of sweat on his brow and came shakily to his feet. The walls seemed to sway in a dizzying circle about the room. Stumbling on feet like clubs, he fought his way through the crowd, pushing aside anyone who got in his path. A girl cried out. A boy cursed Howie and blocked his way; Howie hit him savagely in the chest. The boy folded and fell across a table. Howie saw he had a patch on his eye. He thought he was going mad. He glanced wildly about, and saw nearly everyone there looked the same; they all wore black paper patches on their eyes. The girls wore them too, pretty girls with black paper patches. Howie cried out in anger, and wondered why no one could hear. A waiter with a tray full of mugs loomed up in Howie's way. He ripped the boy's black patch away and knocked him aside, stepped on ale and broken glass, saw the swinging doors ahead and didn't stop.

"Oh, Howie Ryder lost his eye, yes it's true-oh,
But he never lost his courage or his heart.
And now every soldier knows his name-oh,
Every Rebel lad knows his name. . . .

He wasn't really sure where he was. Somewhere on the far edge of town, away from the brightly lit streets. There was a grassy park with a fountain. He washed his face in the cool water and started walking toward the hills above the town. After a while, his heart began to slow to a normal beat. The fear went away, and raw anger took its place. Lord, they were nothing but *kids* who'd never gone without a meal, or gotten anywhere close to the war. They'd never seen a man scream and try to hold in his guts, watched a friend die with a cold rain filling up his mouth. They didn't have anything to do so they played at being soldiers. And singing a song about *him*—maybe coming out to that place every night to put a toy paper patch on their eyes. As if he'd ever been a goddam Rebel or a trooper on either side. Some fool soldier had been looking for a hero after the bloody fight, and stumbled on him.

And worse than that was that even if they had it all wrong, folks knew who he was. He had never even dreamed of a thing like that. Just thinking on it brought the fear back strong. All he'd ever wanted was for people to forget who he was—just leave him the hell alone. He'd lost about everyone and everything he had, and now he didn't even have that. Now he was a goddam song.

It took nearly half the night to walk back up the hill. There weren't any farmers with wagons or anyone else on the road. The big house was dark. Coming across the lawn through the trees, he eased quietly through the front door and started across the hall to the stairs. Ritcher Jones was sitting in a chair in the dark.

"Might I ask where in God's holy name you have been, boy? I have had riders out half the night!"

Howie had seen the preacher angry once before, when he walked in the jailhouse in Alabama Port. Still, that particular event didn't begin to match the fury Howie saw in the man now. Jones didn't raise his voice, but the rage was clearly there.

Howie stood his ground. "What the hell's the big fuss? I went out. You got some rule against that?"

Jones took a breath. His eyes bored into Howie. "*Where* did you go, Cory?"

"I went into town."

"Into town."

"That's right. I had a mug or two of ale, but I don't guess that's no sin."

The preacher grasped the arms of his chair. He wouldn't look at Howie. "I am sure that I reminded you, boy, that California is not like anyplace you've ever been. It is not somewhere you simply—"

"Listen, dammit, I ain't no *boy,* I'm a man," Howie exploded. The night's event had wound him up tight, and a sermon wasn't what he cared to hear. "And I'm not one of your Brothers in a robe. Don't talk to me like some kid, 'cause I ain't!"

"I know that, Cory."

"Well, it don't sound like it. I'll go where I damn well please, mister. You can tell those pie-faced Churchers of yours what to do, but I ain't one of them. And I'm thankin' that *God* of yours for that!"

Jones's face turned the color of port wine, but he held himself back. "I expect you had better get some sleep," he said coolly. "We leave for High Sequoia in the morning."

"Well maybe I'm not going to High Sequoia," Howie said. "Maybe I ain't decided yet."

"Suit yourself, Cory," Jones said. He stood, and left Howie in the hall.

* * *

He waited a long time. He lay awake in the dark and watched the stars shift across the night sky. He stayed awake as long as he could, but Lorene never came.

CHAPTER TWENTY-ONE

THE CARAVAN LEFT FOR HIGH SEQUOIA JUST AFTER FIRST light, four closed carriages accompanied by ten Brothers on horseback. Ritcher Jones acted as if nothing had happened between them the night before. He greeted Howie at breakfast with a smile and seemed to be in high spirts, eager to get on the road. Still, when it came time to go, Howie saw Jones would be riding with Lorene and Camille and Brother Harmon, and he himself was assigned to a carriage with three Brothers he didn't know.

Being left out didn't bother him at all. It sure wasn't worth being close to Lorene if it meant having Harmon on hand for several days. After two or three minutes with the little bastard, Howie was sure he'd either strangle Harmon or get out and walk. Maybe Lorene or Camille had put a bug in the preacher's ear, let him know that he and Harmon didn't exactly get along. That made sense. Maybe it was true that Jones had forgotten about their quarrel, that he wasn't just pretending everything was all right.

Howie didn't believe that for a minute. *He* hadn't forgotten, and it wasn't likely Jones had either. Still, if the preacher wanted to play it that way, Howie was glad to go along. The truth of the matter was, he was more than a little relieved to see the preacher's breakfast smile—real or otherwise. Lying awake the few hours before the dawn, he had cursed himself for losing his temper with Jones, threatening not to go to High Sequoia. Lord, what if Jones had taken him at his word? He'd lose Lorene, and his chance at Harriver Mason—the only two reasons he had for *being* in California in the first place. It was a fool thing to do, spouting off when you ought to be thinking instead.

The road ran nearly due east along the coast. The Pacific was a magnificent sight, a deep and translucent blue. A Brother named Jonas said the mountains to the right were named the Santa Ynez. He seemed proud of the fact that the smooth gravel highway had been rebuilt from one that had existed before the Great War.

"Enjoy the ride," he told Howie. "You won't see many roads like this where we're going."

Half an hour later, the highway turned abruptly north, away from the sea. Brother Jonas pointed out the somber, gray-green heights of the Sierra Madre range to his right. They were pretty to look at, but Howie didn't care about mountains.

"We going to see the ocean again?" he wanted to know.

"No, that's it," Jonas said. "We'll be heading inland from now on." He pointed straight ahead. "North and east to High Sequoia."

Howie felt as if a dark cloud had covered the sun. He knew from the map at the house that High Sequoia wasn't near the sea at all, but he had hoped they wouldn't leave it so soon.

The smell reached the caravan close to noon. Howie knew at once what it was—the all too familiar, unmistakable stench of stock. Still, it was a full half hour before the pens themselves appeared. Long before that, Howie was certain he'd throw up. The Brothers in his carriage dipped handkerchiefs in a clay jar they'd brought along, and Jonas offered one to Howie. The water was saturated with cloves, and when he held the cloth up to his nose, the awful odor nearly disappeared.

Howie had thought the pens near the docks were immense, but they were nothing compared to this. The complex seemed to stretch out forever on either side; it took close to an hour to pass it by. Howie was grateful for the cloth, but there was no way to blot out the sight of the stock, the vast herds of meat that he knew weren't really meat at all, but a lie that had lived a hundred years. He thought of Elena and her handful of hopeless wards, far to the south in Nueva Panama. Had she ever seen a sight like this? It wouldn't much matter, he knew. Elena didn't care if her task was impossible or not. She didn't think about that. Howie wished he could believe in something that much, and knew he likely never would.

In spite of his distaste for the pens, Howie was once again struck by the contrast between the wealth of California and the poverty he had witnessed in the rest of the country.

"Everybody's starving, and you got plenty here to feed 'em," he said, not truly intending to speak aloud.

Two of the Brothers exchanged a look at that, but Jonas seemed to understand.

"It's the way of the material world, I'm afraid. If those who hunger can't pay, they go without. It is not the Lord's way, but it's a fact."

"Yeah, I can see that," Howie said.

"Most of the meat here isn't sold in this country at all," Jonas said. "Practically all of it is bought by the Asians. They ship stock live overseas."

The Brother's statement puzzled Howie. "What for? Why don't they raise their own?"

"They are not agricultural, I understand," Jonas said. "And they pay a good price—better than the merchants can get here." He gave Howie a knowing look. "And even if they *did* want to raise their own meat, the merchants make it hard for them to get a good start on our herds. Every buck that leaves California is cut—and the females as well."

Howie looked quickly away to hide the disgust he was certain Brother Jonas would see. That's what a merchant would do, all right, protect every copper he could. It was likely, too, that the Asians were smart enough to build herds of their own. There were other ports besides those in California state, and ranchers who would gladly sell the Asians a whole fertile herd for a price.

And there was the other way, too, Howie thought grimly. He felt a slight chill at the picture in his head. The Silver Island way. There was likely someone in Asia greedy enough for that, too. . . .

The caravan stopped early in the evening at an inn on the outskirts of a town with the peculiar name of Rust. Jonas said Howie might like to walk over and see it. The old name of the place was Santa Maria, and there were some interesting ruins to see, some buildings nearly intact from before the Great War. Howie thanked Jonas for the offer and begged off, saying the ride had tired him out.

That was mostly true, as he hadn't slept more than an hour the night before. And he was a lot more concerned about finding Lorene than seeing ruins. She had hardly glanced at him at breakfast, and the few looks he got weren't good. Which meant she was mad about something, and it likely had to do with the night before. Maybe she *did* come to his room, and found he wasn't there. Or worse than that, she'd decided to up and quit. Howie didn't want to think about that.

At supper, he saw Lorene across the room with Camille. Harmon was there too, mooning at the girls and stuffing meat down his throat. Howie ate quickly and walked outside, trying to appear as if he was taking in the sights. The inn was built in the shell of a ruin, and there were arches and columns standing about, and gray stone paths that no longer went anywhere at all.

Lorene finally appeared. Howie was relieved to see Camille wasn't tagging along. He stepped into the shadow of a column and called out her name when she passed.

Lorene nearly jumped out of her skin. "My Lord, Cory—you tryin' to give me a heart attack or what?" She glanced warily over her shoulder. "We can't stand talking like this, you know that. Someone'll see."

"There isn't anyone around," Howie assured her. "Listen, I just want to know 'bout last night."

"What about it?" Lorene absently studied the arched stone ceiling, as if Howie weren't there. "You apparently had some other . . . engagement."

Howie felt relieved. "You did come, then."

"Yes, Cory, I did." She turned on him so quickly long hair flew into her eyes. "Only you weren't there. I—felt like a perfect fool!"

"I'm real sorry. I went down into town for a while. I figure maybe Jones has already told you that."

"No, no one told me anything, Cory. And don't give me that *look* of yours, either. We can't see each other on the road, so don't ask. Besides, I'm not too sure I even want to anymore. Not if you—"

Lorene froze, and her eyes went wide. Howie heard the sound too, like something scraping hard on stone. Lorene turned and disappeared into the dark. Howie ran in the direction of the sound, and caught a glimpse of something round and repulsive as it vanished through a door.

Harmon, Howie thought, and clenched his fists at his sides. Looking back at where he and Lorene had been standing, he tried to guess where Harmon might have been. Close enough to see, but not nearly close enough to hear, he decided. And anyway, they were both whispering low and standing close. And of course, he realized at once, that was all Harmon needed. Whispering and standing close. He didn't have to hear a thing.

The trip was long and tiring, with nothing much to see that he hadn't seen before. There were hills, valleys, stretches of empty country, and farms. The farms were green and lush, and Howie wondered if they ever had a drought out here. Apparently even the weather did what it was supposed to do in California.

The second day out on the road from New Los Angeles, Howie noticed with interest that the caravan's outriders were carrying arms—brand-new rifles, and cartridge belts full of brass shells. So much for the ironclad rule against weapons the preacher had lectured him about. Evidently the rule didn't apply here, or the Brothers chose to break it. And why carry guns at all—unless you thought you might need them?

"Bandits," Jonas said. "They hit travelers now and then this far from a big settlement." He gave Howie a reassuring grin. "Don't be concerned. We're too large a party, too well armed. They like to hit poor farmers, folks that can't fight back."

"You ever *see* any of these bandits?" Howie asked.

"Just the dead ones," Jonas said. "Hanging from a tree."

The third night out was the last night they stopped at an inn. Ahead, there were no settlements at all of any size, only open country and the ruins of century-old towns. As Jonas had predicted, the good highway disappeared; the road turned abruptly into a dusty, rutted path that frequently vanished in the weeds. The land looked fertile everywhere, but there was no one here in the wilderness to till the soil. Jonas said folks simply didn't need the land; there was plenty closer in toward the coast, all the farmers could handle at the moment.

Howie tried to keep his mind on the scenery, but there was nothing real interesting to see. He didn't want to think about the girl in the tavern or the song, or the kids with black patches on their eyes. He didn't want to brood on Brother James, and how he might change his mind and tell the preacher what he knew. Or Harmon—what Harmon might have seen. It was a wonder he hadn't run straight to Ritcher Jones with his tale. It was clear that he hadn't, and Howie couldn't guess why. Or maybe he had. And the preacher was simply waiting till High Sequoia to give him hell. There was Lorene, of course. He was more than a little worried about her. Lord, he hoped she didn't mean what she said.

He tried to toss these worrisome thoughts aside and replace them with something more pleasant. For nearly half a day, he replayed every moment he and Lorene had shared in bed. That first hot and sultry afternoon in Alabama Port, the happy days at sea. After that, he made up things he'd like to do but hadn't. There wasn't much left on the list. Lorene was real good at putting aside yesterday's sins, and trying out something new.

Early on the fourth morning out, as they crossed a narrow valley, bandits hit the caravan hard. It was over almost before it began. Shots rang through the hills on either side, sounding like the cracks of a whip in the morning air. Howie reached for his weapon and remembered it wasn't there.

The riders came in from both sides, their mounts trailing red plumes of dust down the hills. Howie thought there were six or eight; there might have been more or less. Before the Brothers on horseback could get their wits together, the riders were in their midst. Two Brothers dropped from their saddles. Howie saw Ritcher Jones leap from a carriage ahead. Grabbing a riderless mount, he rode among the Brothers shouting orders, waving his silver pistol in the air. The Brothers quickly dismounted; one man held the reins of several horses, freeing the others to fight. When the bandits regrouped and came again, Ritcher Jones was ready. The Brothers held their fire till the last moment, then laid down a withering volley. Four bandits flew from their horses. The others turned and fled.

The encounter had lasted nearly eight minutes. Four bandits were dead, and two badly hurt. Jones hung the two wounded men at once. Three of the Brothers were dead. One, driving a carriage, had caught a bullet in the leg.

When the attack began, Jones had left his carriage to take command, and Lorene, Camille, and Harmon had dropped to the safety of the floor. A bullet had whined through the front of the carriage, missed the driver by half an inch, struck a metal bracing in the roof, turned at a perfect right angle, ignored Brother Harmon—who was screaming and trying to burrow under the girls—and buried itself deep in the back of Camille's head.

CHAPTER TWENTY-TWO

FOR A GOOD TWO DAYS AFTER THE TRAGIC EVENT ON THE road, Howie watched the mountains rise up in the east. The pale lavender peaks were capped with snow, and when the afternoon sun touched the heights, the whole range seemed afire.

"It's the Sierra Nevadas," Jonas said. "That's the old name for them. Lawrence calls 'em the Pillows of God."

"Looks kinda like the Rockies," Howie said. "I seen some of those. But not up real close."

"You'll get to see plenty of these."

Howie blinked at that. "We gotta *cross* 'em?"

Jonas grinned and shook his head. "No, thank the Lord. We're stopping just this side. You'll see."

The caravan had been traveling through heavy stands of pine, spruce, and fir for some time, the forests growing thicker as the carriages and riders reached the foothills of the Sierra Nevadas. On the morning of the sixth day out from New Los Angeles, Ritcher Jones called a halt. Brother Jonas and the others in Howie's carriage scrambled eagerly to the ground. Howie joined them, wondering what the fuss was all about. There was forest on every side, and clusters of light green fern against the trees. He knew Jones liked to keep moving and stopped the caravan only for meals.

"What are we doing?" Howie asked. "We ain't been riding for three hours."

Jonas looked surprised. "Why, we're here, Cory. This is High Sequoia."

Howie didn't like to seem a fool, but he couldn't see anything but trees. Jonas caught his expression, took his arm, and led him a few steps to the right.

"Look," Jonas said. "Over there."

At first, Howie saw nothing but dense woods, and that was nothing new. His eye caught something, but rejected it at once. It was clearly a trick of the light; there weren't any trees that big, not anywhere. There were six or eight together, and his one eye couldn't sort them out. Then he saw another, and another after that, great, enormous shapes nearly lost in the dusty green light that filtered down from above.

"Great God A'mighty," Howie cried, staring at the sight. "They're *real*, aren't they? They're really there!"

"Oh, they're there," Jonas said. "Giant sequoias, Cory, the Lord's finest creation. This is hallowed ground you're standing on right now. Don't forget that. There's nowhere like this in the world. Nowhere but here."

"I reckon I'll agree on that," Howie said.

The party walked from the point where the caravan had stopped. Carriages and horses weren't allowed within the compound of High Sequoia. Howie didn't ask why; religious folk had reasons for everything they did, but those reasons didn't always make a lot of sense.

The closer he got, the more he was astonished by the size of the great trees. A few stretched nearly three hundred feet toward the sky, and had to be a hundred feet around. Jonas said they were three or four thousand years old. Howie nodded politely at that, and didn't believe it for a minute. The whole world couldn't be a lot older than that, much less a tree. Still, they were likely pretty old, there was no arguing that.

Past a small clearing, he caught his first glimpse of High Sequoia itself. A gate opened wide in a redwood fence nearly ten feet high. Once the party was through, Brothers with rifles over their shoulders closed the gate again. Low wood-and-stucco buildings in muted shades of yellow-green were scattered like children's toys among the giant trees. The structures were well planned, set among fern and twisting vines, vegetation that had clearly been left undisturbed. Everything man-made seemed a natural part of the scene, as if it might have grown up with the trees.

It was the most tranquil, peaceful setting Howie had

ever seen. Still, the farther he got into the compound, the more obvious it became that within the free and open plan of High Sequoia was a more subtle, nearly invisible network of inner boundaries, unobtrusive gates and vine-covered fences that wound like a floral maze through the grounds, forming a number of different areas and enclosures. Now and then, Howie spotted armed Brothers wandering about. They seemed to be paying no attention to their tasks, but Howie knew better than that.

The party thinned as it neared the heart of the compound. Howie saw Ritcher Jones and Lorene disappear through a stand of green leaves. Jonas led him to a gate where a Brother stood guard, and Howie was issued a yellow wooden button. The button had a number on its face, and Jonas told him to wear it at all times.

"While you're here," the Brother explained, "you can go into any area you like that has a yellow circle on the gate. Some gates will have *all* the different colors—yellow, green, red, blue, and white. Others will have only two, and a very few just one. Roam freely about, anywhere you see your color."

Howie tried not to grin. "For a church, you got rules a whole lot like the army."

Jonas shook his head. He wasn't offended at all by Howie's remark. "Visitors get that idea at first sometimes, but High Sequoia isn't like that at all. We *are* a religious community, Cory, and there's a reason for our needs. In some areas—red, for instance—Brothers and Sisters remain in solitude as a part of their training. Novices have their own compound and work areas, though you'll encounter them nearly everywhere. Initiates, those who wear the white robes, have their areas, too." Jonas spread his hands. "Of course, everyone comes together for services and other occasions. In spite of all the *rules*, Cory, we are a very open society here." Jonas smiled and looked up at the majestic tree overhead. "Prayer and devotion is the order of the day, our whole reason for being. The privacy and peace of the individual is our major concern."

It sounded like a speech Brother Jonas had given before, but Howie could see it made sense. He didn't ask about the Brothers who were armed—as far as Howie was concerned, that made a lot more sense than anything he'd seen in the place. The settlement was a hundred or more miles from any help, and no one had to tell him there were groups of lawless men running free in California.

He thought about Camille then, and wondered why God hadn't shifted Brother Harmon just two or three inches to the right to catch the piece of lead that had found its way into the girl's skull. Two or three inches wasn't any big problem for God, but you never could tell what He'd do.

The room was small, comfortable and clean. A window looked out upon a fence covered with tangled green vines. Jonas got him settled, pointed the way to the visitor's dining room, and left Howie on his own.

Howie tried out his bed. It was softer than he'd expected, and he wondered if the Churchers got to sleep on a soft bed, too. The redwood building was long, built with a narrow hall facing eight or ten rooms. There was an outside door at each end of the hall.

How the hell was Lorene supposed to get in here, with all those gates to pass through, and guards everywhere? Howie wondered what color badge she might have. Probably a good one, seeing as how she hung around with Jones. Maybe she couldn't get here at all. Maybe everything was over, whether she wanted it that way or not.

Howie heard steps in the hall, and looked up to see a thin, dark-haired man with olive skin and funny eyes.

"Hello," the man said with a smile. "I am Chan. All right if I come in?"

"Sure, make yourself at home," Howie said. He stood and shook Chan's hand. "I'm Cory. Just visiting the place."

"Ah. I am a visitor as well," Chan said. He spoke English in a precise, studied manner. Howie couldn't guess his age, but he seemed in his thirties somewhere.

"I am with the trade delegation," Chan announced. From the way he spoke, it was clear Howie was supposed to understand. "There are several of us here."

"I guess you're an Asian," Howie said. "I seen some in New Los Angeles, but never met one before."

Chan laughed aloud. "Well, you have met one now. What do you think?"

"I don't guess anything at all."

"Good." Chan nodded as if he had checked something off in his head. "Then that is out of the way. I will explain about Asians so you will clearly understand. Asia is a very large place across the Pacific. Several large places, to be exact. I am from a country called China. You may think of me as Chinese. There are other countries as well, but we are the biggest." Chan grinned again. "And the best."

Howie found the explanation helpful. In his mind, Asia had loomed as a gray, indistinct mass far away.

"That's like being from California or Alabama," he said. "Only they're both part of America, too."

"Yes. Exactly." Chan sat down in the room's only chair. "And what is it you do, Cory? May I ask this question?"

"I don't do a whole lot right now. I used to be in the army."

"Of course." Chan bowed his head for an instant. "And you have been injured. I am sorry."

"I sort of got acquainted with Ritcher Jones back East. He invited me out here for a while."

"Brother Jones." Chan was clearly impressed. "He is a most high official of the Church."

"I guess so. I don't know much about that."

Chan smoothed the collar of his shirt. "As I have said, I am a part of the Chinese trade delegation. I am a cultural representative, which means I do very little. Like you, at the present. We should get along fine." Chan gave Howie a broad wink. "Actually, what I am is a spy. It is my job to see everything I can in California and write it down. I am quite good at it, too."

Howie was taken aback. "If you're a—what you said you was, how come you're tellin' me?"

Chan shrugged. "Oh, it is no great secret. Everybody knows. There is no delegation from China that does not include a spy. Someone is assigned to tell me lies. I listen quite carefully to these lies, and in this way I learn what it is they wish to hide. It is most interesting work."

Howie was somewhat bewildered. "What kinda stuff

does a spy want to know? I mean, there isn't no army in California. All the fighting's back East, over the Rockies."

"Oh, nothing like that." Chan waved Howie's words away. "I am interested in matters of trade. Shipping tonnage. The price of stock. What sort of goods people in California will find desirable."

"Doesn't look to me like you'd have to spy much to learn that. Seems like you could walk up and ask."

Chan raised a heavy brow. "Ah. You would be greatly surprised what people do not wish others to know. Greatly surprised indeed."

Howie glanced out the window past the bed. This far beneath the great tree's canopy, the light itself was green.

"So what are you spyin' on here?" he asked Chan. "High Sequoia's a kinda church. I don't guess they got a lot of shipping tonnage and stuff."

Chan gave Howie a sly look. "I cannot reveal that, now can I? How can I be sure you have not been assigned to tell me lies?"

Howie frowned. "Well, I ain't been. I just got here, and besides, I'm not a Brother or nothing."

"We shall see." Chan stood. "It is time for the noon meal, I believe. I would be pleased if you would join me. Perhaps I will discover who you truly are."

"Don't count on it," Howie said solemnly. "I've fooled a whole lot of spies in my time."

"Marvelous!" Chan laughed. "We will get along well, Cory."

Howie found he liked his new acquaintance a lot. He was obviously crazy as a loon, and that was a real improvement over the sour-faced Brothers of the Church.

CHAPTER TWENTY-THREE

IN THE DINING AREA, HOWIE MET SEVERAL OTHER MEMbers of the Chinese trade delegation—at least he shook their hands and said hello, and received some sort of greeting in return. None of the seven men and women besides Chan seemed to have more than a smattering of English, though Howie suspected more than a few knew exactly what he was saying.

After the introductions, Chan led Howie to a table across the room. Howie thought this was a peculiar thing to do. Then he began to see that Chan, for some reason he couldn't guess, was clearly uncomfortable among his own people. He ate too fast, and talked too much, and made an effort not to look at the others. Howie thought *he* might be the cause, but it soon became obvious the Asians' chilly looks were directed at Chan, and not him. Howie wondered what was wrong, but didn't ask.

There were no other residents in the visitors' quarters. Howie wasn't too surprised; he hadn't expected to find Loyalist and Rebel officers wandering about. He tried to think of some way to learn where these people might be, without really seeming to care. Finally, he simply asked.

Chan merely shrugged, and said the men on hand for the talks were somewhere else in High Sequoia.

"Well apart from one another, I should think," Chan added without a smile.

"Thanks," Howie said. Hell, he already knew that.

After lunch, Chan offered to take Howie for a walk around the grounds. Howie accepted at once, pleased that he didn't have to bring up the idea himself. Learning his way around the big compound was exactly what he needed to do. The night before, he'd stayed awake for some time, wondering how he might get through the maze of gates and fences and discover where Harriver Mason slept. Bypassing the gates wouldn't be that hard, not in the dark of night; there simply weren't that many guards to go around. Finding *which* fences to climb was something else. The way the compound was laid out, a man could wander around forever and not get anywhere at all.

"It is a truly idyllic setting," Chan said, clearly more at ease outside, away from his friends. "These magnificent trees! It is an unbelievable sight."

"They're big, all right," Howie said.

Even in the middle of the day, the clearing was pleasantly cool, sheltered from the sun. Gold coins of light dappled the ground, and pale green clusters of fern. Chan showed Howie several chapels, small, shaded structures built of rough-hewn wood. He pointed out the various study areas, quarters for Brothers and Sisters, and half a dozen other sites that held little interest for Howie. It was pleasant to be with Chan, but Howie learned nothing he couldn't have discovered for himself. Chan wore one of the yellow visitors' buttons too, and had access to the same places Howie could see if he wandered about alone. Still, he got a fair idea of the areas he *wasn't* allowed to enter, and figured that was helpful, too.

As they walked, Chan rambled on about a number of different things—whatever came to mind, as far as Howie could see. It was clear the man was still unnerved by his treatment in the dining area. He told Howie about China, and the wondrous things his people were trying to do, marvels such as the ships Howie had seen that ran by the power of heated water, a process Howie didn't begin to understand. Chan said that he had seen an old machine that could talk and sing songs at one time, though it didn't anymore. More than that, a device that had once flown like a bird. Howie didn't believe any of this, but it was interesting to hear Chan talk.

"Not as much was destroyed in the Great War as one might think," Chan said. "Many useful devices from the past can be put to work again." He offered Howie a confidential smile. "We know much of such things in China. Ways to keep food in containers for several years. Methods of making many things at once."

"I don't see nothing new about that," Howie said.

"Ah, but I am speaking of craft by miraculous machines, friend Cory. Many things produced at once, without the use of people."

Howie gave Chan a curious look. "And how you goin' to manage that?"

"It is really quite simple," Chan began. "The device used to propel great ships across the sea can—"

Chan stopped, caught himself, and looked thoughtfully at Howie. "I think perhaps I am not a good spy. Possibly my comrades are right. I talk too much, and fail to listen to others."

"Hell, I ain't going to tell no one a thing, if that's what you're worried about." Howie wondered why anyone would *want* to hear such tales. "I don't go spoutin' off what I get from a friend."

Chan seemed relieved. It was obvious to Howie that his new companion's open and amiable manner masked some very real fears. His countrymen had cut him off, left him all alone in a land he didn't know. And whatever the reason for this treatment, it was taking its toll on Chan.

"You have seen what they do in my presence," Chan said abruptly, as if he guessed Howie's thoughts. "I am ignored. They pretend that I do not exist."

"Listen, that's your business," Howie said. "I ain't buttin' in."

"I know. You would not do this. And as you say, it is not your concern." Chan offered Howie one of the quick, peculiar bows the Asians seemed to like to do. "Forgive my intrusion. I did not mean to burden you with my problems."

"You're not burdening me at all. I expect I know how it is to have a whole lot of stuff on your mind, and nowhere to put it."

Chan stopped walking and looked at Howie. "Yes. This is so. I saw this, when I walked into your room. I told myself, 'Here is a man who is also greatly troubled. Perhaps he will be a friend.' Do you think this might be so, Cory?"

"I sure don't see why not," Howie said.

"Good. That is very fine." Chan smiled broadly and

shook Howie's hand. "We will help one another. I am certain that we will."

Howie was sure Chan meant exactly what he said. He wasn't playing any games. The man felt threatened, and wanted desperately to share his problems—even with a stranger he scarcely knew. That wasn't too smart, but then Chan wasn't thinking real straight. He was half scared out of his wits; anyone who looked at the man for a minute could see that. Still, Howie had no intention of baring his thoughts to Chan, or to anyone else he met at High Sequoia. A man could smile and stick a knife in your gut—before you even had a chance to smile back. Chan would likely learn this was true if he didn't stop spouting off to anyone who happened to come along.

Lorene was a pleasant surprise, one he hadn't expected at all. The maze of barriers and fences at High Sequoia had convinced him there was little hope of seeing her again. He heard her outside in the dark, and rushed to the window before she could call his name.

"Lord, I think I stepped on every sharp rock in the place," Lorene complained. "I better not be bleedin' or anything."

Howie helped her over the sill and held her tight. He had been lying naked on his bed, and now the softness and the warmth of her body against his skin sparked a surge of excitement in his loins.

Lorene held him off and grinned. "My heavens, Cory, you sure don't waste any time." She glanced shyly down the length of his body, and Howie saw the color in her face. "Don't guess I have to ask if you missed me. I can kinda see you did."

"I ain't going to lie. I sure been wantin' you a lot."

"Oh, Cory!" Lorene wrapped her arms tightly around his neck. "Lord help me, I can't do without you!"

Howie started tugging at her gown, tearing it past her waist to her shoulders. Everything got stuck around her head, and Lorene laughed and helped him along. When his hands touched her flesh she went limp and cried out; Howie swept her up and carried her to the bed.

"How the hell did you get away?" Howie whispered.

"All those guards and everything. I didn't think you'd come, Lorene. I didn't see how you could."

"I grew up here, Cory, remember? It isn't that hard if you know how. And if you got somewhere you really want to go. I just— Oh, God, it's been such a long time!"

The thought touched his mind, lingered there an instant, then vanished at once, lost in the far greater needs of the moment. It was early in the morning, when he once more lay in his room alone, that he saw Lorene could take him anywhere he wanted in High Sequoia. Through the maze and the guards, right to Harriver Mason. All he had to do was think of some way to ask, some reason why she'd do such a thing. He couldn't figure what kind of reason that would be.

Howie was talking to Chan at breakfast when Ritcher Jones appeared. Chan seemed flustered; his friends across the room were clearly impressed as well. Jones greeted them all and stopped to shake their hands, saying how fine it was to have them all there.

"Cory, if you don't have anything planned for a while, I'd be pleased if you'd join me for a walk. That all right with you? Well, fine, it's a right pleasant morning outside."

As ever, Jones didn't wait for an answer. People always did what he wanted them to do, and asking was just a way to pass the time. He clapped Howie soundly on the back and led him out of the dining room and into the pale forest light.

"I hope you like your quarters all right," the preacher said. "Anything you need, why you let me know."

"Thanks," Howie said, "everything's just fine."

Jones stopped and gripped Howie's shoulders. "Now's as good a time as any to say this, Cory. You and me had a misunderstanding back at the house. It wasn't any more than that. Leastways, not as I see it. I want everything to be right between us. That's real important to me. Are we straight now, son?"

"I sure don't hold no bad feelings 'bout you," Howie said. He was surprised, even touched, by the preacher's concern. "It might be I shouldn't have run off into town like that. I mean, I maybe should have said something to you."

"No, no, not at all." Jones shook his head. "You were right in what you said. You're a full-grown man and I had no business calling you down." Jones let out a breath and screwed up his face in a painful frown. "It's a failing of mine, Cory. I'm used to being a shepherd, and I guess I forgot just who's in my flock and who's not. I suspect that I have, in my mind, included you as one of my own."

"That's a real nice thing to say," Howie said. "And I'm grateful for all you've done."

"Why, I haven't done anything at all," Jones said. "Nothing more than the Lord bids all of us to do, and that's heed our brothers' needs."

Jones looked up, peering at the great tree overhead. He smiled then, as if God might be perched in a branch looking down. "Come along, Cory," he said, "it's time you got a first-class tour of High Sequoia."

With Ritcher Jones at his side, no one cared about Howie's yellow button. The guards couldn't move fast enough. Every gate and doorway opened wide as soon as the preacher came in sight. Howie could scarcely believe his luck. He saw everything he'd ever want to see in High Sequoia—the big main chapel, the offices and dormitories, the surprisingly plain house where Lawrence himself lived. He saw the building where the Brothers and Sisters made fine weapons, like the one Jones carried himself. He yearned for a look inside, but Jones quickly passed the place by.

And, more important than anything else, he saw the widely separated compounds where the Rebel and Loyalist officers were quartered. Jones didn't take him real close, but Howie saw enough. He had what he needed to know. And he learned that everyone was here for the talks. The last group had arrived the nigh before, and the talks would begin in a couple of days.

And how long would they last? Howie wondered. How much time did he have? Asking Jones more about the talks would likely seem innocent enough, but Howie wasn't about to press his luck. Mason was here now. That was all he had to know.

Throughout the tour, Jones kept up a running commentary, and Howie kept his good eye open. A map was taking shape in his head. He was almost certain that he wouldn't have to risk prying answers from Lorene. That had never been a good idea, and he was glad he likely wouldn't have to try. Lorene had a real suspicious nature, and she knew him too well; no matter how careful he was, she'd surely guess he was up to no good.

It was close to noon when Jones walked Howie back to his quarters. The preacher was plainly tired from the tour, and seemed pleased to have a cool glass of tea with Howie in the empty dining room. Jones leaned back in his chair and sighed, dabbing his face with a bright handkerchief.

"I forget how big the place is. I assure you, Cory, that I do *not* cover the entire compound every day." He patted his ample belly and grinned. "Though there are those who think perhaps I should."

Howie wondered just who'd have the nerve to say that, besides Lawrence himself. "I sure do appreciate you takin' me around," he told Jones. "It's about the finest place I ever seen."

"It is all of that," Jones said. He nodded his head in thought. "The Lord's Haven, and that's as true as it can be." He paused for a moment, then turned to face Howie. "We've never really talked, you know. About you, I mean, Cory. What you have in mind for yourself, what you might want to do."

Howie couldn't think of anything to say. "I don't guess I got any plans. I never done a thing except farming, and a little bit of fighting. Don't either of 'em tempt me a lot."

"There's a great deal for a young man to do," Jones said. "The future will be a lot brighter than the past. I assure you of that. Peace is in the offing. Make no mistake about it. With the Lord's help, we're going to see to that."

"That'd be different, all right."

Jones ran a finger along his glass. "You might give some thought to High Sequoia. There could be a good future for you here."

Howie was startled, and Jones caught his expression at

once. "No, no, not as a Brother, Cory." The preacher grinned. "Not every man's cut out for such a life, and I doubt it would suit you at all. I didn't bring you all the way to California to fit you with a robe."

Jones leaned forward across the table and folded his hands. "You know what I saw in you, Cory? Why I wanted you to make the trip with me? I saw a young man who's been hurt somehow, a young man who is confused about where he wants to go, what he wants to be. I felt then, and I feel this now, that the Lord's hand has touched you. That He has a task for you to do. This is what I believe. That you are here because you've been given some wonderful thing to do. You don't know what it *is* right now, but you will. I'm certain of that. The Lord's Truth shall be revealed."

Jones stood. "There are a great many study groups here at High Sequoia. You are free to take advantage of everything we have to offer. And I want you to think about this: Being a Brother or a Sister isn't the only way to serve the Lord. There is a place for you here, Cory."

"I'll sure think about that," Howie said, hoping Jones was too tired to read him well.

"Oh, why I nearly forgot." Jones laughed at himself. "I try to think of everything at once, and usually forget about half of what's on my feeble mind. At any rate, you are invited to dinner tonight. As my guest. You will meet Lawrence himself, Cory. Not many folks are accorded such an honor. I think you'll find the evening to be a blessed event in your life. Well, until then, my boy."

Ritcher Jones turned and walked off through the early afternoon. Howie wondered what Lawrence would be like. From everything the preacher said, God's Light followed him around all the time. If that was true, it'd sure be something to see.

CHAPTER TWENTY-FOUR

HOWIE HAD NO IDEA WHAT A STUDY GROUP WAS FOR, and didn't much want to find out. The words *study* and *group* told him all he cared to know. Still, Ritcher Jones had said he ought to give this activity a try; Howie figured it was smart to let the preacher think he might like to stay at High Sequoia. Acting normal right now seemed the right thing to do—especially if you planned on killing someone real soon. Do something like that and it wouldn't be a good idea to stick around. Which he might just have to do for a while.

This new idea began to work its way into his thoughts after Ritcher Jones's tour. Maybe running was the wrong thing to do. Even if he got lucky and stole a horse, there was a damn good chance of getting caught. He didn't know the country, and everyone at High Sequoia did. If he *stayed,* though—simply killed Harriver Mason and went back to bed—why would anyone suspect him at all? No one knew who he was, or why he'd vowed to kill the man who ran Silver Island. There were Rebels at High Sequoia, on hand for the talks, and that's where the Brothers would look first. Some high-ranking Loyalist killed off by a Rebel. That's what everyone would think. And later on, when things had a chance to cool off, Howie could tell Jones he'd decided not to stay.

It sounded all right. Howie just wondered if he had the nerve to do it. To stick around and wait for everything to die down. It'd take more guts than running off.

There was only one thing, or maybe two or three, thoughts that worried at the edge of his mind, and they mostly had to do with Ritcher Jones. The preacher had treated him right, and Howie felt bad about that. And killing Harriver Mason would mess up the peace talks for sure. Could he live with a thing like that, knowing that he'd maybe kept the war going on, and gotten a lot more folks killed? No, not if he thought there was even a chance in hell of the peace talks doing any good. He never had believed that. Ritcher Jones could spout off about love and the Light, but he didn't know beans about war. He didn't know men like Lathan, and Colonel Jacob. Men like that didn't have any *Light* in their hearts. They had an awful taste for power and for blood. They wouldn't give that up because a bunch of folks in robes said peace would be a fine idea. Killing Mason wouldn't hurt anyone except Mason himself, and that bastard had it coming.

There was one other thing—a possible threat, but nothing he could do much about unless he called the thing off. Ritcher Jones knew he had been in Tallahassee when Slade, the *other* big hero of Silver Island, had gotten his throat cut. Would he think about that when Mason turned up dead? Maybe, and maybe not. Still, there was no reason Jones would connect one killing with the other. It was the preacher himself who'd said Rebel guerrillas from the 'glades had gotten Slade. If he'd blamed the Rebels then, he'd likely look to them again.

Howie told himself this was exactly how it would be. And if it wasn't? If Jones just happened to think about him? Howie wondered if the preacher would want to tell old Lawrençe that he, Ritcher Jones, was the man who'd brought a killer all the way across the country to High Sequoia. Most likely not. Ritcher Jones hadn't gotten where he was by playing the fool.

Three hours of Ethics for the New Tomorrow put Howie fast asleep. Chan poked him awake now and then, but Howie simply drifted off again. Stuff like morality and sin, salvation and remorse, failed to compete with pleasant visions of Lorene.

Finally, the seemingly endless lecture ground to a halt. More than one Brother and Sister glanced coolly at Howie as they left. The teacher, a white-haired Brother who had to be eighty, said nothing at all, for he had scarcely noticed Howie was there.

Chan seemed vaguely irritated at Howie's classroom behavior.

"That was not a wise thing to do," he told Howie. "I am certain you will be promptly reported. These people take themselves quite seriously, friend Cory. They do not appreciate signs of contempt."

"I didn't intend no *contempt*," Howie said, stifling a yawn. "I just couldn't stay awake, that's all. What the *hell* was all that about, Chan? You got any idea?"

Chan tried to suppress a smile. "I think perhaps a stimulating beverage is in order. In my room I have a small but potent bottle from the East that will—"

Chan stopped. He stared past Howie, his broad smile vanishing at once.

Howie turned, and saw the somber figure of Brother James by the classroom door.

"May I speak to you a moment, young Cory?" James said. "I hope you'll excuse us, Master Chan."

Chan looked stricken. He glanced once at Howie, and vanished down the hall.

Howie hadn't forgotten about James; he had simply hoped the sour-faced Brother had forgotten about him.

"Well now," James said, "I see that you are not greatly interested in the scholarly life."

"I gave it a try," Howie said. "Guess it didn't take. I sure didn't mean to offend no one."

"No, certainly not," James said. He stared absently at the ceiling. "I expect the, ah, *ceremonial* aspects of the Church are more to your liking."

Howie ignored the remark. James was trying to bait him, and Howie was determined not to let him get his way.

"You said you wanted to talk. What about?"

"We spoke, you and I. Before we left New Los Angeles." James paused. "About—*obligations*, as it were. The return of a certain favor."

"I ain't forgot."

"I am pleased to hear you haven't. Because I am asking you to repay that debt to me now." James studied Howie a long moment. "It is a very *small* task, really. Very small indeed, considering what I have done for you.

Withholding my knowledge of your most grievous offense against the Church."

Howie was wary at once. "Maybe I better just hear how small this favor of yours is."

"I simply want you to tell me something, young Cory. Nothing more than that. You have the honor of meeting Lawrence tonight. There will be a Brother Michael at this gathering. A short, rather obese person with, ah, very little hair. I merely wish to know what Brother Michael says and does during the evening. I am especially interested in what he might say to Lawrence."

Howie frowned. "That's all? Just what this Michael feller says?"

"Particularly to Lawrence. I hope I have made that clear."

"All right. If that's all." Howie didn't care for the business, but didn't see how he could refuse.

"Good. Then we are agreed." James tried to smile. As ever, the result didn't seem worth the effort. "We can trust each other now, boy. I shall not betray you, and you will not betray me. There would be no advantage in that, now would there?"

Before Howie could answer, Brother James turned and quickly walked away. Not for the first time, Howie cursed himself for pulling such a damn fool stunt back in New Los Angeles. Peeking in a window like a kid. Now he was chained to Brother James, and he didn't need that. Not now. He wondered for a moment what the business with Brother Michael was all about, and decided that he didn't want to know.

Chan was waiting in his room, and it was clear he had already started on his mysterious Asian drink. There was a glass bottle of straw-colored liquid on the table, and a third of it was gone. Chan was slightly flushed, and his eyes didn't seem to work right.

"Whatever that is," Howie said, "I think I'll have me a cup. Maybe two."

Chan stared suspiciously at Howie. "I do not like that man. How is it that you know him? What is he to you, Cory?"

Howie was getting tired of answering questions. "I

met him down at the house 'fore we left New Los Angeles. He isn't nothing to me at all."

Chan leaned forward. "Do you know who he is, what he does? No, I think that you do not. I can see that is so." He poured himself a generous drink, and one for Howie. "This Brother James that you know and yet do *not* appear to know is a Church enforcer. This, in fact, is his official title. He is the Grand Enforcer for High Sequoia."

Howie felt a slight chill at the back of his neck. "And what the hell is that supposed to mean?"

"It means he is the law in this place. In effect, the head of the Church's police. All the armed guards are under his command. The security of High Sequoia is his responsibility. But he is far more than that, I assure you. I am not so poor a spy as you might imagine. I know that this James is a dangerous man. He watches his own people as closely as he watches visitors such as ourselves."

Chan paused, and nervously wet his lips. "I would ask what it is he wants of you, friend Cory. Of course, I cannot demand that you answer. But it might be wise to tell me. It may be that I can help."

Howie was taken aback by Chan's words, and the very real fear in his eyes. It was an effort to show he wasn't concerned at all.

"To tell you the truth," he said, "I don't *know* what he wants. What he said out there was it didn't look like I was going to take to learning. I said I figured he was right."

"And that is all?"

"He kinda give me the idea I wasn't acting the way I should. That I ought to least try and stay awake, and not go insultin' the Church."

"Nothing more. Just that."

Howie looked pained. "For God's sake, Chan, you're worrying about nothing, you ask me. James has been eyeing me since I got to California. Now that you tell me what he is, I figure I know the reason why. If he's a snoop for the Church, lookin' is what he's likely going to do. I don't like him much either, but I'm not goin' to let him get me down. I haven't got anything to hide."

Chan clearly wasn't convinced. "He is not to be trusted. Have nothing to do with the man."

"Well, that's sure up to him, not me." Howie wondered just what the hell he'd gotten himself into with James, and how he could get himself out. He poured himself another drink. The stuff tasted a little like wine, only better, and seemed to have an immediate effect. The fumes were as potent as the liquid itself.

"What do you call this drink?" he asked Chan. "It damn sure packs a punch."

"*Sake,*" Chan said. "It is from the Japans. There is no such place anymore since the war, but fortunately, the drink has survived."

Howie set down his cup. "Sounds like you've learned a whole lot 'bout High Sequoia," he said. "This James and all, what goes on around here."

"No. I know very little." Chan's answer came too quickly.

"No offense, friend, but I don't believe that."

Chan flushed, a slight hint of anger in his eyes. "You must forgive me. I have things I must do. I—" Chan looked at the floor, then at Howie. "I am sorry. I do not mean to be rude. I am certain you are my friend. It is simply not—wise, to be discussing such things."

"If we're friends, like you say, why's that, Chan? I thought friends were supposed to help each other. That's what you were telling me a while ago." Howie knew he ought to stop, but didn't want to do that. "You ever hear any talk about how High Sequoia was before? I know for a fact it wasn't the same place 'fore Lawrence took over. Even Ritcher Jones says that. And I knew someone who was here. A girl name of Kari. She got away from High Sequoia when it wasn't near as *holy* as it is now—"

Chan came halfway out of his chair and stared at Howie. "You must never—speak of such things! Not to me or anyone else. Whatever you may have heard, put it out of your mind at once."

Chan's reaction took him totally by surprise. The man was flat scared, and Howie couldn't say why.

"Well, thanks for the drink," Howie said at the door, but Chan clearly didn't hear a word he said.

CHAPTER TWENTY-FIVE

AT SEVEN, TWO BROTHERS ARRIVED TO LEAD HIM TO HIS appointment with Lawrence. Howie figured he was supposed to be impressed; instead, the appearance of the pair made him angry all over again. He was still irritated by an incident that had occurred an hour before, and the "escort" merely added new fuel to the fire.

Close to six, a boy in a yellow novice robe had knocked on the door, handed Howie several neatly wrapped packages, and left. The packages contained brand-new trousers, the finest cotton shirt he'd ever seen, a black jacket with metal buttons, and new boots. Howie spread the items out on his bed and simply stared. The clothes were far better than any he'd ever worn, and he knew why Ritcher Jones had sent them: The preacher didn't think Howie looked good enough to meet the great high and mighty Lawrence.

The idea filled him with sudden rage. He knew it was a damn fool thing to even care what Jones thought about, but that did little to curb his anger. For an irrational moment or so, he thought about wearing the worn-out shirt and pants he had, and seeing how Lawrence liked that. He knew at once that it would be a stupid thing to do. He'd come to High Sequoia to get Mason. Riling up Jones wouldn't bring him any closer to that.

Howie's escorts turned him over to two armed Brothers at Lawrence's door. One of the guards knocked and stepped in, then came back shortly with Ritcher Jones. Jones beamed and shook Howie's hand.

"Well now, this is certainly a fine occasion," Jones said. "Lawrence is looking forward to meeting you, Cory. I've told him all about you."

"Thanks for the clothes," Howie said. The words tasted awful in his mouth. "You didn't have to do that."

"No, no, nothing at all." Jones looked at Howie. They stood in a narrow hallway with polished walls.

"There are several things you should know about, ah—being in Lawrence's presence," Jones said. "Although you are not a member of the Order, there are courtesies to be observed. Lawrence is a Holy Person. This may not be your belief, Cory, but you will be expected to act as though it were while you are here. Speak to Lawrence *only* when he addresses you. Answer him plainly and without undue elaboration. But—and please remember this—do not *initiate* a conversation yourself. That's important. If you feel you have something you'd like to say, tell it to me. I will decide if it is something Lawrence might care to hear. When you speak, address Lawrence simply as *Lawrence*. Nothing more. We consider that as both his title and his name."

Jones spread his hands. "It's very easy, really. Just remember what I've said. I'm certain you'll do quite well."

"I guess so," Howie said. He wanted to ask Jones if it was all right to breathe inside, then recalled the preacher liked his own jokes, but didn't much care for other folks' attempts at humor.

Jones led the way, past a beaded curtain and through another wooden door. Howie took the room in at a glance. There wasn't much to see. The floor was sanded wood, walls painted white. The room was stark, with no decoration at all. People were seated at a long dining table, and they all looked up as Jones and Howie entered. There were two men from the Chinese delegation. And Lorene, and an attractive brunette Howie hadn't seen before. Harmon was there too, next to the good-looking girl. Howie recognized Michael at once, from James's description.

Lawrence himself was a surprise. He sat at the head of the table, and looked for all the world like an ordinary man. Middle-aged and gaunt, with hollow cheeks and thinning hair. Howie looked for shining lights, and didn't see anything at all.

"Lawrence, may I present Master Cory," Jones said, stopping a respectful distance from Lawrence's chair.

Lawrence looked up, staring for a moment, as if he hadn't noticed Howie before.

"Welcome to our table," Lawrence said simply. His voice was a weary monotone.

"Thank you, sir," Howie said. Ritcher Jones didn't pass out cold or anything, so it must have been the right thing to say.

Jones took a seat next to Lawrence, across from Brother Michael. Howie sat next to Jones, directly across from Lorene. Jones introduced him to Brother Michael, Sister Marie, and Mr. Wang and Mr. Chen.

"Of course you know Sister Lorene and Brother Harmon," Jones added.

Lorene smiled politely. Harmon scowled at Howie and filled his mouth with food. Howie let his eyes linger on Marie a second or two longer than he should. Marie blushed and looked away.

Howie couldn't take his eye off Marie. She was pretty, but that wasn't it. He realized then that she reminded him of Camille, Lorene's friend who'd died of a bandit's bullet on the way. They didn't *look* all that much alike, but they were both dark-haired, with the same sharp features and liquid eyes. Howie felt a little guilty. He'd meant to say something to Lorene and Ritcher Jones when they got to High Sequoia, but there had never seemed to be a right time. It was the polite thing to do; they hadn't brought it up either, so maybe they were waiting for him.

"I believe you are acquainted with our Mr. Chan."

Howie turned, and saw the Chinese by his side watching him with curious eyes. He wasn't real surprised to hear the man spoke English, with hardly any accent at all. He'd guessed Chan wasn't the only member of his party who knew the language. Howie decided he was Wang, and the other one was Chen.

"We've talked a couple of times," Howie said. "Off and on."

"Yes. I have seen this." Wang looked about sixty; his head was perfectly bald. The skin stretched tight across his face was the color and texture of old paper.

"Chan is a very able young man," Wang said. "Most

intelligent and alert. We are expecting much of his abilities."

I heard some different, Howie thought. "He's a real fine person, all right," he said aloud. "Interesting feller to talk to. I didn't know nothing about China. Sounds like a real nice place."

Wang looked up from his plate. "Indeed it is. And what did young Chan tell you about China?"

Howie took a bite of melon while he tried to think what he ought to say. What Chan might have said that he shouldn't.

"Mostly, he talked about the country. Rivers and lakes and such. Trees and birds. Sounded right pretty."

"Yes. I see." Wang was clearly disappointed. "China is a beautiful place. And a most progressive nation as well. Many things have been accomplished there that have not yet appeared in the West. I imagine Chan told you of such things."

"No, not a thing," Howie said. "I'd sure like to hear about 'em, though."

"Yes. Perhaps we will talk sometime." Wang nodded curtly, and showed a sudden interest in his food.

By God, Chan was right, Howie decided. For whatever reason, his friends were trying to bring him down.

"Cory . . ." Jones poked Howie sharply in the ribs.

"Uh, what?" Howie turned. Jones was staring at him, plainly irritated.

"Lawrence is *speaking* to you, Cory."

"Oh." Howie looked at Lawrence. "I'm real sorry, sir."

Lawrence didn't smile. "I understand you were in the war."

"Yes, sir. I was."

"You lost an eye. How did this occur?"

Howie tried to remember the story he'd told before. "A cannon exploded. A piece of hot metal caught me right in the eye. The other fellers there was killed outright. Guess I was lucky."

Lawrence turned to Brother Michael. "I think this unfortunate incident must be dealt with at once. I see no other alternative."

"Yes, I am afraid this is so," Michael said. "I shall see to it, Lawrence."

"As soon as possible, Michael. No delays."

"Yes, of course."

"I regret this, Michael. It should never have happened." Lawrence turned to Jones. "Nothing can be accomplished by waiting. Is this your conclusion as well?"

"It is, Lawrence," Jones said.

"The Lord has brought this to be," Lawrence said. His dark eyes closed for a moment. "We shall not oppose His will."

Howie felt cold all over. He stared at Lawrence, wondering which "unfortunate matter" they were discussing, and how they'd found him out. It dawned on him then that no one was even looking his way, that whatever it was, it had nothing to do with him. Lawrence had simply tired of the conversation and gone on to something else. Like he wasn't even there.

Well by damn, Howie thought, just because you talk to God all the time don't mean you got to be impolite!

Howie looked around the table. Lawrence, Jones, and Michael were still deeply engrossed in weighty conversation. Maybe he'd tell Brother James what he'd heard, or maybe not. He might just make something up. Lorene and Marie had their heads close together, whispering over something and grinning now and then. Harmon was stuffing his face. Mr. Wang and Mr. Chen were exchanging rapid gibberish across the table.

Howie wondered about the Chinese, and what they were doing at High Sequoia. Chan said they were a trade delegation. But what were they trading *here?* He hadn't asked Chan when he first brought it up, and there wasn't any chance to later. Not after his new friend started acting real funny.

And that was downright peculiar, too. Chan had flat gone to pieces when he, Howie, had just mentioned High Sequoia. And especially *old* High Sequoia, the way it used to be. That didn't make a bit of sense, yet Chan was flat scared out of his wits. What was he scared *of?* Howie wondered. Brother James was likely the answer, he decided. That cold-eyed son of a bitch had Chan completely cowed, and Howie couldn't much blame him. You let a man like that get a start . . .

Howie looked up, and caught Lorene watching him from across the table.

"It has been some time since we spoke, Master Cory," Lorene said. "I trust you find High Sequoia to your liking."

Howie tried not to grin. "Never had a better time in my life. It's about the prettiest place I ever saw. Still can't get over them trees."

"Yes, they . . . are quite magnificent." Lorene squirmed uncomfortably in her chair. She knew he was talking about the two of them, no matter what he said.

"I got a real pretty view outside my window," Howie said. "I sit there and look out at night."

"Is that so?"

"You can hear all kinds of things. Birds, leaves rattling in the trees." Howie was suddenly aware that several others at the table, including Harmon, had started listening to the conversation. He decided he'd maybe gone far enough and should shut up, or say something normal to Lorene.

"I ain't had a chance to say how sorry I am about Sister Camille," Howie said. "I should've said something before. That was a real awful thing, and I—"

Lorene's expression stopped him cold. Her eyes went wide, and all the color drained from her face. What the hell did I do now? Howie wondered.

He didn't have to look. He could feel Lawrence's eyes suddenly upon him.

"You are clearly not aware of our ways," Lawrence said bluntly. "I hold you blameless for what you say. But understand, young man, that we do *not* mourn the passing of a Brother or a Sister. We rejoice that the Lord has chosen one of our own. Death is the beginning of our finest work for God. Pray for the day when you can begin this task yourself. Do not feel sorrow for Sister Camille."

Howie wished he could sink beneath the floor. "I hadn't thought it out the way you explain it," he said. "That—makes sense to me." He remembered, too late, that Lawrence hadn't *asked* him to speak.

Lawrence didn't seem to care. "There is much you can learn at High Sequoia," he said. "A single day beneath God's Holy Trees will strengthen your soul beyond measure. Prepare yourself for the Joy and Light to come."

Then, just as he'd done before, Lawrence turned abruptly back to Michael and Jones, leaving Howie hanging on a limb.

Howie downed a whole glass of wine. It tasted awful, and his throat still felt dry as sand. He couldn't stand to look at Lorene, or anyone else. Damned if this place wasn't getting more peculiar by the minute. People tryin' to hurry up and die and grab hold of more joy and light—when they hadn't used up what they had right here.

• • •

This time he was listening for the sound; he sat up quickly and walked naked across the room. The white gown appeared like a ghost in the dark, the slender figure and raven hair . . .

Howie blinked. Lorene didn't *have* dark hair, and her face wasn't like that at all.

"Well, you going to help me in or not?" Sister Marie leaned in the window, watching curiously as Howie searched for something to cover himself.

Marie sighed. "Listen, I can go away if you like. I sure don't have to stay."

"No, I mean—here, lean in a little more." Howie tried not to think real hard. He grasped Marie around her waist, noting at once that she was somewhat lighter than Lorene, that everything about her was soft and hard at once.

Marie slid her hands around his neck as he lifted her into the room; once inside, she continued to hold on, standing very close to Howie, studying him in the dark.

"Lorene couldn't come. Brother Jones had some things for her to do."

"She—I mean, she knows about you bein' here?"

"Now who you think sent me here, Cory? Of course she knows I'm here."

"And she doesn't mind?"

"Good heavens, why should she?"

Howie was both excited and alarmed by this slender girl who pressed herself boldly against him. Excited, because she was there. Alarmed, and a little disturbed, because Lorene apparently didn't care. She couldn't make it, so she'd simply sent Marie in her place. Like that was the polite thing to do.

"You know what?" Marie said. "I got an idea you think too much. You got that look. I've seen it once or twice."

Howie could smell her skin. Her lips were no more than an inch away. "I just—wouldn't want to do some sin, or anything like that," he told the girl. "I know how you folks feel. Now, if it's all right with you, and 'course you're already here . . ."

Marie laughed in her throat and kissed him hard. Howie didn't know what to say and didn't care. Still, in some small corner of his mind, a very small corner not concerned with Marie, and what she was doing with her body and her hands, Howie told himself he had to do what he'd come to do, and get *out* of High Sequoia. Sin and religion, and folks looking forward to being dead—it was getting too hard to understand. There was too damn much going on, and the rules kept changing all the time.

CHAPTER TWENTY-SIX

HOWIE WAS AWAKE WHEN SHE LEANED ACROSS AND kissed him; her hair brushed his face and he could smell the sweet scent of her skin. He watched her as she slipped out of bed, careful to keep his breathing at the slow, even pace of sleep. In the near darkness of the room, she drew the white gown over her head, making no sound at all. For a moment, she stood by the window, listening to the night, then she quietly slipped over the sill.

Howie was on his feet at once, thrusting his legs into

his pants and grabbing up his shirt. There was no time for boots—every second he wasted gave Marie a chance to get farther ahead, to vanish into the dark. Climbing through the window, he moved quietly along the side of the building. He guessed it was close to one in the morning. There was a moon up there somewhere, but very little light made its way through the trees. Darkness was a blessing and a curse. If he lost her, he'd simply have to—

Howie stopped. There, a patch of white against the night. His heart hammered against his chest. Marie moved swiftly along the vine-covered fence that surrounded the visitors' quarters. As Howie had expected, she wasn't going through the gate; she was headed the other way, toward the eastern side of the fence.

Howie watched. A moment later, Marie vanished. He smiled to himself and let a silent breath escape his lips. Keeping to the ground, he made his way quietly to the fence.

Howie suffered a few seconds of panic before he found it. He was sure this was the spot where Marie had disappeared yet the boards of the fence seemed solid as iron. There was nothing loose, no opening at all. Dammit, this had to be the place, he told himself. The girl wasn't here, and that meant she was on the other side—maybe vanishing again. If he missed her, he'd have to climb the fences and pray the guards couldn't see any better than he could in the dark.

Suddenly, a board gave slightly under his touch. He squatted down and found a section of the fence had rotted through near its base. Lowering himself to the ground, he forced himself through. It was a tight squeeze at best; he wasn't even close to being as slender as Lorene or Marie.

Parting the vines on the other side, he caught a quick glimpse of Marie before the night swallowed her up once again. He had seen this section of the compound during the day. It bordered the vistors' area and was used as an exercise ground by the novices. A guard would be at the gate, twenty yards to his right. Howie couldn't spot him, but that didn't mean he wasn't there. Following the shadows of the fence would take too much time. He'd lose Marie for sure. Still, the place was flat and open, and there was little cover at all. To hell with it, Howie decided. He drew in a breath and raced low across the ground.

He knelt in the shadows along the fence. The building was a long wooden structure with an entry at both ends. Inside there would be a narrow hall, and a door to each room. The building was identical to the one where Howie was quartered—except for the presence of an armed Loyalist trooper at the door.

He had fully expected that. Armies posted guards whether they needed to or not. It gave the poor troopers something to do instead of sleep.

There was a guard at the front and the back, but Howie figured he wouldn't have to deal with more than one. He was sorry about the guard. The man was a soldier, doing what he was told to do. Howie didn't want to kill him, and maybe it wouldn't come to that. Searching about in the dark, he found a good-sized rock beneath a thick stand of fern. He waited until the trooper was looking the other way, then went to his belly and started across the dark.

The idea had first come to him talking to Lorene. He'd been astonished that she was able to get to him past the guards and the maze of fences and gates. Lorene had laughed at that, telling him how it wasn't that hard for a girl who'd grown up in High Sequoia.

Howie had given that a lot of thought—Lorene, and some of the others too, playing here as children, finding secret places, ways to get through fences and go anywhere they liked. It had struck him then that Lorene had grown up here *before* there were Brothers and Sisters at High Sequoia, before Lawrence came. She'd been here when High Sequoia was something else, not anything like it was now. Hell, she had probably been here when Kari was here too, and those were bad times. Kari had gotten away, but the old High Sequoia had left its mark. Something awful had happened to her here, and all the time he'd known her in the war, she had never said what.

Lorene had come through all right, and Kari hadn't. Why was that? Howie wondered. He had wanted to ask Lorene about the times that had gone before, but he knew that was a poor idea. Most of what they'd shared was in bed; he didn't know much more about Lorene.

And that was why he'd never seriously considered asking her to show him how to get through High Sequoia in the dark, without using any gates. It was only when he had lain awake next to Marie that the answer struck home. He didn't *have* to ask. All he had to do was follow the girl when she left. The Sisters' quarters weren't that far from the building where Harriver Mason slept. Marie couldn't lead him all the way, but she could take him close enough. He'd take his chances with the last few fences himself.

He was sure he hadn't hit the trooper hard. He would sleep off the blow and be fine. Howie was relieved to find they followed the same pattern here as they did in the building where he stayed. The name of a Loyalist officer or high official was written on a small piece of paper and tacked to each door. The hall was nearly dark, but he could still read the names. Mason's room was the third door down.

He stood there a moment, but couldn't hear a thing. Carefully gripping the knob, he quietly opened the door, stepped inside, and shut the door behind him. He could hear Mason breathe. A faint light came through the window, enough to show him a man's shape in the bed. Going to his hands and knees, he made his way across the room. Mason's clothes were drapped neatly over a chair. On the table by the bed was a pitcher of water, Mason's army pistol, and a knife. Howie was glad to find the knife; a blade was easier and quicker than having to use your hands. He slipped the knife from the table and stood.

Mason was on his side, turned toward the wall. Howie eased one knee on the bed, then jerked Mason over on his back, straddling him quickly, using his knees to pin the man's arms to his sides. At the same time, he clapped a hand firmly across Mason's mouth and pressed the point of the knife just below Mason's eye.

Mason came awake at once. He stared wildly at Howie and tried to jerk away. Howie pricked him harder with the knife.

"You do that again and that's it," Howie said quietly. "You get what I'm saying?"

Mason nodded and tried to talk through Howie's hand. Howie jabbed him hard, and Mason went quiet.

"I ain't got a lot of time," Howie said. "I wish I had all night, but I don't. My name's Howie Ryder. I want you to know who I am and why I'm here. You had my sister at Silver Island. I know what happened to her there, and to all them other folks, too. I know what you did. I don't reckon you bothered with names in that place, but she *had* a name, mister. It was Carolee Ryder. You think on that. Think on it good. That's how I want you to go. Thinking on her."

Mason screamed, the sound all but lost under Howie's firm grip. He touched the knife to Mason's right eye, then drove it in hard with all his strength. Mason shuddered once. Howie waited a moment, then drew his hand from the man's mouth. A long, final breath escaped Mason's lips. Howie turned him back to the wall and drew the covers about his neck. He left the knife where it was.

Seconds later, he was out of the window and on the ground. He listened, but heard nothing but the sounds of the night. Moving quietly below the other open windows, he made his way toward the front of the building. The fence he'd climbed was twenty yards away, lost, for the moment, in the shadow of a giant tree. Howie moved toward the fence, keeping low to the ground.

They were on him in an instant, coming out of nowhere at all. He couldn't tell how many, but it was enough. He fought as best he could, kicking out and taking one blow after another on his arms. He struck back until something hard as iron found the base of his skull, and he didn't have to fight anymore. . . .

CHAPTER TWENTY-SEVEN

WHEN HE WOKE, HE WAS AWARE OF THE LIGHT AND THE pain. The hurt was centered in the back of his head and throbbed clear down to his eye. The light came from a lantern somewhere off down a hall out of sight. The light was broken up by lines, vertical stripes of black like a fence where the boards are spaced wide. He looked at the lines for a while until his eye was working right. Bars. They weren't lines, they were bars.

He tried to move, but nothing worked. He couldn't feel his arms or his legs. When he moved his head and looked at himself, he saw he was sitting in a chair. In a chair in a room, with his arms and his legs bound painfully tight. And that was the moment when his head started working, and it came to him what he had done, and what the bars were for.

Howie woke with a start, the sudden motion bringing the pain alive again.

"Here," the voice said. "I expect this will help."

The cup touched his lips. Howie drank cool water until he choked.

"Easy now."

The cup went away. Howie looked up and saw a Brother he didn't know.

"What—what are they goin' to do to me?" The moment he opened his mouth, he knew it was a fool thing to say.

"I have to do this," said the Brother.

"Do what?"

The Brother leaned down and pressed Howie's cheeks hard, forcing him to open his mouth.

"Dammit, wait—!"

Howie tasted a mouthful of cloth. The Brother stuffed it in tight, then wrapped another length across his mouth and tied it behind his head. When he was done, he stepped back and looked at his work.

"I think that will do. Can you breathe all right through your nose? Good."

The Brother turned and left. Howie heard the harsh, final sound of iron as the bars clanged shut.

He was wide awake when the Brother came again. No, not the same one—this one was taller and had a rifle strapped across his shoulder. He opened the bars and stood aside. A Loyalist trooper came into the room. He hung a lantern from a chain a few feet from Howie's chair and turned the wick up high. A moment later, two troopers came in with a small wooden table and three chairs. They set the chairs and the table in front of Howie, then everyone left except a single armed soldier. He stood at the open cell door and looked straight ahead. He never glanced at Howie.

Howie heard boots on a stone floor. The trooper looked quickly to his right and snapped to attention.

Three men came into the room. Howie's heart sank when he saw them. They were high-ranking Loyalist officers, two colonels and a cavalry general. They all wore clean dress greens with rows of medals on their chests.

The general was heavyset, with thinning gray hair and leathery skin that had seen the sun. He took the center chair; the colonels stood until he was seated.

The general cleared his throat. One of the colonels handed him a folder; the general opened it, glanced at it briefly. He looked curiously at Howie, then turned his attention to the contents of the folder. He never looked at Howie again.

"This is the defendant named Howie Ryder, also known by the alias of Cory?"

"Yes, sir, it is," said the colonel on the general's right.

"Defendant Howie Ryder is charged with the mutilation and subsequent murder of Colonel Eligh Jacob, late of the Second Army of the Western Expeditionary Force of the United States Army, this action having occurred in or about the state of Colorado. Is this a true and valid charge?''

''Yes sir, it is a true and valid charge.''

''So noted, then. Said defendant Howie Ryder is also charged with the murder of Senior Administrator Harriver Mason, this action having occurred in High Sequoia, in California state. Is this a true and valid charge?''

''It is a true and valid charge, sir.''

The general closed his folder. ''Said defendant Howie Ryder has been charged and tried on two counts of murder; these charges have been deemed true and valid. Therefore I declare this hearing closed.''

The general stood. The two colonels rose quickly and came to attention. The three officers turned and walked stiffly out of the room. Troopers entered at once and removed the table and the chairs. The soldier closed and locked the barred door and disappeared, and Howie was alone once again.

Howie tried not to think. There wasn't a whole lot to think about. They had caught him red-handed, there wasn't any way out of that. The *trial* was over and done, though why they'd even bothered, Howie couldn't say. Except the army liked to write things down.

The business with Colonel Jacob—that had surprised him somewhat, but not a lot. They'd caught him for killing Mason, and while he was out cold, some trooper or officer who'd been in Colorado had recognized his face and the missing eye. Probably got a promotion for it, too. Better than what the trooper who'd spotted him in Alabama Port got for his trouble, Howie thought.

That little problem had worked out fine. Only this time, Ritcher Jones wouldn't likely walk in and get him off with a bribe. Even if he did sit right next to Lawrence at supper. Lawrence wouldn't forget who'd brought a killer into High Sequoia, and someone would have to pay for that.

Howie didn't look forward to facing Jones. Saying he was sorry for the trouble he'd caused wouldn't do a lot of good. The thought suddenly struck him: Lord, what was Lorene going to think? Finding out the man she'd been loving every night was a man she didn't know.

The thought of Lorene brought Howie a sense of sadness and regret. He'd thought about them maybe going off somewhere, dreamed about it, anyway, thinking how it might turn out to be true. Would she cry a whole lot when he was gone? Dying was supposed to be a fine thing to do, the Church had taught her that. But he figured that she'd cry some, too.

Somehow, knowing it was going to happen soon didn't bother him at all. Dying just hadn't hit home. It likely would, he decided, when they took him out under a tree. A bunch of troopers with a rope would get a man's attention quick.

No one had bothered with windows in the place, and Howie had no idea if it was daylight or dark. Sometime after the officers left, the Brother who'd stuffed a gag in his mouth came back and took it out. He fed Howie soup and another cup of water, and checked to make sure the ropes weren't cutting off his blood. Howie said he appreciated that; he didn't think it looked right for a man to have a case of gangrene when they took him off to hang. The Brother paled at this remark and hurried quickly from Howie's cell.

He tried to stay awake, but the dull, throbbing presence in the back of his head seemed determined to pull him under. He dozed off again and again, waking each time with a start. His head felt heavy, as if it might be full of sand. The light from the lantern was fuzzy, strangely indistinct. He wondered if the blow had done something real bad to his head, maybe damaged vital stuff inside. He'd been hit once or twice before, and the hurt had gone away, so maybe this was temporary, too.

He caught himself and tried to laugh. The effort sent a sharp surge of pain through his skull. What the hell difference does it make? Howie thought. I'm temporary all over, it ain't just in my head.

He drifted off again, then came awake abruptly as a key clicked sharply in the lock of his cell. Howie looked up, blinked, saw the blow coming and couldn't jerk away.

"Damn your filthy *soul,* boy!" Brother James struck him again across the face. Howie sucked in a breath.

James grabbed him by the throat and brought his face close to Howie's. "God's mercy, what have you done to me? I've nothing to do with this business!" His voice trembled with rage. Howie could smell his sour breath, count the beads of moisture on his flesh.

"I haven't done nothing to you," Howie said. "You ain't even—"

James hit him again. Howie groaned and thought his head was coming off.

"What have you told them?" James said. "What did you say about me?"

"I didn't say a thing about you. Why the hell should I?"

"I am not involved in this foulness of yours," James said. His hand closed tightly about Howie's throat. "My name . . . must *not* be spoken. It will *not* be spoken by you."

"I told you, dammit. What the hell's the matter with you, mister?"

"You have spoken to no one about our—little agreement?"

"No, honest. I—"

"I think I shall have to make certain of that." James showed Howie a terrible grin. "I think I must be sure."

James brought both his hands to Howie's throat. He pressed his thumbs hard, cutting off Howie's breath at once. Howie tried to cry out. Bright spots of light began to dance before his eyes. He strained at his ropes, knowing it would do him no good. The face before him began to fade. An odd, almost comical expression appeared on Brother James's face. His eyes rolled up, and one corner of his mouth twisted awkwardly toward his jaw. He released Howie's throat, backed away a step, and tried to turn around. Something happened to his legs and he collapsed to the floor.

Howie gasped for air. Ritcher Jones stepped over James. Concern spread over his features; he found a cup of water and brought it to Howie's mouth. Howie threw up half of the water, and drank again.

"Thank the Lord," Jones said. He wiped Howie's

face with the edge of his robe. "Are you all right, son?"

"I reckon so," Howie said. His voice sounded like a frog's. "Thanks—for getting here."

"You're going to be just fine," Jones said. He turned and spoke over his shoulder. "You'd best take him out the east door. Use Samuel and Micah."

Howie looked past Jones and saw Brother Michael. He held a pistol in his hand. Something long was attached to the end of the barrel; it looked like a piece of black pipe.

"You won't need me here?" Michael asked.

"No. Tell Samuel to come back when you've disposed of James. Tell him to stay here, outside the room."

Michael nodded and disappeared. Ritcher Jones turned to Howie.

"You came rather close, I'd say. We've been trying to find Brother James. I had no idea he'd turn up here." Jones looked curiously at Howie. "Can you tell me why he *did* come to you? Why he was so interested in your silence?"

"I don't have any idea," Howie said. "He just came in here and—"

"No." The preacher shook his head. "I want the truth now, boy. I must know what passed between you two."

Jones turned as two Brothers came into the room, picked up the limp form, and left.

"I have to know this," Jones said gently. "It is very important to me."

Howie looked at the floor. "He caught me doin' something once. I ain't going to say what it was. It don't matter. He—wanted me to tell him what Brother Michael said. Whatever he said to Lawrence."

"Ah, I see." He shook his head and laughed quietly to himself. "And he enlisted you in his scheme. Poor Brother James. What a tragic mistake."

"I don't know nothing about any schemes," Howie said.

"No, of course you don't." The preacher let out a breath. "I fear our dear Brother had delusions of higher station. He wished to take Michael's place. We knew about it, of course. And you're right. It had nothing to do with you or your own . . . intentions of violence here."

Howie's mouth felt dry as dirt. He forced himself to look at the preacher. "I don't guess nothing I can say is going to help. I'm sorry I brought trouble on you. I didn't want to do that. It's just I had to do what I—"

"You had to kill Harriver Mason," Jones interrupted. "Yes, I know you did, boy." He paused and studied Howie a long moment. "You owe me no apology, Howie Ryder. None at all. You did what you had to do. The Lord spoke, and He delivered your enemy unto your hands. His will is done, and you have served Him well."

Howie stared in disbelief. "What the hell are you trying to say? You don't *care?* You don't think I did nothing wrong? I kill a man and mess up your peace talks, and that don't bother you at all?" He laughed aloud at Ritcher Jones. "I hope you'll tell them army bastards out there that *God* said everything's all right. I got an idea they haven't thought about that!"

Jones sighed and looked at Howie. He found a stool in the corner and brought it around before the chair.

"There is much here you don't understand, young man," Jones said. "I know you cannot mean the things you say. You mock the Lord's words, because you lack the knowledge to know them. You are His instrument, son. You were brought here by Him to do this deed, and no power on earth could have stopped you."

Jones leaned in close to Howie. "Why do you think the Lord placed me in Tallahassee, exactly at the moment you yourself would be there? He did, and He lifted the veil from my eyes and I *knew* you. I knew you had to be Howie Ryder. These things do not happen by chance, they are willed by the Lord."

Howie felt cold all over. "You—knew who I was? You knew right then? But how could—"

Jones shook his head and smiled. "A great many people know who you are and what you look like, Howie. You are quite a legend in some circles. Most especially those who fought on either side in Colorado. I should think you would know that, from your venture in New Los Angeles.''

''Goddam, what are you pullin' on me?'' Howie blurted.

''Word reached me soon after you left for town. I was most concerned, Howie. You had the Lord's plan to fulfill, and I didn't want you to come to any harm.''

The preacher's words struck Howie like a blow. ''You—you *brought* me here. You son of a bitch, you *wanted* me to stick a knife in Mason!''

''I was only an instrument, like yourself.''

''Don't give me no Church talk, mister,'' Howie said. ''Just tell me *why*. It don't make any sense. If you wanted the bastard dead, you could've had him killed yourself. Why'd you need *me?*''

Jones looked pained. ''What good would that have done? Harriver Mason dead by any hand but yours would serve no purpose at all. Howie, I don't pretend to know why you killed Anson Slade—yes, I know you did it, though I didn't see it done. But I did see the plain look of murder in your eye when you saw him, when I told you his name in the tavern. I knew the truth of what happened at Silver Island, and I guessed, at that moment, that you knew as well. Later, of course, I saw your aversion to meat. But that instant, that moment when you first saw Slade—there could be no other reason for your obvious hatred of the man. I knew then, Howie, that the Lord was speaking clearly to me. That His Light would show me the way. If you hated Anson Slade, if you were driven by such a need to see him dead, then you would certainly wish the same for Harriver Mason. By the way, the Loyalist people here know nothing of Slade. I saw no reason to add another murder to two. Two is quite enough.''

Ritcher Jones paused and frowned thoughtfully at Howie. ''Who was it, boy? A girl you knew, a brother or a sister who went to Silver Island?'' He waved the words away. ''No matter, and that is not my business, now is it? That's a personal matter with you.''

Howie wanted to throw up, but there was nothing in his belly. ''It ain't right,'' he said, squeezing his eye shut. "It don't make sense. Dammit, you can't do stuff like this to people. Just—*using* them for something."

"It *is* right, son. God's plan is always right, whether we see His way clearly or not. It was all written plainly in His hand, waiting to be read. Before I left California, I knew, from things I heard from important men in the Loyalist camp, that Mason was out of favor. He had risen too high, and wished to rise higher still. And more than that, he was becoming an embarrassment to the Loyalist cause. A secret is hard to keep, and too many of Lathan's Rebel officers knew of Silver Island, and disapproved of what had taken place there."

Jones spread his hands. He seemed to be looking at some wonder far away. "Do you see it all clearly now, Howie? How the Lord saw a need, and brought this all to pass? Mason stood in the way of peace. The Loyalists would shed no tears at his passing, but they dared not do the deed themselves. Mason still has friends in high places, including the President himself. But if an outsider should kill Mason, a man already wanted for the murder of one of their own, Colonel Jacob . . . Do you see how the Lord works His will? I knew, soon after we met, that you would play a part in His work. And you *have,* boy. A very important part. When the Loyalists announce that Mason is dead, the Rebels will be pleased, and more amenable to bringing about the peace. They won't have to know who did the deed itself, only that it was done. There are certain—*incidents* they desired as well, and the Lord has provided for their needs. That doesn't concern you, of course, but I will tell you that all has been achieved. High Sequoia means to bring about the peace. And you must not, in any way, Howie, feel that you have damaged the upcoming talks. Dear boy, you have helped to make them *work.* The Lord has blessed you, son. I hope you see that He—"

"You goddam fool!" Howie exploded with such a fury that Jones rose from his stool and backed away, forgetting that Howie's ropes bound him to the chair.

"All that *talk* you fed me about having a future at High Sequoia, how you wanted me to do something with my life. And all the time what you had in mind for me was dying. You didn't want me to *be* anything except dead!''

Jones looked startled, as if Howie had somehow betrayed him. ''But I meant what I said to you, boy. Every word. I wanted you to have a part in High Sequoia, to achieve your goals here. And you *have*. Don't you see? This is what I wanted for you, to do something with meaning, something that would bring you true glory. What does it matter if you gain that glory on this side of life or on the other? God Himself put the words in your mouth at supper last night, Howie. When you said you felt a sorrow at Camille's passing. And He spoke again through Lawrence to bring you the answer—that the Lord has far greater tasks for us on the other side. You have done your work here, and you shall receive His glory for it. I envy you, Howie. How I yearn to stand before Him!''

''Let me loose from this chair and I'll sure as hell send you on your way,'' Howie said.

Jones smiled. ''If I can offer any further spiritual guidance before it is—time, I would welcome the chance.''

''You can get your ass out of my sight,'' Howie said bitterly. ''I had about all the damn sermons I can take.''

Ritcher Jones straightened his robe and moved to the door of the cell. He stopped then and looked at Howie.

''You haven't mentioned the matter, Howie, but I know it's on your mind. While Sister Lorene's attentions toward you were initiated at my request, her—*feelings* for you became quite real. I assure you this is so. She is a most loving person, full of God's Joy and Light.''

''Get out of here,'' Howie shouted. *''Goddam you, get out!''*

Howie yelled at the preacher's back, cursing him long after he disappeared. And when rage gave way to sorrow and the hot tears scaled his cheeks, he knew he didn't ever want to know, that he didn't want to face Lorene and search her eyes, and see if he was there, or maybe learn there was nothing there at all. . . .

CHAPTER TWENTY-EIGHT

MOMENTS AFTER RITCHER JONES LEFT, A BROTHER CAME in and let Howie loose from his chair. Another stood guard, just outside the bars, a rifle held loosely in his arms. Once Howie's bonds were gone, the Brothers who'd cut him free retreated quickly from the cell, and the pair disappeared down the hall.

Howie had to laugh at the gun. They'd had him in the chair maybe eight or ten hours—even with the ropes cut away he couldn't move. His whole body felt dead. Gripping his knees, he tried to stand up straight. Pain tore down the length of his spine; he choked back a cry and fell helplessly to the floor. He didn't try to move again; he lay quietly in the dirt, cursing Ritcher Jones and everyone else at High Sequoia.

He tried to bring it all back, think what he might have done to make it turn out different from the way it had. It was shameful to think how simple it had been to draw him in. Jones had played him for a fool from the start. Once he'd found out who Howie really was, the rest had been easy. The preacher had simply held out Mason as bait, then hooked him with Lorene. After that—

No, now that ain't right, he told himself quickly. I would've come anyway. I did it for Carolee. To get even for her. It didn't have nothing to do with Lorene. . . .

Only it did, he knew that. It was too damn late to start denying what was true. And the cold truth was, he didn't care what she'd done or why. He wanted her again, wanted desperately to hold her and love her as hard as he could. Touch her all over just once before they took his life away. Maybe Jones had lied. Maybe

Lorene was just doing what he'd told her to do, and she didn't feel anything at all. Hell, Jones had lied about everything else.

That didn't matter anymore. Feeling bare flesh next to his was a hunger he couldn't put aside. And Ritcher Jones knew it, too. He knew Howie Ryder better than Howie knew himself. The thought brought a sudden burst of anger and shame. Ritcher Jones knew. There wasn't a son of a bitch alive knew more about sin, and what it could do to a man. He knew Howie had to have Lorene. And if Lorene wasn't there, why, Marie would do as well. That was the worst part of all. That the preacher could look inside his head, and see stuff Howie didn't want to see himself.

He knew it had to come. He'd hear their boots in the hall and then the troopers would appear. Three, maybe four. There'd likely be an officer, too. And when he saw them, he'd know. That there wasn't any time left to live, that everything was over and done. So he let himself think about it coming, walked through it in his head, thinking maybe that would make it work, that it wouldn't be all that bad if he knew just how it would be.

And when it happened, nothing helped at all. He didn't feel courageous or resigned; instead, he was scared out of his wits, numb all over with fear. When the soldiers appeared, he retreated to the far end of his cell and pressed his back against the wall. They would have to come and get him. That was the thing to do. Make them come the extra ten feet. Steal an extra minute of life. Maybe two. Something would happen and everything would change from the way it was.

There were two troopers and an officer. The troopers held their rifles at port arms before their chests.

"You going to give us any trouble?" The officer stopped a few feet inside the cell and gave Howie a wary look. He wore captain's tabs on his freshly pressed greens. "It's goin' to happen either way, you know that. We can leave here easy or hard."

"I won't give you any trouble," Howie said.

The captain looked over his shoulder. The troopers stepped forward smartly, one on either side of Howie.

"Let's go," the captain said. "Just keep between them two."

Howie didn't move. "Listen, is it a hanging or a gun? I want to know that."

The captain nodded, as if he fully understood this concern. "It's a hanging."

"I been inside here a spell. I don't even know if it's daylight or dark."

"It's day. About sunup."

"Thanks," Howie said. "I kinda figured it was."

The hallway was dimly lit and smelled of earth. The passage curved sharply to the right, and Howie had to duck to avoid a root as thick as a man. They were underground, then. He had been out cold when they brought him in. Somehow, he felt better knowing where he was.

It made a lot of sense, Howie reasoned. Everything looked real nice at High Sequoia. The Church would want to keep something ugly like a cell out of sight, so they'd burrowed beneath one of the giant trees. Lawrence was good at that, hiding all the bad stuff where no one could find it.

The first sight of daylight hurt his eyes. The greens were too harsh; even the muted sunlight from high above was too bright. A high wooden fence circled one side of the giant tree. The path was scarcely four feet wide; Howie couldn't see past the trooper and the officer ahead. Where would they do it? he wondered. Out of sight somewhere, a place where most of the Churchers would never go. Hell, Ritcher Jones would find them a good spot.

Howie didn't doubt for a minute that few of the Brothers and Sisters had any knowledge at all of the events going on in their midst. Ritcher Jones and Michael, Lawrence, a few others they could trust. That was the thing about a place like High Sequoia. Lawrence and God told you when to eat and pee and go to bed. You didn't ask questions and you did what you were told. There were rebels in the ranks now and then, like Brother James, but he didn't count. James didn't want to change anything, he simply wanted a place at the top of the heap.

Howie's thoughts were on James, and the sound of a pistol he'd never even heard, and the picture was so clear in his mind he imagined it was happening again. It happened so fast he had no time to blink, no time to even move. Three rapid sounds, as if someone had coughed close by. The trooper ahead of Howie stumbled, tried to catch himself, and dropped to the ground. Howie saw the captain on his knees, moaning and trying desperately to crawl away. The coughing sound came again and the officer collapsed and lay still. Howie stopped cold. He heard another stifled cry and jerked around. The other guard was flat on his back, staring at the sky. Chan stood over the trooper, a pistol in his hand. It was the same kind of weapon Brother Michael had carried, a revolver with an awkward black pipe on the end of the barrel.

"Hurry, this way," Chan said, gesturing with his weapon.

Howie stared at Chan as if he'd never seen him before. "What—what the hell happened?"

"This is no time for talk," Chan said. "We must go!"

Chan stepped over the dead trooper, gripped Howie's arm, and shoved him roughly down the path.

Howie balked. "Listen, friend, this is the way they was taking me to string me from a tree."

"Fine. You are free to take any path you wish," Chan said sharply. "I am going *this* way. I wish you good fortune on your journey."

Chan trotted off quickly down the path, leaving Howie behind. Howie hesitated only a moment. He glanced back once at the carnage, then followed after Chan.

It seemed to Howie they were doing nothing more than circling the giant tree. Chan paused every few yards to search the thick patch of ferns to his right, poking the foliage with his weapon. His face was strained, the skin taut across his cheeks. Howie didn't figure this was any time to poke around plants, but managed to keep his silence.

A man shouted in the distance. Another answered, crying out in alarm. Howie was ready to take his chances, climb the fence and run, do anything but stay where he was.

"Ah! I have it," Chan said. "In here, quickly!"

"In where?" Howie said.

In answer, Chan stepped into the stand of ferns and vanished. Howie looked curiously at the spot where his friend had disappeared, then stepped into the greenery. Chan tapped his ankle. Howie started and looked down. Chan was halfway down a hole, a narrow cleft at the base of the tree.

"Be careful," Chan said. "It is quite steep."

Howie gripped Chan's shoulder and followed him through the darkness. He smelled earth and the scent of wood. Touching the sides of the tunnel, he felt wet roots and dirt.

In a moment, the passage widened. Chan stopped. The air was cool and wet; Howie heard the steady drip of water somewhere. Chan handed Howie his weapon. Howie could hear him searching about. A spark lit up the darkness; a flame came to life in Chan's hands. He moved the flame to a lantern, and turned the wick up high.

The tunnel came to life. Howie stared in wonder at the sight. Tangled roots gripped clots of stone and earth. Everything glistened with beads of moisture. The passage was narrow, and no more than six feet high.

"I have only been here once before," Chan said. "We are fortunate to find my lantern. I was afraid I had left it in another passage."

Howie stared at Chan. "You been here before? How'd you *find* this place?"

"As you recall, I am a spy," Chan said patiently. "Spies are supposed to find things. There are maps, drawings, from a time even before the days of old High Sequoia. This place is not supposed to exist, but it does. As you can see. We are fond of saving old things in China. That is where I discovered the map, and many other ancient things. Do not ask me how it came to my country from here. We know little of that terrible time, but it is my belief that men hid in this place during the Great War."

"And the Churchers, they don't know about the tunnels?"

"Certainly not." Chan looked sternly at Howie. "We would not be here if they did. For a man who is supposed to be hanging from a rope at this moment, you ask a great many questions."

"I ain't ungrateful," Howie said. "I just like to have some idea what I'm doing. I don't see nothing wrong with that."

Chan leaned back against the damp earth. He closed his eyes a moment, then looked thoughtfully at Howie. "Yes, you are right. I cannot blame you for being curious. I am quite curious about a number of things myself. I am especially curious about a friend named Cory, who also seems to be a person called Howie Ryder. This Howie Ryder is a person who has killed a very prominent member of the Loyalist delegation. I learned of this event from a Churcher who is Lawrence's cook. I have paid this Brother well for some time, in order to gain certain information. Finally, he earns his keep, and I am able to vanish from my quarters with seconds to spare. If I had not been warned, I would now be dead." Chan shook his head. "It is not healthy to be a friend of this Howie Ryder. People who know this person seem to suddenly disappear."

"What—what are you talking about?" Howie stared at Chan. "*Who's* disappeared?"

"Howie Ryder, everyone who knew you is dead," Chan said gently. "The Churchers have eliminated any person who had anything to do with you. A Sister named Lorene, another named Marie—"

"God, *no!*" Howie cried out. A terrible fear gripped his heart. "Aw, they wouldn't! They wouldn't murder them girls!"

"Yes," Chan said, "They would, my friend. There is also a Brother named Jonas. He is dead as well. And several more."

"I rode in a carriage with him from New Los Angeles. All I did was *talk* to him."

"That is apparently enough," Chan said. "This thing

you have done, it is clearly of great importance, something the Churchers are determined to keep to themselves."

Lorene, Lorene! Tears blurred Howie's good eye. He tried to hold back the sorrow, but all he could see was Lorene, her face and her shining hair, her mouth when she laughed.

"I am sorry," Chan said. "I do not pretend to understand all this. I only know that it is so."

"They—Ritcher Jones," Howie said, "He knew I wanted Harriver Mason dead. The thing is, *he* wanted the bastard out of the picture, too, and he used me to get it done."

"Ah, the peace talks. Yes." Chan nodded in sudden understanding. "This explains a great deal." He looked soberly at Howie. "There is much here I do not know, but the picture is growing clear, Howie Ryder. High Sequoia is determined to maintain control of this war between the Loyalists and Rebels in your country. I know this is so. And to do this, they must control the peace talks as well. It is they who will decide the points of compromise. The two opposing forces will imagine they have agreed upon terms—but those terms will truly come from High Sequoia itself."

Howie looked confused. "The Churchers have got that much clout in California? They can really do that?"

Chan showed Howie a weary smile. "I see you are unaware of the truth, friend Howie Ryder. This is not surprising. It is what you, and everyone else, is supposed to think—that High Sequoia is a small religious sect and nothing more. That is not so. Lawrence has a great deal more than this *clout* you speak of. High Sequoia *is* the ruling force in California. Its people are in key positions; they have been there for many years. Public officials are elected, yes—but it is men like Ritcher Jones and Lawrence who make the real decisions."

Chan paused. "That is the true danger to your country, and to the rest of the world as well. This *new* High Sequoia is new only on the surface. It grew from a haven for the lawless, where men could get anything they wanted for a price. Arms, women, food. Anything, if you could pay. Now the men who rule High Sequoia wear robes and call themselves a church. But nothing has changed. It is the same. Lawrence's 'new tomorrow' will be subtly but rigidly controlled. He has manipulated the war to his liking by controlling the source of supply for both armies. He will manipulate the peace as well. The war will end when High Sequoia wishes it to end. Then the people Lawrence has placed within both the Loyalist and Rebel governments will form a *new* United States. High Sequoia will rule not only California, but your entire nation as well."

"God A'mighty," Howie said. He was startled by the enormity of what Chan was saying. The whole country, run by men like Lawrence and Jones. Chan was right—they were far more dangerous than Lathan or Colonel Jacob, or a bunch of damn generals out for glory. All the armies had was men and guns. Lawrence had *God* whispering secrets in his ear, and that made everything fine. If you were crazy as a loon, it was *right* to kill Lorene or Marie or anyone else who got in the way, because dying was the greatest thing anyone could do. You were doing a person a favor, sending him off to the Lord. A terrible picture appeared in Howie's head—Lorene and Marie, lying cold and still, all the color gone from their cheeks, their lips pale as chalk.

"My friend, we have very little time," Chan said, as if he guessed Howie's thoughts. "There are things I must know. Things that perhaps you can tell me."

"I figured there was a lot of things I knew," Howie said bitterly. "It don't appear like I know hardly anything at all."

The lantern began to flicker, and Chan turned the wick up higher. "There is much here that *few* people know," Chan said. "High Sequoia has covered its tracks well. And they are not the only danger, my friend."

Chan laughed, a quick, hollow sound laced with anger. "If I had not been marked for death through my friendship with you, my own companions would have managed to murder me before we returned to China."

"I got an idea there was a problem," Howie said. "I just didn't know what."

"It is a great deal more than a *problem,*" Chan said shortly. "If you have been to New Los Angeles, you have seen the great stock pens there, and you know that Asia is a major market for meat. There are factions in China that strongly oppose these dealings. Unfortunately, these factions are weak. The people you met at our quarters represent the party presently in power. These men care little for China; they are blinded by the lure of great profits."

Chan hesitated, then placed his hands on his knees and leaned closer to Howie. "In China, we have long raised other kinds of—stock. Creatures, animals, that have not been seen in your country since the Great War. This stock is still in short supply. The stock from your country is *not.* It is shipped to my country—live—then butchered in remote areas and sold in markets throughout Asia. My friend, the people who eat meat from California do not *know* that it comes from stock with two legs. They are not aware that such a horror has taken place in your country since the Great War."

"My God . . ." Howie stared at Chan.

"Ah, I was almost certain that you knew the truth," Chan said with some relief. "I see that it is not necessary to convince you."

"I know stock's the same as people, if that's what you mean," Howie said darkly. "I know a whole lot about that."

"It is an appalling secret," Chan said. "And one that the trading powers in my country will go to any length to protect. They share this interest with the few in your country who know the truth. I will tell you, Howie Ryder, that I was sent to California to spy on *my* people, not yours. I was sent to attempt to stop what is almost certain to begin—here, at High Sequoia."

Howie shook his head. "If you're goin' to try to stop this trading in meat, you got a damn near impossible job on your hands. Especially right now."

"No. You do not understand," Chan said. "What I came to stop has not yet *begun.* But it will, if High Sequoia and traders from China have their way." Chan gripped Howie's shoulder. "There was a place in your country called Silver Island. It was not what people believed it to be. Things were done in this place that—"

Howie cut him off. "I know all about Silver Island," he said harshly. "What the hell do *you* know about it?"

Chan raised a brow. "You are full of surprises, Howie Ryder."

"You didn't answer my question," Howie said. "What do you know 'bout Silver Island?"

"I know that High Sequoia was the silent partner, the major force behind the breeding experiments that took place at Silver Island. I know this is why my people are here—they are willing to pay any price to learn how to set up such a facility in China. They have come to California to learn these procedures firsthand."

Howie was puzzled. "Firsthand *how?* Silver Island's gone. Hell, I been there. The whole thing's burned to the ground!"

"The place you saw is gone, my friend," Chan said. "But the terrible things that happened there are not. Silver Island is *here.* At High Sequoia."

CHAPTER TWENTY-NINE

HOWIE FELT AS IF A GREAT AND AWESOME PRESENCE HAD risen up within him, a surge of pain and anger that threatened to consume him. He heard himself cry out, felt his fists tighten until his palms began to bleed.

Chan was startled by the sudden, frightening change in his friend; the face he saw in the dim light was a face he didn't know, a man he'd never seen before. He waited, held his breath until the storm began to subside.

"You *know* this," Howie said finally, staring at his hands. "You sure what you're saying? Silver Island's here?"

"Yes. It is here."

"Where is it? How far from here?"

"Not far. Two, perhaps three miles to the west. The

Brothers and Sisters are told it is a private retreat for Lawrence and the elders of the Church. No one who is not supposed to be there goes anywhere near it."

"I expect they got some guards."

"Some. Not many. Obedience is the guardian at High Sequoia."

Howie looked wearily at Chan. "They start out here with new people and stock, or did they bring some with 'em from Silver Island?"

"I cannot say. I know where it is—I have certainly not been inside." Chan looked curiously at Howie. "What is it, my friend? Why do you wish to know these things?"

"Because Silver Island took my sister," Howie said harshly. "They took her away when she was a kid to their goddam better tomorrow. That's why I came to this place, 'cause Ritcher Jones said Mason was here."

Chan was silent a long moment. "Yes, of course. I am most sorry, my friend. It is little wonder you have such anger in your heart." He laid a hand on Howie's arm. "I believe I know what you are thinking. But you must not allow yourself to dwell on this. Your sister could not be here. You know this isn't so."

"How do I know she's not here?" Howie's eyes blazed with sudden anger. "I don't know nothin' at all. They didn't murder everyone at Silver Island. Some of 'em got away. A few down Mexico to Nueva Panama. And some others hid out in the 'glades. I *talked* to them, Chan. They *knew* her. A girl there told me she was good with little kids. She kept them from getting scared."

Howie touched his chin and closed his good eye. "Only everyone who got away from Silver Island figured there was nothing but killin' going on. There wasn't no reason they'd think anything else. Nobody knew they were going to keep Silver Island going here." Howie looked at Chan. "It makes sense, now don't it? They wouldn't have any reason to flat out slaughter everyone—specially the people they were using for breeding, or folks who were useful somehow. Why would they want to start over? Dammit, they must've brought some of 'em here."

Chan shook his head. "She is gone, my friend. You know this is so!"

"I reckon you're right. But I got to find out." Howie looked soberly at Chan. "Listen, I owe you a lot. I'm thanking you for what you've done. You ain't involved in this, Chan. Just show me where to go. If I make it back out, maybe there's someplace we could try and meet up."

"That will not be necessary," Chan said. "I will show you the place myself."

"I don't want you doing that. It isn't your concern."

"This is so," Chan said. "And I assure you I have made a solemn vow. In the future, I will be most careful in the matter of choosing friends. It is clear that I lack understanding in such things."

Howie parted the ferns carefully and looked out across the clearing. The fence was a little higher, and the guards seemed somewhat more alert; other than that, the area looked no different from many others he had seen at High Sequoia. Chan was right. Lawrence didn't need to make a big fuss about the place. No one was going to walk up there and ask what was going on inside.

"There's just two guards," Howie said. "That won't be a problem. Inside's where I'll likely have trouble."

"Your reasoning is astute," Chan said dryly. "Again, if you insist on this folly, I suggest you wait until dark. Noon is a very bad time to enter a place you have never been before."

"It's got to be now. They got people out lookin' for us everywhere but here."

Howie looked curiously at Chan's peculiar weapon. Chan handed it over, and Howie hefted it in his hand.

"This thing's a wonder," Howie said. "That business on the end's what keeps it from making noise?"

"It is called a 'quieter.' It muffles the sound of firing."

"Brother Michael had one like yours. When he used it, I didn't hear a thing. Those bastards know their arms, you got to give 'em that."

Chan looked appalled. "This is *not* an achievement of

the Churchers," he said stiffly. "We sold it to them. It is Chinese."

"Yeah, well, it's some fine gadget," Howie said. "You don't mind, I'd like the loan of it awhile."

"I will expect you to bring it back intact," Chan said. His eyes, though, told Howie that Chan never expected to see the weapon again.

Getting in would be easy. Getting back out again was something else, and there was no use thinking on that. Chan had gotten them clear of the main compound, leading Howie through a branch of the ancient tunnels that took them several hundred yards from the base of the giant tree. Maybe there was another path through the tunnel, one that would take them even farther? No, Chan said; if there was, no such route appeared on his map. They would have to find another way.

Howie studied the gate across the clearing. There might be a better way, another entrance somewhere, one considerably less exposed. He thrust the thought aside. There was no time for that. He'd have to backtrack a good half mile through the trees to avoid the clearing, and come upon the compound from the east, the only direction that offered cover. A frontal approach was clearly the only way. And that meant taking out the two guards.

Howie had few qualms about that. The two Brothers had to be a part of Lawrence's trusted inner circle. They knew what was going on inside. As far as Howie was concerned, that stripped them of their innocence. Hell, no one was innocent at High Sequoia, he decided, whether he knew what was happening or not.

He listened once more for sounds of pursuit. Nothing. Only the distant rush of wind in the branches overhead. The guards were less than twenty yards away. A pistol was always a risk at any distance past a few feet, and Howie was concerned with the unwieldy quieter on the barrel. Standing slowly, he held the weapon steady in both hands, let out a breath, and squeezed off his shot.

The revolver made a soft, barely perceptible sound. The first guard dropped on his face. His friend looked surprised. Setting his rifle aside, he kneeled down for a look. Howie shot him in the back of the head.

Racing across the clearing, he dragged the two Churchers to a thick stand of greenery by the fence. The first man he'd shot was bleeding badly. A red stain spread across his robe. Howie took the second guard's garment and slipped it on, slung one of the rifles across his shoulder, and jammed the pistol in his belt out of sight. The robe would help some, but not much. Everyone inside would know everyone else. Howie worried about the gate; the first person who came in or out would see the guards were gone. But there was nothing he could do about that. Taking a deep breath, he opened the gate and walked into the compound.

The grounds were smaller than he had imagined. There was a long barracks-type building to the left, the back set close to the fence, and another smaller building to the right. And past that, at the far end of the fenced area, a covered shed that had to hold stock.

Howie ducked quickly to the left, into the narrow aisle between the rear of the larger building and the fence. This operation was nothing like Silver Island. One hurried glance told him that. It was smaller, with only limited facilities, a single pen for meat. The *people*, the ones they'd use to strengthen the herd with new blood, were likely housed in the barracks—breeder males, pregnant mothers, and the offspring of people and meat. Maybe the smaller building was used by the Churcher personnel who worked in the area.

Howie felt a sudden surge of anger. He had a good idea what this facility was for. Chan's guess was close; it was a model for setting up larger operations like Silver Island. Throughout the country, and in Asia as well, if the Chinese delegation had their way. And High Sequoia would control the whole thing—the breeding, the trading, the great wealth of the herds. They would feed a hungry nation—on Lawrence's terms. The nation would be grateful, and would likely never learn it was feeding upon itself.

* * *

Howie stopped halfway down the narrow path. He had hoped for windows at the rear of the building. The back wall was bare. He would have to try the front, and risk being spotted by a Churcher. Cursing his luck, he turned and went back, out into the open, keeping his face averted from the compound itself.

Two Brothers came toward him from the right. They were deep in conversation, and neither looked up. Howie opened the first door he came to and closed it quickly behind him. There was a window on either side of the door; both of the windows were barred. Beds lined the walls. Sleeping quarters, then. The room was orderly and neat. Howie swallowed his anger. High Sequoia took good care of its breeding stock.

There was another door on the wall to the left. Howie felt a quick sense of relief. Good. Maybe there were interior doors all through the building. He wouldn't have to go outside again.

Opening the door carefully, he peered through the crack. A naked, pregnant girl lay on a table, her arms strapped securely to her sides. Two Churchers, a man and a woman, bent over the girl's swollen belly. The man heard Howie. He looked up, startled, and backed toward the outside door.

"*Don't!*" Howie said.

The man stopped. The woman started to scream. Howie took one step toward her and hit her hard with his open hand. The woman sank to the floor. The man cried out and bolted for the door. Howie cursed, jerked Chan's pistol from his belt, and shot the man twice.

The outside door had a heavy metal bolt, and Howie slammed it tight. The girl on the table followed him with her eyes. Her slack, incurious expression told Howie she was stock. She lacked the capacity to wonder what was going on; she wouldn't cry out, or do anything else.

There was a stack of sheeting on a shelf. Howie tore the cloth in strips and bound the Sister's hands and ankles. He found a pitcher on a table and emptied it on her face. The women came to her senses at once, spitting water and kicking her legs. Howie straddled her and jammed his pistol in her mouth. The Sister's eyes went wide with fear.

"You maybe got a girl here," Howie said. "They'd have brought her from Silver Island. She's people, not meat. If she's here, you probably got her takin' care of kids. That's what they had her doin' there. Her name's Carolee, and she'd be about fifteen now. I'm going to let you talk. Try anything else and you're dead."

Howie drew the barrel from the Sister's mouth. She made a face and worked her lips.

"There are—a couple of girls here. I don't know any Carolee." She gave Howie a haughty look. "We don't give them any *names.*"

"Where would the girls be?"

"Two—two doors down. That's where the children are. You're going to kill me, aren't you?"

Howie ignored the question. "What's in the room next to this one?"

"We keep records in there. That's all."

"How many people work in there?"

"One, I don't know. I hope the Lord damns your soul for what you—"

Howie slapped the woman hard. The Sister groaned and sucked in a breath. Howie shoved a wad of cloth in her mouth and turned her roughly on her belly. He glanced at the girl on the table. She watched him with the same vacant stare.

Howie opened the door to the next room. There were shelves stacked high with papers. A man looked up from a desk.

"You want to live or not?" Howie said.

The man stared and nodded quickly.

Howie walked to him and slammed the barrel of the pistol down hard on his skull. The man sighed and relaxed.

Howie paused for a moment and felt through his pockets for Chan's extra shells. Five. That would have to do. He reloaded the two empty chambers. He didn't want to have to use the guard's rifle. One shot would bring everyone in High Sequoia.

Howie looked at the door. All he had to do was walk

in and he'd know. He wasn't sure he could handle that at all, because he knew Chan was right. There wasn't a chance in hell she was here, still alive after all this time. Lord, they'd slaughtered so many at Silver Island! She was dead and that was that. Only a damn fool would think any different. He didn't have a sister anymore; Carolee Ryder was a thousand miles away, her bones picked clean on a patch of white rock. That was how it was, whether he wanted to see it or not.

And when he opened the door she was there. The room was full of children, and she held a small boy in her arms. She looked up at Howie and smiled, and he saw it at once in the smile and in her eyes, saw his sister was gone, saw that Carolee had shut out all the hurt and the horror she had seen.

Howie wanted to cry out, release all the sorrow and anger in his heart, open the door and just stand there and kill every Churcher he could find. Only that wouldn't help. It wouldn't change a thing. He could kill Harriver Mason a hundred times over and it wouldn't bring her back. Nothing would do that. Nothing could make up for what they'd done.

"Hello," said Carolee. "I don't think I know you, do I? *You* haven't been here before."

Tears filled Howie's good eye. She had to be fifteen, but she spoke like a well-mannered child.

"No, I—haven't been here before," Howie said. He choked on the words. God, she looked so much like Ma, the same corn-yellow hair, the fine blue eyes. She was a tall, full-figured girl, just as pretty as she could be, only that was all there was.

"Are you going to help with the children? Oh, I *hope* so. We can certainly use the help. What's your name? I'm Carolee."

"Carolee, I'm Howie." He pulled up a chair and faced her, his hands on his knees. "Don't you remember? Don't you remember me at all?"

Carolee squinted her eyes in thought. "I don't *think* so. I don't guess. Oh, I'm so sorry about your eye. Did you hurt yourself bad?"

"No, I'm all right. I'm just fine. I—"

The door to the compound opened and Howie came to his feet, bringing the pistol out fast. A boy stopped in his tracks, stared at Howie, then looked at Carolee.

"Get in," Howie said. "Close that door!"

The boy did as he was told. He had sunburnt hair and dark eyes, and looked to be the same age as Carolee.

"Who are you?" the boy demanded. "What are you doing here? Carolee, you all right?"

"I'm *scared*, Tommy." Carolee held the child close to her breast and looked fearfully at Howie. "He's not going to take the children, is he? I don't want him doing that."

"Now, everything's fine," the boy said. He patted Carolee on her shoulder and looked defiantly at Howie. "Mister, what the hell do you want?" He wasn't afraid of the gun.

"You're not one of them, are you?" Howie said.

"What do you think? Look, you've got no right to—"

"My name's Howie Ryder. She's my sister."

The boy looked stunned. "My God—!" He glanced at Carolee, then back to Howie. "What are you *doing* in here? You out of your mind, mister? If they find you, we're all dead. Her too."

"Nobody's going to do any dying, 'less they're wearing a goddam robe." Howie waved his gun at the door. "Listen, I ain't got time for talk. You know this place and I don't. They got horses somewhere? I didn't see any. Is there another way out besides the front?"

"There's a gate out back. I think maybe there's horses. Sometimes, anyway." He looked at Howie. "What are you going to do?"

"I'm taking her out of here. Right now."

The boy's eyes went wide. "No, you can't do that. She won't—she can't make it on the outside. She doesn't *know* anything else. She's got the children here. That's all she has. I know you think you're doing the right thing, but—dammit, look at her. You see how she is!"

"We're going," Howie said.

The boy glared at Howie. "She won't go with you.

She doesn't know anyone but me. I take care of her. I've been with her all along."

Howie let out a breath. He looked at Carolee, saw her clinging desperately to Tommy's arm. He knew the boy was right.

"All right. Then you're going too," Howie said.

For the first time, the boy showed fear. "I—can't do that. I wouldn't know what to do out there. Any more than her. They treat us all right in here. It's not real bad. You got to see that. We—"

Howie heard the shots then, three sharp cracks of a rifle. Someone answered with a pistol, two shots and then nothing after that. Howie wondered who the hell was fighting who. There wasn't anyone on his side except Chan, and he had Chan's only gun.

CHAPTER THIRTY

HOWIE MOVED QUICKLY PAST CAROLEE AND THE BOY, opened the door a crack, and looked out at the compound. Churchers were running aimlessly about, shouting at one another, apparently wondering what to do next. Howie heard another burst of gunfire. The sound came from the gate. He turned to the boy.

"Stay right here. Take care of her." He poked his finger in Tommy's chest. "Don't think about bein' nowhere else when I come back."

Tommy nodded. Every muscle in his face was taut with fear. "What—what are you going to do? Where are you going?"

Howie didn't answer. Taking the guard's rifle from his shoulder, he raced toward the gate. A heavyset Brother ran toward him, shaking his fist. Howie hit him with the butt of his weapon and kept going. The gate was half open; Chan lay prone behind it, squeezing off shots at the clearing. A bullet splintered wood, and Howie dropped quickly to the ground.

"What the hell are you doin' here?" he asked Chan. "I told you to stay out of this."

"I forgive your insulting remark," Chan said. "You are clearly under great stress." Chan fired again; the stock of the rifle slammed hard against his cheek. "You left your rear unguarded, Howie Ryder. Very poor strategy. Fortunately, you left one of the guard's rifles as well."

"How many out there, can you tell?"

"Not many. But be assured more will come."

"Come on. We ain't staying here." Howie grabbed Chan's shoulders and lifted him to his feet. Chan protested as Howie pushed him toward the safety of the fence. Setting his rifle aside, Howie pushed the gate shut, then shoved a heavy timber through the wooden lock.

"Ah, now we are safely inside," Chan said.

Howie shot him a look. "Just follow real close and don't talk." He ran toward the building, Chan at his heels. A Churcher appeared at the door of the smaller building, waving a pistol in his hand. Howie fired twice, and the Churcher sprawled on the ground.

"Wait here," Howie said. "Keep those bastards off my back."

Chan went to his knees, sweeping his weapon across the open compound.

Howie found Tommy and Carolee crouched in one corner of the room. Carolee was crying. She still held the baby in her arms. Howie knew better than to waste time asking. He went straight to his sister, took the child from her, and lay it in one of the small beds. The child squalled and kicked its tiny legs. Carolee made a terrible sound in her throat and rushed past Howie for the child. Howie bent low, grabbed her waist, and lifted her easily to his shoulder. Carolee kicked and screamed.

Tommy stepped boldly in Howie's path. "Don't—don't do this. Please. Just leave us alone. I can take care of her here. I know how to do that."

Howie thrust his rifle at the boy. "You want to take care of her, do it with this."

Tommy stared at the weapon. "I never ever touched one of these things before!"

"Point it. Pull the trigger. That's all you got to do." Howie opened the door and stepped out. Chan blinked in surprise. Howie waved his questions aside and looked at Tommy.

"You said the Churchers have horses."

"I *think* they do," Tommy said. "I don't know. Out back. There's another gate past the pens."

"Howie!" Chan turned and fired. Howie saw a Churcher scramble quickly off the top of the fence.

"That ain't going to keep 'em out long," Howie said.

"A keen observation." Chan kept his eyes on the wall. No one else appeared. All the robed figures who worked in the compound had vanished. The place looked suddenly empty.

Howie spotted the rear gate, just behind the stock shed. He tried not to look at the naked figures crowded inside, the slack expressions and empty eyes. They were all young, none of them more than twelve or fourteen, the right age for breeding.

"Let 'em loose," Howie told Chan. "That'll give the Churchers something to do."

Chan nodded, walked to the shed, and unhooked the wooden gate. He waved his arms and yelled; the stock began to wander aimlessly into the compound.

Tommy had gone ahead to open the timbered door at the rear of the compound. Howie passed him quickly, and breathed a sigh of relief. A small corral stood ten yards past the fence. There were seven horses and a covered feed shed. Howie found saddles and harnesses inside. He turned Carolee over to Tommy and stepped over the fence. The mounts shied away, and he talked to them gently and calmed them down. There was no time for saddles. The Churchers could send a party around the fence at any moment. He rigged three of the best horses with bits and reins, opened the gate, and shouted the other mounts out.

"You and me'll ride single," he told Chan. "That keeps us free to shoot. Tommy, you take care of Carolee."

The boy stared at the horses and shook his head. "No, sir. I'm not getting on one of those. I won't do it."

Howie looked at the boy, and knew at once Tommy had never even been close to a horse before. Hell, he hadn't thought of that.

Howie handed his reins to Chan, walked over to Tommy, picked him up bodily, and lifted him to the back of the mount. The boy sat frozen in fear. Howie thrust the reins in his hand.

"Listen to me," Howie said. "You kick it when you want to go. Not hard, real easy. Pull them things when you want it to stop. You learn how to do that *fast* or one of them fine Brothers will put a bullet in your back. You got that?"

The boy didn't answer. He closed his eyes tight and gripped the reins. Howie mounted up, and Chan lifted Carolee up behind him. Carolee whimpered at his back and wrapped her arms tightly around his waist, more frightened of the horse than she was of Howie.

"Which way?" Chan said.

"North. I figure that's the quickest way out of California. Canada's up thataway a piece."

Chan gave Howie a sober look. "I would say four hundred miles. That is indeed a piece."

"Hell, you got any better ideas?"

"I do," Chan said. "And if we are alive at this time tomorrow, I will discuss them with you further."

Howie lay flat on the stone outcropping and studied the darkening valley. The sun had just dropped behind the hills to the west, and the rock was still warm. A river ran through the valley, some three hundred feet below. Trees lined the river on either side; past the trees, grassy plains swept steeply up the sides of the surrounding hills. Howie could see the whole valley clearly for miles to the south and east. If pursuers were there, they were keeping to the trees and not building any fires. And they were there, all right, he knew that. They'd keep on coming.

They wouldn't give up. Ritcher Jones wouldn't let them do that.

Howie knew they wouldn't have made it four days without a little good luck at the start. Chan figured the Churchers had stumbled on them at the compound—four or five men, maybe bringing something to the facility. Or maybe they'd left the place earlier and were simply coming back. They didn't have horses, and that gave Howie's party a chance. A good hour's start, maybe more than that, before the Brothers could get back and start riders from High Sequoia on the move.

Howie and Chan spotted their pursuers at the end of the first day. A dozen or so Churchers, maybe seven or eight Loyalist troopers, making their way through the woods. Howie had taken his mounts up high as soon as he could, getting out of the forest where horses left a trail, finding hard and rocky ground. It made for rough riding, especially for Carolee and the boy. Still, once Tommy had gotten a good look at their pursuers, he started learning horsemanship fast.

The troopers worried Howie a lot. They knew what they were doing, and every time he threw them off, they backtracked and found the trail again. They had food and plenty of arms, and the army always took remounts along. That put them way ahead of their quarry. Howie knew if he couldn't shake them off real soon, the army and the Churchers had to win. The odds were simply stacked too high. He didn't have to tell Chan and the boy. It was clear they already knew.

Chan had a small fire going under a rock overhang. The horses were close by in a shaded hollow, and the camp was high enough to be relatively secure.

Chan looked up sharply as Howie came through the trees, then relaxed. "You see anyone?"

Howie shook his head. "Didn't figure I would. They're out there, though."

Chan had caught a few small fish and managed to snare a large bird. The bird tasted awful, but Howie ate it anyway. Chan said it was an owl.

"I never ate an owl," Howie said. "I reckon I know why."

"I would not complain if I were you," Chan said. "I may not find an owl tomorrow."

"The kids already eat?"

"I gave them most of the fish. The boy was hungry. Your sister eats very little."

Howie looked past the fire at Carolee. She sat hunched in the shadows of the rock. He could hear her singing softly to herself. Tommy had made her a doll out of part of his shirt, and stuffed it with dry grass. Carolee hugged it close, and it seemed to keep her happy and quiet.

Tommy sat close by Carolee, holding the rifle in his lap. Howie had shown him how to lever fresh shells into the chamber and pull the trigger. At first the boy had refused to have anything to do with the weapon. Then Howie explained that if he didn't want to learn how to shoot, he didn't really give a damn about watching out for Carolee. That did the trick. Tommy practiced his dry-fire routine every night, and wouldn't quit until Howie made him stop.

"He is very good with Carolee," Chan said, guessing Howie's thoughts. "I do not think she would have survived in that place without him."

"I reckon he's all right," Howie said. He poked a stick at the fire and began taking his rifle and Chan's pistol apart. "They're going to know when we stop goin' north and turn west," he told Chan. "They'll figure that one out real quick, and guess we're making for the sea."

"It is the only thing to do," Chan said. "There are many Chinese in the northern ports of California. We will get a ship." He showed Howie a weary grin. "I promise you that. Get us to the coast, and I will get us a ship."

Howie didn't look up. "Soon as they track us headin' west they're going to know. That's when they'll split up their forces. Keep one bunch on our tail and send the others off fast to cut us off." He made marks on the ground with a stick. "They take us, and I ain't able to do it, you got to promise me they won't take Carolee. Tell me you'll do that."

"We will make it. It will not come to that."

"Dammit, you don't know that at all," Howie said harshly.

Chan stood. "I know that I intend to get some sleep. I suggest you try to do the same."

Howie sat by the fire and finished cleaning his weapons. Once he looked up and saw Tommy watching him from the shelter of the overhang, and wondered if the boy had heard him talking with Chan. Carolee was still singing to her doll, and Howie knew Tommy would stay awake until she slept.

The sharp blast of sound brought him straight up out of sleep. For an instant, he was certain the troopers had found them and were firing into the camp. Then a bright fork of lightning lit the sky and the sound struck again, shaking the high ground.

Howie was up before the first heavy drops of rain splattered the dry earth, yelling for Chan as he ran through the brush for the mounts. The sky opened up and he was drenched before he made a dozen yards. He laughed and turned his face up to the rain, raised his hands, and shouted at the sky.

Chan caught up with him at the makeshift corral. The mounts were spooked by the lightning and the sound. Howie calmed them as he led them out of the hollow.

"Get Carolee and the boy," he shouted over the rain. He laughed again and clapped Chan soundly on the back. Chan looked startled, and Howie leaned in close to his face.

"Hell, man, don't you see it? The *rain*. That's the break we need. We're turning west right now, out of these hills and down to flat ground. Ain't anyone alive can tell where we're heading after this!"

Chan looked appalled. "We will surely fall into holes in the dark. Very deep holes, perhaps."

Howie grinned like a fool and pushed Chan ahead down the path. By the time they reached Carolee and Tommy, everyone was thoroughly drenched. The boy was used to riding, and Howie had been leaving Carolee in his charge.

This time, though, he took his sister on behind him. He didn't want anything to happen to the boy, but if it did, it wouldn't happen to Carolee as well.

A hundred small rivers rushed down the hill, turning the earth to mud. Once Chan's horse lost its footing and panicked, and Chan had to fight to keep the frightened mount from bolting. Howie blessed the ragged lightning and prayed for more. Without it, he knew they'd never reach the flats in one piece. He kept everyone together, testing the treacherous ground first, shouting back orders if the way looked too dangerous ahead. The rain pounded Howie's skin like tiny stones, and lashed out at his good eye. He heard Chan shout above the storm, turned and saw his friend's mount tumble down the slope and disappear. Howie started back, fearful of what he'd find. Another flash of lightning turned the darkness into day, and he saw Chan pick himself up from the mud and climb up behind the boy.

It suddenly struck Howie that the hill didn't seem so steep anymore; his horse was holding his footing well. It dawned on him then that they were onto the plain. He yelled and shook his fist in the air. The ground was still wet, soaked by the rain, but it was flat as a board, stretching out toward the west. Howie kicked his mount and trotted back to Chan and the boy, urging them forward through the rain. He stopped then and peered back up the hill. He couldn't imagine he'd ever had the nerve to try it, or that he'd gotten them all down through the storm. Chan was right. It was a damn fool idea, and he was relieved it was over and done.

The rain didn't stop until morning, and even then the dark clouds hung ominously low, sweeping nearly to the ground. Howie didn't let them rest until the rain was completely gone. He knew every mile he put behind them made it that much harder for the troopers. They'd have to guess now—give up the trail and send riders out in every direction, hoping to catch sight of their prey. Howie figured he'd put ten, maybe fifteen miles at their backs. And every inch without leaving a single mark. The country was big, and the troopers would have to cover it all.

He'd let the mounts rest for an hour or two, no more than that. Then they would head for the coast. For the first time since Howie had left the compound at High Sequoia, he knew they could make it, that the ship wasn't simply in Chan's mind, it was real.

He woke and looked up at the sky. Clouds still masked the sun, and he guessed it was maybe noon. He felt a moment of alarm, knowing he'd slept longer than he'd planned. They needed to get moving, eat up some more miles.

When Howie stood, everything hurt. He tried to remember how it felt to be dry. Chan had found a grove of trees that morning, a spot slightly higher than the flats. There was no standing water, but the earth was anything but dry. He felt hollow and light-headed, and wondered where they'd find any food. Most likely they'd do without for a while.

Chan was still as death, and Howie let him sleep. He couldn't find Tommy and Carolee, and guessed they'd found a reasonably dry spot farther back in the trees. He checked the horses, and saw they were doing fine. They wouldn't be anxious to get to work, but there was nothing he could do about that. He'd have to try to run them easy, keep them alive till they reached the coast.

Walking to the edge of the grove, he looked west. The land sloped slightly to the north, and he could see white croppings of stone in the earth. Good. The ground would be dry enough and hard enough to ride. They would make good time.

As Howie started back, he spotted color in the trees and saw it was Carolee. She was sitting under a stunted pine, talking to her doll. When Howie approached, she looked up and smiled.

"Well, I hope you got some sleep," Howie said. Carolee's hair was half dry, but her dress clung to her like skin. She didn't know what modesty was all about, and the thin skirt hiked up to her thighs.

"That was some rain we rode through last night. I'm real proud of you, Carolee. You did good."

Carolee stuck out her lower lip in a pout. "My baby got all wet. It doesn't look nice anymore."

"Say, now, I bet we can get her all dry." Howie held out his hand. Carolee hesitated, then handed him the doll. There wasn't much left except a patch of wet cloth. Most of the dry grass stuffing was gone.

Howie made a show of patting the grass in place, and handed the doll back to Carolee. "There. That's a little better. We'll find some nicer clothes for her soon. Get her all fixed up."

Carolee made a face. "It's not a her, it's a *he.*"

"Oh, well, see, I didn't know that," Howie said.

"Boy babies are better than girls."

"And why's that?"

" 'Cause boys don't have to lie down and do bad things, and get all swole up."

Howie felt his throat go dry. He wanted to reach out and hold her, bring her close, tell her everything would be fine, that everything she'd seen, everything they'd done to her, would go away. Only that wasn't so. She'd always be what she was right now, that wouldn't ever change.

"Your eye's *real* scary," said Carolee. "Only I'm not as 'fraid of it now as I was."

"I'm sure glad you're not," Howie said. "I don't want you being scared of me. I don't want you to ever be scared of anything again."

"I *like* riding a horse now. I'm not afraid any at all. Tommy says I might learn to ride all by myself."

"You just might."

"Are you scared of anything, Howie?"

"Well, I guess sometimes I am."

"Like the dark?"

"No, not the dark. But I—"

Howie froze as he heard a twig snap behind him. Carolee's eyes went wide, and she brought a hand to her mouth.

"Don't even move, boy. Don't even think about it."

Ritcher Jones stepped quickly to the left where Howie could see him. He held the long-barreled silver gun in one hand. His robe was dark with mud, and the white hair was plastered across his face. Howie felt his gut twist up in a knot.

"Where are the others?" Jones said sharply. "That Chinese fella and the boy?"

Howie's mind raced. Jones had spotted the two horses. He hadn't been up in the grove. Howie had loosed all the other mounts at the compound, and Jones didn't know how many they'd ridden off. His trackers had likely told him three or four, but he didn't know for sure.

Howie forced an easy grin. "They rode on ahead. You just missed 'em, preacher."

Jones frowned at that. He gave Howie a piercing look, as if he might see right into his head. He backed away a foot, and glanced quickly to the west. Howie knew he was figuring how far ahead Chan and the boy might be, when they'd likely come back.

Jones studied Howie another moment, then smiled at Carolee. "You caught me napping with the girl, son. I guessed you'd lost family at Silver Island. But finding her, out here . . ." Jones shook his head. "Now that's a miracle of the Lord's own making. Your sister, I'll bet. Looks like you."

"Leave her be," Howie said. "I won't give you no trouble. Just leave her be. You bastards done enough to her!"

Jones didn't seem to hear. "You have caused me a great deal of grief, Howie Ryder. A great deal of anguish and pain. I have prayed long and hard these last few days, prayed that God would allow me to make amends for the mistakes I've made with you. And last night, He gave me that chance. The rains came down from the heavens, and all the men about me were dismayed. But *I* knew. The Lord let me see that you would *use* that rain, that you would flee at once to the sea." Jones smiled again. "The Chinese take pride in their ships. They covet their fine craft and love the water more than the land, and I knew the heathen would take you there, guided by Satan himself."

That goddam heathen's going to sleep all day, Howie thought miserably. That's what he's going to do.

"All I'm askin' is you leave the girl alone," Howie said. "That's all. You got no need of her, it's me you—"

"Shut up!" Jones said sharply. "Move away from her. Over there. I'll decide about the girl in time." Jones thumbed back the hammer of his weapon and aimed it at Carolee's head. "Do it, Howie Ryder. Or I'll come to that decision right now."

Howie stood. He made himself move slow, thinking what it might take to get to the gun. Ritcher Jones would get off a shot, and likely hit him true. He was too damn good to miss. But the shot would rouse Chan, and maybe Chan could save Carolee.

"Don't consider anything foolish," Jones said. He backed off another step and leveled the gun at Howie's chest.

Carolee began to cry. "It's all right," Howie said, keeping his eye on Jones. "Just sit still, Carolee."

"Now that's a right fine thing to do," Jones said solemnly. "A good man takes care of his kin. And I feel you're a good man, Howie Ryder. We've had our differences, you and me, but we've served the Lord together, and that's the thing. When you stand before Him, boy, you'll see what I've been saying all along. That true glory comes to a man when he steps from this life to the next, when he—"

Howie saw him a split second before Jones. Tommy came out of the trees, firing the rifle as fast as he could, going through the steps he'd practiced every night—fire, lever another shell in the chamber, fire again. Ritcher Jones jerked up straight, a startled expression on his face. Bullets whined all about him, slicing off twigs and digging dirt. Jones danced aside, snapped off a shot and missed. Tommy kept coming, squeezing the trigger every second, doing everything right. The only thing Howie hadn't taught him was to aim. Lead hit everything but Jones. The preacher bent his knees and fired again. Tommy cried out and went down; without pausing an instant, Jones swept the long barrel toward Howie.

Howie threw himself at the preacher. White fire blinded his eye and a sound like thunder filled his head. His shoulder struck Jones solidly in the gut and sent him sprawling. Howie heard the pistol hit dirt. Jones cursed him and pounded him with his fists, cutting Howie's cheek and bringing blood to his eye. Howie couldn't see Jones but he knew he was there, knew when his hands got past the hurting fists and found the preacher's throat. Ritcher Jones kept fighting, lashing out wildly at Howie's head. Howie didn't care. All he could feel was the rage in his heart, the sorrow for Lorene and Marie, for his mother and his pa, for boys he'd seen die in the war, and everyone else who was gone that he wouldn't ever see anymore. All the hurt and the pain flowed through his hands, and when Chan tried to pull him away, he saw there was nothing he could do but turn away and take care of Carolee, and see what could be done about the boy. . . .

EPILOGUE

CHAN SAID TOMMY WOULD LIKELY MAKE IT, THAT IT was fortunate indeed Chinese doctors were the best in the world.

"He would not have a chance if he were left to the butchers in your country who call themselves physicians," Chan explained. "If one is shot in the toe in America, the leg will most probably be amputated at once. If a finger is afflicted, the arm itself must go. On the other hand, I have seen miracles of healing in China. Even if a limb is nearly severed—"

"Fine," Howie said, "as long as you get him back on his feet. He's a good kid and worth saving, and I sure ain't anxious to give Carolee bad news."

Howie sat up and stretched, left Chan below, and made his way to the forward deck. The sky was an awesome shade of blue, and a gentle wind swept in from the east. A giant of a man who belonged to Chan's faction back home was sitting cross-legged on the deck, facing Carolee. He had taught Carolee a game that involved colored marbles. It made no sense to Howie, but seemed to delight Carolee.

When the Chinese saw Howie, he stood and bowed solemnly, and walked back along the deck. Howie knew he wouldn't go far. Chan had carefully explained to the man that Carolee was a sacred person, as anyone could see from her innocent manner. Chan's friend took his job quite seriously and seldom let Carolee out of his sight.

"Hello, Howie," Carolee said. "You want to play?"

Howie eased himself down on the deck. "Not me. You're too good. You doing all right?"

Carolee leaned forward. Sharing secrets was one of her

favorite things to do. "I have been *trying* to make Mr. Huan smile. I don't know if I can."

Howie grinned. "You keep trying. He'll come around." He looked at Carolee, at the fine mist of hair across her face, then past her to the east. Chan assured him California was a good four hundred miles away, but this failed to set Howie's mind at ease. High Sequoia was still there. Lawrence was there too. He had the power and the will; he'd do whatever he wanted with the country, until someone else got big enough to stop him, and do something different. Things would get better or worse. Howie wondered if that was the way things had to be. Maybe it was. It seemed like you could fix things good sometimes, get everything going real fine, and then someone else would come along and tear it down. Like they did in the Great War. Everything was supposed to be nice before that, but you couldn't tell it now. There wasn't much left to show.

"You want to tell me a story?" said Carolee. "Huan tells me real good stories."

"I ain't much good at telling stories," Howie said.

"Please!" said Carolee.

"All right," Howie said. "But don't expect a whole lot." He stretched his legs out on the deck and leaned against the high wooden rail. "There was these two people, and they had 'em a real nice farm. There was all kinds of stuff growing, wheat and corn and everything. They worked real hard. And one day they got the notion to get all dressed up, and take the younguns to the Bluevale Fair. They figured on having a whole lot of fun."

"Was the younguns girls or boys?" asked Carolee.

"One of each," Howie said. "There was a boy, and he had a real pretty sister who looked just like her ma."

"A boy *and* a girl!" Carolee clapped her hands in delight. "Just like you and me."

"That's right," Howie said. "Kinda like you and me."

ABOUT THE AUTHOR

Neal Barrett, Jr. is the author of over thirty books. He is a graduate of the University of Oklahoma, where he received a degree in professional writing. In addition to writing, Mr. Barrett has worked as the Director of Public Relations for the Dallas Chamber of Commerce and in the U.S. Army Counterintelligence Corps. He currently resides in Fort Worth, Texas, with his wife, Ruth, and their five children.